HIS AUCTION PRIZE

Brides By Chance
Regency Adventures
Book Eight

Elizabeth Bailey

HIS AUCTION PRIZE

Published by Sapere Books.

20 Windermere Drive, Leeds, England, LS17 7UZ,
United Kingdom

saperebooks.com

ISBN: 978-1-80055-325-5

CHAPTER ONE

The gaggle of giggling girls waiting their turn on the dais was thinning at last. Raoul Ruscoe, Marquis of Lynchmere, standing aloof from the noisy game, passed the remaining debutantes under critical review.

He had so far refrained from adding his voice to those of the enthusiastic bidders. Resigned irritation plucked him from the threatening tedium that dogged his life. He must either participate or endure an earwigging from his cousin. Trust Angelica to think up an idiotic charade of this nature.

If he had known about the auction, nothing would have induced him to present himself at the Latimer ball. Why in Hades had he not followed his instinct when Angelica pressed him to attend?

"You must go, Raoul. I shall not forgive you if you don't."

"Good God, why? You know I never attend such affairs."

From under the pretty cap she wore, Mrs Summerhayes rolled her eyes. "Such a poseur you are, my dear, of course I know. But this time you will, if you please."

"And if I don't please?"

The accusation nettled. Angelica, a social butterfly, could not understand the intolerable boredom the pointless round induced in him. He had long abandoned any hope of persuading her that the *pose* she complained of was real.

"It makes no matter." She set a hand on his arm and dropped her tone to a confiding note he recognised. "You will not repeat this, I know, but the Latimers are in desperate straits. Margaret Latimer is my dearest friend and I must do everything I can to help."

Raoul groaned in spirit. "By dragging me into the business?"

"You will lend a much-needed cachet. I have thought up such a scheme as will make this party the talk of the Season."

Which was the point where Raoul's instinct kicked in. He was all too well acquainted with Angelica and her schemes. If his cousin had set one trap to try to induce him into dropping the handkerchief, she had set a dozen.

"I'm having nothing to do with one of your schemes, Angie, I thank you. Consider me out of the picture."

Her merry laugh had rung out. "You need not panic, Raoul. I'm not trying to marry you off to one of the Latimer twins. Not but what it is high time —"

"Angelica!"

The warning note had its effect. "Oh, very well, but if my dearest aunt had still been alive, you would have been wed long since."

"Enough! Start on that and I'm off."

She seized his arm. "No, don't go. Pray, Raoul, do me this one kindness and I swear I will not ask you for another."

He all but snorted. "Until the next time."

"No, I mean it. In any event, I don't intend to remain in Town once the Latimer do is over. Summerhayes is fretting to be gone, and Nurse sent to say little Sally is missing me and both Hugo and Nicky are driving everyone demented."

Mention of his obstreperous godsons caused Raoul an inward shudder, but the prospect of Angelica's departure from the metropolis induced him to relent. He regretted it now, eyeing the young females who had yet to engage a supper companion by means of Angelica's ingenious ploy to raise the stakes for this confounded event. The Latimer twins were still waiting, presumably having held back to allow their guests to have an early bite of the cherry. If he did not make a move, he would find himself obliged to partner one or other out of sheer courtesy. Was this Angelica's intention after all? Hell and the devil, had she tricked him?

He glanced from one to the other of the girls. They were alike, but not identical. One had a trifle the superiority in height and hair a lighter shade of brown. Silvestre, was she? An outlandish name for a girl. The other was Henrietta, if he recalled correctly, a shy female and less conversable than her sister. He had danced with both on occasion, to little effect. Would one of them do?

Raoul was conscious of a drop in spirits. Marry he must, no doubt, and in the not too distant future. If the Latimers were all to pieces, as Angelica seemed to suggest...

He was contemplating the unwelcome prospect, glancing from one to the other of the twins in hopes of discerning a preference, when his eye caught on a little redhead hovering at the back of the depleted group.

Who in Hades was that? He put up his quizzing glass, but she was too far away for it to help. Raoul skirted the edge of the crowd about the dais, from where several as yet unaccompanied gentlemen were gallantly bidding for the unprepossessing Maria Ambleside, in her third season and still not betrothed.

The fresh vantage point enabled Raoul to get a better look at the girl with a mop of ill-dressed red hair twisted into some kind of topknot. He could not recall seeing her before. A wispy creature with an elfin face, marred by a profusion of freckles. Had not her mama the sense to use some sort of cosmetic deterrent? He dropped his gaze to the low-cut gown, showing far too much freckled flesh for her scant bosom, and made up in ubiquitous white. Disastrous. She ought to be in jonquil or peach, perhaps green with those copper locks.

Almost as if she felt his critical gaze, the girl turned her head and glanced in his direction. He could swear her eyes widened briefly as they met his. Then she turned quickly away.

"Miss Ambleside is won!"

Lord Nalderwood, the bright young spark presumably inveigled by Angelica into taking the part of the auctioneer, invited young Tarporley to approach and claim his prize. The Ambleside wench was handed down and one of the Latimer twins pushed the little redhead forward. Was she reluctant, or did he imagine it? She certainly hesitated as Nalderwood came to hand her up. A whispered conference ensued and the murmurs of the crowd ceased as the girl took her place on the dais.

The momentary lull seemed filled with a collective oddity. Instinct told Raoul the girl's identity was universally questioned. The increase of candlelight upon her face showed a wash of colour momentarily drowning the freckles. Then she put up her chin and it faded again. Raoul was conscious of a prick of admiration.

"Now then, gentlemen. Who will offer the first bid for Miss Felicity Temple?"

Confronted with the battery of eyes under the dazzle of the huge chandelier, Felicity struggled to keep her countenance. Her pulse, already awry, bumped so uncomfortably in her chest she feared she might lose her senses. She had only fainted once in her life, but the memory of waking to confusion stiffened her spine. She must not swoon in this assembly.

She hardly heard the man who was asking for bids. She scanned the faces, looking for the one she knew. Or at least she knew it well enough after this short week to be able to recognise Mrs Sprake, even in this motley crowd. The creature

8

had promised she would not be far away. Felicity had not seen her guardian either for at least an hour. Where was he?

"Five guineas, sir!"

Felicity's stomach lurched. Heavens, someone was bidding!

"Ah, thank you, Mr Finglesham, a fine beginning."

Her mind flittered in tune with her uneven heartbeat. Five guineas? A poor start, rather. Others had begun at ten. Even fifteen for the blonde beauty. Sophia, was it? Still, it was more than was offered for the poor girl who had preceded her. Not that it mattered a jot. What in the world was she doing here?

"Come now, gentlemen, no hanging back," came the auctioneer's encouraging tones. "Who will raise Finglesham's stake for the lovely Miss Temple?"

Lovely? Felicity bit back the threat of hysterical laughter. Or no, why? It meant nothing. He had said the same for all. Different words. *Delightful?* Yes, a dark girl had been delightful. Oh, and that Sophia was *delectable*.

"Seven guineas!" A different voice.

Felicity caught sight of a chubby countenance, grinning from a coterie of young people. Oh, heaven help her, she would go mad in a minute!

"My lord Abinger enters the lists. Excellent, sir."

"Ten!"

Felicity looked quickly back to the first bidder who had countered. An ordinary face. Nothing remarkable or frightening about it. Her alarm lessened a trifle. She might manage to fend him off if he pried too closely.

"Now you are talking, gentlemen." The auctioneer gestured to the new bidder. "Don't let her slip through your fingers for a mere ten, Abinger."

Mere? Ten guineas? A fortune! Not that Felicity would receive a penny of it. As far as she could see, no money changed hands. Each winning gentleman took his prize to a table at the side and wrote a chit. She had watched it happen during the long wait, desperate for any distraction from anxiety. Had Lord Maskery known all this? Could he not have warned her? Where had he got to?

"Twelve guineas!"

Her gaze darted back to the chubby-faced creature, who was laughing as the company about him encouraged him with both word and gesture.

"Go to it, old fellow!"

"An intriguing prize, if you can get her."

Catching the murmur, Felicity felt the warmth leap into her face. Intriguing? Dear heaven, if they knew the truth! She should never have consented. She should have stayed at the academy where she was safe. Dull, yes. But secure at least. This was fast turning into a nightmare. Where in the world was Mrs Sprake? All the other duennas or mothers had watched over their charges while they took their turn.

"Fifteen!"

"Sixteen!"

"Sixteen and a groat!"

"Sixteen and sixpence!"

Laughter rang in Felicity's ears as the vying gentlemen fell into a ridiculous game, raising the stakes by a few pence each time. They shifted out of their spheres, moving to confront one another, taunting bids at each other face to face. It ceased to be about Felicity at all, and she breathed more easily. If only she could slip away right now. But that would make her even more conspicuous, raise more questions.

When they reached seventeen, the auctioneer intervened.

"Enough jollification, gentlemen! Come, we have more young ladies to put up. Let us have a solid bid, sirs."

The two fellows laughed, and the chubby one cuffed the other on the shoulder.

"You take her, Finglesham, I'm done."

"No, I concede, Abinger. You said seventeen, not I."

"Did I? I thought that was you."

The heat of embarrassment enveloped Felicity. Neither of them wanted her at all! Her heart sank. The mockery was justified. What else did she expect?

"Gentlemen, gentlemen, if you please. Allow me to be the judge." The auctioneer was moving across to join them when a deep voice spoke.

"Enough of this folly, Nalderwood. I will give twenty guineas for the lady."

Felicity followed the sound as all eyes turned towards the speaker. She glimpsed a tall man, darkly shadowed. As he moved into the light, the breath stopped in her throat. It was the gentleman she'd glimpsed before she took the dais. Watching her. Or so she'd thought. Heavens, it was indeed he! Lean and powerful, with strong, stark features and shaggy, raven hair.

A thread of discomfort snaked through Felicity and her mind clouded. The whole scene slipped into unreality and her head felt light. Panic gripped her. *Do not faint, do not faint.*

"My lord Lynchmere wins it," cried the auctioneer, throwing up his arms. "Miss Temple is yours, sir!"

Felicity watched his approach, only half aware of the hush that fell upon the room. Rendered speechless by this wholly unforeseen outcome, she met the hard stare in a pair of steel-grey eyes.

"Miss Temple?"

A hand was offered. Felicity put out quivering gloved fingers and a strong clasp closed over them.

11

The girl was trembling. She almost tripped as she stepped off the dais and Raoul had to reach out his free hand to help her down.

"Steady!"

She threw a glance up at him out of those unexpectedly candid eyes that had stared at him as he came up. "My thanks."

Low and unsteady. Conscious of a sliver of sympathy, he guided her away from the dais. But as he moved towards the table where he must pay for this folly, he saw Angelica bobbing about behind it, evidently trying to catch his eye. He hardened his heart.

"Am I so formidable, Miss Temple? Or is it the experience of putting yourself up to the highest bidder?"

Another glance. Eyes of a colour intense yet indeterminate. Green? Blue? Grey? A mixture. Apprehensive, certainly. But her words belied it.

"Both, sir. You would scare anyone to death and the ordeal dismayed me."

Raoul almost laughed out. "You may blame my cousin for both. This was her notion and she insisted upon my presence."

Angelica had heard him, just as he intended. She moved in, smiling at the girl as she gestured to the table. "Sign your promise, Raoul. He is a very lucky man, Miss — Temple, is it? I don't believe we've met."

The girl removed her hand from his arm and dropped a curtsey. "We have not, ma'am."

"I am Angelica Summerhayes, and this ill-mannered boor who has won you is my cousin Raoul. He is the Marquis of Lynchmere, you must know."

Raoul was signing his IOU for twenty guineas, presented by a clerkly fellow who was keeping the tally. He threw down the quill and straightened. "I consider Miss Temple a bargain, Angelica." He offered his arm. "I believe you are mine for the evening. Is that not so, dear cousin?"

"For supper, Raoul. You need not monopolise poor Miss Temple all night."

"What, my twenty guineas buys me only supper? For shame, Angelica. I shall claim a deal more than that."

He produced a wolfish smile for his cousin's edification and swept Miss Temple away from the table. She did not appear to be either flattered or troubled as he guided a path for them, skirting the low chattering crowd as the bidding started up again. She was scanning the room searchingly.

"You have lost something, Miss Temple?"

Her gaze came back to his. "My chaperon."

"Ah, I was wondering why I had not been accosted by a worrisome mama. They are usually very eager to seize the day."

Her eyes raked his face. Was there still anxiety there? If so, it was overlaid with faint question. Or was it disapproval?

"I suppose you are excessively eligible. Oh, wait. Marquis? I was not attending very closely, I'm afraid. My head still feels a trifle cloudy."

She was either pert beyond words or too innocent for her own good. Raoul suspected the latter. A suspicion burgeoned. "Do you know anyone in this assembly?"

"Only my guardian and Mrs Sprake." Consternation entered her eyes. "Oh, he told me not to say that."

Intrigued, Raoul eyed her. "Who is your guardian?"

"Lord Maskery."

That fellow? He knew him, too well and with good reason. Raoul hesitated, reluctant to release the words hovering on his tongue. He kept them back. "Let us find a quieter spot, Miss Temple," he said instead.

13

She made no demur, but her gaze continued the hunt as he eased her around the back of the crowd and out into an adjoining saloon. It was by no means empty, being occupied by several partnered couples from the auction, along with a few elderly persons who preferred to sit and talk rather than watch the farce inside the ballroom.

Raoul found a free sofa and obliged his prize to sit, taking his place beside her and signing to one of the hovering waiters. "You will take a glass of something, Miss Temple?"

She was fiddling with her fan, her eyes on the uncarpeted floor, but she looked up at this. "Yes, if you please. Not wine. I must keep my wits about me."

He wondered if she meant against himself and was amused again. Or was there once more a touch of apprehension in those eyes?

"Lemonade for the lady," he told the waiter who was bowing before them. "I'll take Burgundy, if you have it."

Evidently the Latimers could still afford a decent cellar, for the man made no demur. The moment he departed, Miss Temple turned a little towards him.

"You may as well know now as later, sir."

Startled, and reluctantly interested, he raised his brows. "Know what, Miss Temple? Are you about to reveal some dreadful secret?"

Her direct gaze did not flinch. "Yes."

This girl was singularly intriguing. He attempted a light note. "But why not keep the feminine trick of maintaining an air of mystery?"

"I cannot."

Was there a note of anguish? The scent of danger was in his nostrils. Was this a ploy? Almost he did not ask, but the words slipped out. "Why not?"

She looked away and back, then down to the fan, now folded and clenched between her fingers. Her voice dropped to a murmur. "Because I suspect I have been tricked."

It was so unexpected Raoul simply stared at the bent head for a moment. What in the world did this mean? He recalled her confession that she knew no one here beyond Maskery and a duenna of sorts. Instinct urged him to extract himself from a threatening imbroglio, but this wretched little redhead had touched a nerve. Innate chivalry? He was not quite a monster, though Angelica was apt so to condemn him.

"What is it you fear, Miss Temple?"

His tone of careful quiet seemed to soothe her for she looked up, meeting his gaze in that candid way she had. "I think they have abandoned me. I have not seen either for more than an hour." Her fingers fiddled, spreading the fan open in her lap and closing it again, her eyes registering discomfort as they flicked away and back again. "I beg your pardon. I suppose I should not trouble you with all this. I ought to engage you in light-hearted banter. Is that not how it is done? I'm afraid I have no feminine arts."

He was oddly touched. "Light-hearted banter bores me. I am besides inured to the lure of feminine arts." A tiny smile flitted across her face, wrinkling the freckles. Raoul watched them straighten again. He raised his quizzing-glass to his eye. "Fascinating."

Her eyes grew wide. "I beg your pardon?"

"When you smile, your freckles shift like a dance of tiny creatures on your cheeks."

Her mouth dropped open and a little peal of laughter escaped, transforming the piquant face. Her eyes warmed.

Raoul was conscious of a flitter of something in the region of his chest. Dropping the glass, he suppressed it swiftly, adept through long habit.

Miss Temple's brief instant of merriment disappeared equally fast. "Is that meant for flirtation, sir?"

He raised his brows. "Did it sound like it?"

She gave a little sigh. "I really have no idea. I have no experience of such things."

"Good God, where have you been, Miss Temple?"

Once again her clear gaze confronted his. "In an academy, my lord, teaching girls deportment and how to behave."

"A schoolmistress? You don't look old enough."

He said it before the oddity of it struck him. But the inevitable question was balked by the arrival of the waiter with refreshments. Raoul took the glass of lemonade presented on the tray and handed it to Miss Temple, taking the wine for himself. He sipped, watching her lift the glass to her lips and gulp down quite half the liquid in a bang. She lowered the glass and touched her gloved fingers to the corners of her lips, drawing breath.

"I needed that so very much."

He was amused. "So I perceive."

She hesitated, fiddling now with the glass instead of her fan, which lay folded in her lap. He awaited what next she might say with barely contained impatience. Miss Temple was so very unexpected. She did not disappoint.

"Would you object very much if I were to slip away?"

"From my company or this party?"

"Both."

"Yes, I should." He surprised himself with the vehemence of his response. He prevaricated. "I will have pledged twenty guineas to no purpose. Why do you wish to slip away?"

"Because they may perhaps have returned to the inn."

"They being this guardian and duenna, I presume?"

"Lord Maskery and Mrs Sprake, yes."

He frowned. "Are you sure they are not still here? Either or both may have gone into another room."

She studied the glass in her hands, or so it seemed to Raoul. Then she lifted her eyes to his and there was hurt in them. "She promised to remain within sight. My guardian was adamant she should. I know very well I could not attend without an older female, even though I am no green girl."

"You may not consider yourself a girl, but you are undoubtedly green, Miss Temple. What do you know of Maskery?"

She flinched. "Not very much. I've known him as my guardian for years, but he did no more than see that I was placed in the academy in Bath. I believe it was he who arranged for me to become a teacher there when I should be old enough."

Raoul was reluctantly disturbed by this snippet of history. Dumping the girl in some school was in keeping with what he knew of Maskery. This begged the question of why he had dragged her out of it and foisted her on an unsuspecting public. Yet he was hanged if he wanted to become involved. He hedged. "How old are you, if I may ask without seeming impertinent?"

She looked him in the eye again. "I am two and twenty, sir."

"You look younger. I would not have taken you for more than eighteen."

The brief smile appeared again. "I've been told so before. But I can assure you I am all of my years and I have been a mistress at the academy since I was fifteen."

Startled, he eyed her with keen interest now. "You've been teaching for seven years?"

"You perceive why I have had no time to acquire feminine arts, no doubt."

He had to smile. "You don't need them, Miss Temple. I must beg you will refrain from trying."

She neither smiled nor laughed. "I should doubt whether I will have the slightest use for them, my lord. I foresee an early return to the academy, for I cannot think my career in the *Ton* is likely to last beyond this night."

CHAPTER TWO

A loud cheer from the ballroom distracted Felicity's jumping thoughts. Lord Lynchmere glanced towards the sound, a wry twist to his lips.

"You need not repine. To be obliged to endure this sort of thing is, I assure you, more a penance than a pleasure."

The tone was dry, and Felicity recognised a cynical note she had heard before. It was in keeping with her first impression of him. He had proved oddly contrary, like one of the academy pupils in recalcitrant mood. At one moment perfectly amiable, at another decidedly alienating.

She struggled against the increasing sensation of oppression. She ought to be flattered by his lordship's attention. He was a marquis, after all. Felicity found it hard to care. She had never expected to be obliged to curry favour in society and could not conjure the falsity of being impressed with rank. She certainly had no reason to do so. The girls in her care had uniformly misbehaved, regardless of whether their fathers were dukes or mere gentlemen.

"You are very thoughtful, Miss Temple."

Startled out of her preoccupation, Felicity blinked at her companion. "I beg your pardon. Is it rude of me?"

"Very."

"Yes, I suppose it is." She eyed him, trying to find words that had no bearing on her disturbing situation. They would not come. "I'm sorry for it, sir. I know it ill becomes me to return your attentions with nothing but worrisome plaints, but I find it hard to think of anything but the predicament in which I now find myself."

There was a frown in his gaze, which was unwavering. He paused a moment, and then shifted his stance so that he faced her more completely. "I acquit you."

Perplexed, Felicity frowned back. "Of what, if you please?"

"Rudeness, for one. For another, engaging in an ingenious ploy to capture my interest."

A rush of heat took Felicity unawares. She acted on it before she could think of the wisdom of her words. "Oh, indeed? You supposed I was setting my cap at you? Heavens above, my lord, if I were ninny enough to think myself worthy of the honour, I would be stupid indeed to suppose I might attract a man by behaving in a fashion which might well make him suppose me to be demented! I am aware I have been all too distracted, but I promise you I have no slightest desire to capture the interest of you, or any other gentleman — of whatever rank or eligibility."

His brows rose and he lifted his quizzing glass to his eye, regarding her through it in a manner as patronising as it was infuriating. "But what a heat!"

"What an arrogance!"

The quizzing glass dropped and he laughed out. "Excellently done, Miss Temple. You are an original, I'll give you that."

"Thank you. I am flattered beyond words."

An oddly attractive crinkle at the corners of his eyes lent warmth to his otherwise harsh features. Felicity's ruffled temper began to cool, allowing her underlying agitation room to return. On impulse, she threw him a smile. "Well, you succeeded in turning my thoughts for a moment, my lord. I will thank you for that."

He bowed his head, the amusement still visible in his face. "An estimable pleasure, ma'am." He glanced again towards the ballroom from where, Felicity realised, the noise of chatter and laughter was increasing. "I apprehend this foul auction is now over. Should you care to stroll the rooms in search of your errant guardian?"

He rose on the words and Felicity followed suit with alacrity.

"Yes, if you please." She set her hand on his proffered arm and threw a glance up into his face, which had returned to a set look of jaded boredom. Felicity strongly suspected it was habitual. She recalled an earlier notion she'd picked up from his conversation. "You know Lord Maskery, sir?"

The cynical look reappeared as he turned and met her gaze. "Too well."

She spoke her thought aloud. "You don't like him."

"Not in the least." He began to lead her in the direction of the ballroom. "Does it trouble you?"

"No, my lord. I do not like him either."

He glanced down, amusement once more in his eyes. "How extraordinarily well we agree on so many things, Miss Temple."

Nettled, she snapped back. "We do not. I wish you will not talk to me in that flirtatious way."

"You find it flirtatious?"

"Isn't it?"

"Not intentionally, I assure you."

"Well, I'm glad of that at all events. Please may we simply look?"

His brows lifted. "I thought we were looking. So far, I am drawing a blank. Do you see your duenna anywhere?"

They had arrived at the open double doorway that let into the ballroom, if it was one. For the first time, Felicity glanced at the proportions of the room. She had been too agitated to take in more than a general impression of elegance, light and vastness. Now she saw that the size of both room and crowd was exaggerated by several pier-glass mirrors at either side.

21

The guests were beginning to disperse, moving in a purposeful direction through the doorway and following, Felicity saw, a bowing and gesturing major-domo. The purpose of this exodus was explained by Lord Lynchmere.

"It would seem supper is the next order of business. Would you care to join the throng?"

She was not conscious of hunger. Rather of a growling empty hollow that spoke of bewilderment and despair. There was no sign either of Mrs Sprake or her guardian. "I suppose there is nothing else to be done." Was there a faint hope either one or other might be found in the supper room?

"We could starve instead, but I would not advocate it."

Her mood lightened briefly as she laughed. "Are you always as sarcastic as this?"

"It is an art, Miss Temple." He gave a small bow but his lips twitched. "I do my poor best."

He drew her into the line of chattering, laughing guests, thinning by this time. Felicity could not refrain from checking faces as the line crossed the rapidly emptying saloon with its couches about the walls, traversed a short hallway and entered a dining-room set with several tables already occupied. The moving line brought Felicity within sight of sideboards containing a selection of viands piled high on serving dishes, which were being rapidly demolished.

"They are not in such sore straits they cannot afford to feed their guests in a lavish fashion."

The murmur from her companion startled Felicity and she looked up. "What did you say, sir?"

"Nothing." He was frowning, clearly preoccupied, but as he met her gaze the frown cleared and he produced a smile she found superficial. "Allow me to procure you a repast before the lot disappears. Chicken?"

His purgatory was coming to an end, he hoped. With supper over, the business of the evening could be said to be complete. There was to be no dancing, Angelica had informed him in a brief moment as she passed from couple to couple in the supper room, merely a conversable evening against a background of music provided by a string quartet. "To give our auction partners an opportunity to get to know each other," as his cousin put it.

In the event, it was obvious this plan fell sadly flat with the guests after the excitement of the bidding. A number of them were finding excuses to leave and the groups were growing sparse in the saloon, the chatter desultory. Raoul was tempted to emulate several gentlemen who had ruthlessly abandoned their prizes. But since Miss Temple had no duenna to re-join as several forlorn debutantes had been obliged to do, it would be churlish to leave her flat.

Thrust into the thick of things in the supper room, the girl had lost all the charm of her unexpected candour. Raoul found her subdued, her responses to his sallies mechanical. She ate sparingly and if she looked about her it was only, he was persuaded, to satisfy herself that her errant duenna and guardian had not made an appearance.

There had been a brief instance of animation when she had paused with her fork halfway to her mouth, her gaze riveted upon the doorway.

"Miss Temple?"

She glanced at him but immediately trained her eyes back to where a couple of footmen stood either side of the open door. "I thought I saw him."

"Who?"

"My guardian."

"Maskery?" She half rose from her chair. Raoul set down his napkin. "Stay where you are. I will go and see."

It had taken several minutes to weave a path through the noisy tables and by the time he reached the door, Maskery had vanished. If he had been there at all. Raoul made a cursory sweep of the immediate area beyond the door, even venturing into the gallery and checking the stairwell and what he could see of the hall below.

"I believe you must have been mistaken, Miss Temple," he told her when he had managed to wend his way back.

She had accepted this, but the interlude rendered her more distrait and silent than before.

Creeping tedium threatened. Yet it was overlaid with an irritating snake of concern Raoul found impossible to shake off. Had the fellow indeed looked in? If so, where the devil was he? And why in heaven's name had he left the girl without support?

It was none of his affair and he had no desire to become involved in whatever shambles was brewing here. Especially with a girl under Maskery's care. Although, if she was of age, presumably she might do as she pleased.

Yes, return to this academy of hers to teach ghastly young madams how to comport themselves in public, whispered an infuriating voice in his head. As if Miss Temple herself had any notion how to behave. She had treated him with none of the deference due to his position — though he must admit to a preference for that. He loathed the toad-eating simpers of your average debutante. Miss Temple did not simper. Nor was she arch. But neither was she animated. At least, she had been, but no longer.

"I am poor company, I'm afraid," she said suddenly, as if she echoed his thought.

"Not at all," he returned, as mechanically as she had spoken earlier.

Her open gaze met his. "You are being polite."

"I do know how."

A shadow crossed her face. "Which is as much as to say I don't. Alas, I know it." She fidgeted with her fan, glancing absently about the room, and then looked at him again. "I dare say it would be best if you were to escort me downstairs and ask someone to procure me a hackney."

Release? Perversely, Raoul's conscience kicked in. "I shall do no such thing."

"Why not, when you are wishing me at Jericho?"

The resumption of her earlier manner had the effect of driving off his irritation. "I am, of course, but I have more civility than to acknowledge it." Her face broke into laughter and a tiny crack opened in Raoul's defences. Aware of it, he summoned them back. "A better plan, I believe, will be to inform Angelica of your difficulty."

"Your cousin?"

"She's a resourceful creature, I'll give her that. She is bound to think of some scheme to succour you."

The girl's eyes dimmed. "I thank you, but I have no need of any scheme. Mrs Jeavons will take me back."

He frowned in an effort of memory. "I thought you said she was Mrs Sprake. And since she is nowhere to be found —"

"I don't mean that creature. Mrs Jeavons is the headmistress at the academy. My only difficulty is finding means to travel back to Bath, but I think I can manage to pay my way on the stage."

An unwelcome image entered his head, of Miss Temple, squashed in a corner of one of these rumbling stagecoaches for hours as she returned to a life of drudgery. Raoul dismissed it.

"That would be quite ineligible. Let us go in search of my cousin."

Angelica was discovered, after some scouting about the main rooms, deep in discussion with the clerkly fellow in the deserted ballroom.

"Then you will send to the gentlemen who have not made good on their pledges, Gawcott." She looked up at Raoul's approach. "Ah, here is my cousin. I don't suppose you carry any money on you, Raoul? No, I thought not. Gawcott will send to your secretary. How are you faring, Miss — Temple, was it?"

"Yes, it was," said Raoul, seizing her by the elbow and drawing her away from the clerk, "and she is faring ill."

Angelica's blue orbs exhibited instant sympathy as they turned on the girl. "Dear me, are you feeling unwell, my dear? I am so sorry. Do you wish to go home? Raoul, why have you not called for Miss Temple's carriage?"

"She does not have one," he said, exasperated. "For heaven's sake, hold that rattling tongue of yours for a moment, Angie!"

"Well, really, Raoul, there is no necessity to be —"

"There is every necessity. Miss Temple is not sick, but she does need your help."

To his chagrin, the girl cut in. "I did ask him to arrange a hackney, ma'am. I have no wish to trouble you with my difficulties. I need no assistance."

"Yes, you do. I won't have you gallivanting off on a stagecoach," Raoul snapped.

"It is hardly gallivanting, and it's none of your affair!"

"I am making it my affair. Be quiet!" He became aware of his cousin's open-mouthed astonishment and checked himself. "She's lost both her guardian and her chaperon and she does not know anyone. I have no notion why, but evidently Miss

Temple has left her post at some academy in Bath at the behest of Maskery, and she is now at a loss. I told her you would think of something."

Angelica, looking both bewildered and entertained, if he was any judge, fastened on the last point. "Of course I will think of something. I always do. But Maskery, did you say?" She turned to the girl. "Do you tell me that awful man is your guardian? How dreadful for you!"

"Angelica!"

But Miss Temple's freckles were shifting as she laughed. "You and Lord Lynchmere are much alike, I perceive, ma'am."

Angelica threw up hands of mock horror. "Do not say so! He is quite a boor while I am perfectly amiable. I utterly reject any comparison at all."

"Ditto." Raoul eyed Miss Temple. "I shall not ask in what capacity you descry a resemblance, but instead request you both to stick to the res. What are we going to do with you?"

Miss Temple sighed. "Really, sir, there is nothing you can do. As I said before, the best plan will be for me to return to the inn. At least I may discover some news of Lord Maskery. Besides, everything I own is in my room there."

The last held a note of anguish, and Raoul was again plagued by an unwanted stir of compassion. Before he could say anything, Angelica butted in again.

"My poor dear girl, whatever do you mean? Have you no home to go to? Why in the world are you staying at an inn with Maskery? It is not at all the thing, you know."

"She wasn't alone with Maskery, but this Sprake woman has also disappeared." Raoul made up his mind. "I had best take you to this inn of yours, Miss Temple."

She appeared at once relieved. "Oh, would you indeed?"

"Certainly not," chimed in Angelica. "Without a chaperon? It is not to be thought of."

Raoul sighed. "Angelica, don't start to make a lot of difficulties."

"I am not, but you know perfectly well it is quite improper for you to escort Miss Temple, and I cannot possibly leave yet. Margaret is depending upon me."

About to argue, Raoul was forestalled by Miss Temple.

"Ma'am, pray don't disturb yourself. Once I am deposited at the Black Swan, I may fend for myself. I have no intention of compromising Lord Lynchmere, if that is what you fear."

Raoul laughed. "The boot, Miss Temple, is on the other leg."

"Exactly so," agreed Angelica.

"Then I shall slip away by myself."

"That you won't." Raoul took her by the elbow as she showed signs of walking off. "I will take you. Don't fret, Angie. Nothing will come of it."

"But I thought you wanted me to think of something."

"Not at the moment. Let us first find out what the devil is going on."

The drive, in Lord Lynchmere's well-appointed carriage, did not take many minutes. But they were minutes fraught with question. Felicity sat bolt upright, clutching the hanging loop to steady herself with one hand, and with the other holding together the edges of her cloak retrieved for her by a footman.

Lost in dark thoughts, she had half-forgotten the presence of the figure beside her until he spoke from the darkness.

"What troubles you the most, Miss Temple?"

Startled, as much by his perception as his voice, she answered with truth. "That I have been betrayed."

"By Maskery? How?"

Her breath caught in her throat and she struggled to sound normal. "He said he had a new life planned for me, that I would be as his daughter and enjoy the pleasures of society."

"You believed him?"

She caught the sceptical note and turned to look at Lord Lynchmere, seeing only a shadowed face where he sat at his ease against the squabs. "No, if you want the truth. I had doubts from the outset. He had not previously led me to suppose he entertained any desire for my happiness."

"Then why did you agree?"

She shivered and turned away. "You may well ask. He was insistent, plausible in some ways. And Mrs Jeavons added her persuasions. She said bluntly I ought to take this chance to escape the life she'd had to live or I would regret it my lifelong. In the end, it seemed churlish and stupid to hold out."

"But your doubts remained."

She drew a shaky breath. "They grew worse." Somehow it was easier to talk of her folly in the dimness of the coach. "To be housed at an inn was a shock. Lord Maskery explained he owned no house in town and could not with propriety take me to his lodging. When he installed Mrs Sprake —"

She stopped, feeling anew all the revulsion the creature had evoked in her. It was not merely the twang she detected beneath Mrs Sprake's over-refined speech. Nor yet the falsity of her overtures of affection. Felicity's skin had crawled at the assessing look in the woman's eyes as they went over her, at the darting tongue that wetted her lips whenever she exchanged a glance with Lord Maskery.

The carriage was slowing, dragging her mind out of the memory.

"I believe we have arrived. You may tell me the rest later."

If there was to be a later. The thought flitted through Felicity's head and was gone as the coach lurched through an archway and came to a standstill. She could see through the window the flicker of light and motion in the yard of the Black Swan.

Grinding anxiety returned and Felicity had to force herself to move as the door opened and one of Lord Lynchmere's liveried servants let down the steps. He moved beside her.

"Let me go first."

She sat back to give him room to pass. Next moment, he had jumped down and turned to hand her out of the coach. She climbed down and looked up into his face, his features harsh in the half-light of the yard. "Thank you, sir. I can manage now."

"Don't be ridiculous. I am coming in with you."

She was hit with a flurry in her bosom, part gratitude, part apprehension. "There is no need, I assure you."

"I'll be the judge of that. Come."

He picked up her hand and tucked it into his arm perforce. Why in the world he should take it upon himself to assume responsibility, Felicity could not imagine.

"I can't think why you must needs be so masterful about it."

One of his wry laughs came. "Am I being so?"

"Decidedly."

"Long habit, I expect."

She did not answer. They were approaching the rear entrance to the inn, and his lordship's lackey slipped ahead to open the door, affording her a glimpse of the very different lifestyle a marquis held to that of a lowly schoolmistress. But the thought was fleeting as remembrance of her predicament returned.

The landlord was apologetic and obsequious, a circumstance Felicity at once attributed to the presence of Lord Lynchmere. Her room, it appeared, was no longer available for her use.

"I regret infinitely, madam, but I had not anticipated your return. I assumed, when his lordship paid his shot, that the whole party had departed."

Aghast, Felicity stared at the man. "But my belongings! I had not packed. You cannot have allowed another to occupy the room!"

The landlord, a portly fellow, spread his hands. "Unfortunately, madam, this is indeed the case. I apprehend Lord Maskery appropriated anything left in your chamber since he and the — er — lady sent down several portmanteaux."

The words began to dance in Felicity's head, making no sense. She could not think. An image of the room as she had left it at the start of the evening played in her head, her personal accoutrements, meagre as they were, scattered about, her valise standing near the dresser, less than half its contents having been taken out.

"Allow me, Miss Temple."

She had forgotten her escort, who had remained in the background while she questioned the landlord in the vestibule below the stairs. He moved past her to confront the landlord.

"I presume you have a lady wife? Fetch her, if you please."

"Of course, of course, my lord." The landlord bowed himself out of the vestibule, disappearing down a narrow hallway.

Felicity was beyond asking what Lord Lynchmere would be at. Numbness threatened to rob her of every faculty. She was hardly aware of speaking. "My things! If they are gone, I have nothing but the clothes on my back, and they are not mine."

"How did you come by them? Maskery?"

There was no vestige of sympathy in his tone and, curiously, Felicity found its matter-of-factness bracing. The feeling of unreality began to recede. "Mrs Sprake furnished the gown. My undergarments are my own. The cloak too. But that is nothing

31

to the purpose, sir. Clothes may be replaced, though how in the world —" She broke off and started again. "What I mean is there are personal items, mementoes, articles I cherish."

The miniature of her mama and the locket with the curl of her own infant hair; Papa's journal, which was all she had left of him now. If these were lost to her, then she was lost indeed.

"It may yet prove that your belongings have not been removed, Miss Temple. Or if they have, perhaps Maskery had at least the decency to secrete them somewhere. The landlady will know."

The rise of grief engendered by the thought of her loss receded. "You suppose he may have left my valise with her? I cannot think it. The landlord must have known if he did."

"Let us wait and see. One thing at a time, Miss Temple."

It made sense, but all too many things were crowding into Felicity's head all at once. If her valise was gone, she had no money either. What little coin she possessed was secreted in an old leather glove and a couple of stockings, pushed to the bottom of the case. She had now no means of travelling to Bath, let alone anything suitable to wear for the journey. Where was she to sleep? How was she to eat? The hideous truth came home to her.

"I am destitute." She did not know she spoke aloud. "Why has he done this to me? To what end? If he meant to abandon me, why fetch me from the academy at all? Why not leave me there to earn my keep as I could? Instead, he has lured me with false promises and reduced me to penury. Why? I don't understand."

Two strong hands took her by the shoulders and Lord Lynchmere's harsh tones struck at her. "Enough! Falling into hysterics will not help. All these questions may be addressed in due course. For this present, let us find out the position of affairs and then we will decide what to do."

The panic began to leave her. She drew a breath and pulled herself out of his hold. "You are right, sir. I am glad you are here. I fear I have no choice but to throw myself upon your mercy. Or rather, that of your cousin, if she will be so good."

"Now you are talking like a sensible woman. Angelica will be delighted. Nothing pleases her more than to run other people's lives. She will embrace the challenge with alacrity."

Felicity produced a smile more mechanical than real. She had never felt more bereft, even when she became an orphan, but in the face of his lordship's avowals, it would be ungrateful to say so. "Thank you, my lord, you are very good."

"I'm not, and I much prefer your acerbity. I don't doubt you are too much oppressed to be capable of it at this moment."

She was touched by his understanding, and once again surprised at his perspicacity. The landlord returning at this moment, accompanied by a stout dame in a mobcap, she let the matter drop. Her eager expectation was disappointed.

"No, ma'am, I'm afraid there was nothing left."

"No note, nor any message?"

"None, sir. And the room is taken. We have no other tonight, I'm afraid."

Felicity's heart sank, and she could only be relieved that Lord Lynchmere took this on her behalf.

"Thank you, but Miss Temple will be staying with Mrs Summerhayes. She has no need of a room."

A sensation of cold was seeping into Felicity's limbs. She watched without really taking it in as coin changed hands and without demur allowed herself to be ushered out of the inn and handed back up into the waiting coach. She sank against the squabs and closed her eyes, feeling the shivers start up as Lord Lynchmere gave the direction to his lackey.

The vehicle shifted with his weight as he jumped in and then settled when he took his seat beside her. Felicity tried to control the tremors now fighting for supremacy, hoping he would not notice. In vain.

"Are you cold, Miss Temple?"

She tried for a calm tone, though her teeth chattered. "Not c-cold, sir. It's the-the shock. I've seen it in one of the girls b-before. It will p-pass in a moment."

He seemed to hesitate. Then, to Felicity's combined dismay and reluctant gratitude, he put an arm about her shoulders and pulled her into a powerful embrace.

CHAPTER THREE

Locked in the alien arms, Felicity felt only warmth and the needed comfort of a temporary haven while the tremors shook her frame. They receded in time and she became aware of the rocking of the carriage instead of her shaking body.

She made a move to free herself and the embrace loosened, yet keeping a steadying hold.

"Better?"

Abruptly conscious of the indecorous nature of her position, Felicity tugged gently away and sat back. "Much, thank you."

"Had I my flask on me, I would have administered a tot of brandy."

She gave a little laugh that broke in the middle. Suppressing the urge to sob, she summoned as ordinary a tone as she could manage. "Where are you taking me? Not back to the party, I trust?"

"I have no choice." The deep voice came at her from the darkness, throwing a fleeting remembrance of the early part of the evening into her mind. "Angelica will not have left. She considers herself a hostess there, having assumed in some sort responsibility for the Latimers."

"A family trait, then?"

A faint laugh came. "Come, you begin to be yourself again."

Felicity had no answer. She felt, on the contrary, as though she occupied some other plane. But the thought of entering into public again was real enough. "Must I go in? Could I not await you in the coach?"

"What, and give every fool in London food for gossip? Besides, I should imagine most of the guests will have departed."

Felicity said no more. She was in his hands and grateful for it. Though she must suppose his lordship would be thankful to hand over the charge to his cousin. She would be obliged to depend upon Mrs Summerhayes, at least for tonight. Perhaps she might borrow suitable garments and enough money for her journey to Bath, if not tomorrow then the day after. She could post the clothes back once she had acquired her own, although how she was to do so remained a question. There might be something wearable in the trunks in the attics, a jumble of items forgotten over the years when girls left the academy. As for her fare, she could ask for an advance upon her salary. It would leave her seriously short for months, but what other option was open to her?

An access of light drew her gaze and she glimpsed the bobbing flambeaux and the blaze of candles from the house she had so recently left. A patter arose in her bosom as her thoughts shifted to the immediate future and her ignominious reduction to the status of beggar.

Respecting her silence, Raoul found room for the questions he would by no means force upon Miss Temple. She had fastened upon the salient point at once. What the devil was Maskery about? If he did not know the man so well, his conduct would be inexplicable. Not that Raoul could explain it, except to know it was not a random act of insanity. His actions were deliberate and smacked of a plot with all the hallmarks of the kind of villainy to be expected from a man with few moral limitations.

Raoul knew him for an inveterate gamester with a regrettable addiction to drink, women and the fleshpots. His reputation was unsavoury, to say the least, and it was rumoured he lived on a constant knife-edge of ruin. Certain it was he had not yet paid the IOUs Raoul himself held from an evening at Faro when he had held the bank. Maskery had asked for time and that was more than a week since.

Was Miss Temple's involvement to do with some scheme to avoid disaster? Exactly how Maskery sought to use her was unclear, but if he had driven himself to *point non plus* even the embarrassment of a dependent ward might be too much.

Although was she dependent? She said she was able to pay her way. Then what? How could he gain from leaving her friendless and alone, destitute as she had said? Or had he anticipated some such outcome as had occurred? Was he relying on the compassion of his world? Or, no. Was Maskery expecting or hoping Miss Temple might be compromised? He could then reappear to play the outraged guardian and demand recompense.

A niggle of regret snaked into Raoul's head. Why had he to give in to a moment's impulse and make that bid? What the deuce had he got himself into?

The arrival at the Latimer establishment was welcome. Once he had handed the girl over to Angelica, he could wash his hands of the business.

The door opened and he made to alight. Miss Temple put out a hand. "Stay, my lord."

"Yes?" She hesitated, peering at him. Raoul noted a faint line between her brows and cursed inwardly. He had not meant to sound harsh. "What is it, Miss Temple?"

She shook her head. "Nothing."

He did not pursue it, conscious of a disquieting mixture of guilt overlaid by irritation. At himself rather than Miss Temple. This was not her fault.

He got out and helped her down. Her hand was cold even through the glove and the inner disturbance increased. The sooner he extracted himself from this situation the better. It was shaping up to prove a confounded nuisance.

At least the rooms were virtually empty, those guests still remaining clearly in the process of making their farewells. Raoul guided his unwanted charge swiftly past the coterie around Mr and Mrs Latimer and hastened in search of his cousin. He found her sitting in the smaller saloon, in animated discussion with the twin daughters of the house.

The two girls looked round and the more outspoken Silvestre chirped up at once.

"Oh, Lord Lynchmere, there you are! We thought you had gone, and I did so want to ask you —" She broke off, her gaze travelling to the cloaked figure at his side.

Raoul's irritation increased. There could be no doubt of where her curiosity had been tending. She wanted to ask about the mysterious Miss Temple.

"I need a word with my cousin, Miss Latimer, if you will be so good."

His repressive tone had its effect as Silvestre's cheeks flew colour. But he found himself called to order by Angelica, who rose to meet him.

"For shame, Raoul, how can you? You have no need to dismiss Silve and Hetty, because they have very kindly offered to take care of Miss Temple tonight, should it prove necessary."

Infuriated, Raoul glared at her. "You told them? For God's sake, Angelica! Why didn't you just announce it to one and all?"

At this, Silvestre blushed again, but the softer Henrietta jumped up, frothing expostulation. "Oh, no, I assure you, my lord, we would not dream of saying a word. So horrid for poor Miss Temple!"

"There, you see, Raoul. You may trust them implicitly."

"Yes, indeed. Pray don't fear our tongues. Why, we are obliged to be discreet on our own account." With which Henrietta put out her hands to his companion. "Dear Miss Temple, we are so very sorry. If we'd had an inkling of the truth, we should not have put you forward as we did. I do hope you were not overly embarrassed."

Raoul found himself relegated to the background as Henrietta and Angelica between them drew Miss Temple into their circle and obliged her to sit. She was looking bemused, as well she might, and she had not yet spoken a word. At least, he recalled a vague murmur. Had she said his name?

A faint resentment at being ousted attacked him, but he crushed it. He had wanted to be rid of the business, had he not?

"Did you not find Lord Maskery then, sir?" Silvestre Latimer had come up. "Mrs Summerhayes said you had gone in search of him."

The last was added in a placatory tone, as if she sought to excuse her previous lapse of tact. A trifle ashamed of his earlier rudeness, Raoul offered an abrupt apology.

"Forgive me, Miss Latimer. It's been a difficult evening and my temper is rubbed."

She made no comment on this. "But what did you find at the inn, my lord?"

39

"Nothing. Maskery had paid his shot and left, along with Miss Temple's chaperon and all her belongings."

"He abandoned her?" The hushed tone spoke her shock. "How cruel! And why? Why would he do such a thing?"

"That is what we all wish to know, Miss Latimer." He had no intention of airing his views on the subject. "Not a word of this, if you please."

"No, indeed. But what will she do? How can we help her?"

His opinion of her rose. "It would seem you are already helping. As for what she will do, I dare say you will find Miss Temple has her own views on the subject."

Silvestre's unexpectedly intelligent gaze raked his face. "And you, my lord? You will allow her to do as she chooses?"

A wholly unwanted rush of protest threw him back to his cynical tone and he raised his quizzing-glass, looking through it at her face. "I cannot imagine why you should suppose otherwise, ma'am. I have neither control nor authority over the lady."

Silvestre looked baffled. "Oh. But you escorted her, did you not?"

"I could scarcely do less." He dropped the glass. "For the rest, I am depending upon my cousin's good offices."

"And so you may," came in Angelica's robust tones. She had left the girl seated with Henrietta. "We have settled it she will stay here tonight, since the servants are all awake and it will not cause so much of a stir as it would at home. I shall come over in the morning to fetch her to my house, where you may wait upon us in the afternoon, Raoul."

This disposition of his time annoyed him, but he could scarcely refuse. He would be little better than Maskery if he rejected Miss Temple's call upon his chivalry at this point. Not that she had made any such call. Indeed, she had made efforts not to involve him at every stage. He entered only one caveat. "Is Miss Temple suited with these arrangements?"

"Of course she is." Angelica lowered her voice. "To tell you the truth, I think she would be suited with anything that rescued her from such a hideous situation. She is in shock, poor girl, and who shall blame her?"

Not Raoul, that was certain. He was in fact already of the opinion this was only the beginning of the shocks in store. He too dropped his voice, glancing at Silvestre. "You do realise she has nothing but the clothes she stands up in? You can furnish her with what she needs for tonight?"

The Latimer girl threw a sympathetic look towards the sofa and also spoke in a murmur. "You need have no apprehension, Lord Lynchmere. We will do all we can to make her comfortable."

The small voice in the back of his mind tempted him to say it was no concern of his, but he swept it away. "Excellent. Then I leave her in your hands with a clear conscience." He moved towards the sofa, raising his voice. "Miss Temple!"

She looked up, her eyes narrowed a little as if she found it difficult to hold the lids open. In the stronger light, her freckles emphasised her pale skin. She looked exhausted. And altogether vulnerable. A twinge of something other than mere compassion attacked Raoul. He acted on instinct, leaning down to capture one of the gloved hands lying loosely in her lap. It quivered briefly in his hold and lay still.

"You are not alone." He smiled. "I won you, remember. I pledged my twenty guineas and I make it a rule to extract value for money."

The freckles danced as a trickle of laughter escaped and an echo of her customary animation entered her face. "I did not do my part, did I?"

"Decidedly not. But you may make up for it presently. Try to sleep. Things always look better in the daylight."

With which, he executed a bow and walked away with swift steps, wondering if he had taken leave of his senses.

Felicity's head throbbed. She sat up in the truckle bed, dutifully swallowing down the warm milk brought up by a maid, and tried not to mind the fussing and chatter of the Latimer twins. She would much have preferred to be left alone to brood, but she could not repudiate their kindness. At least she had held out against taking up one of the places in the big four-poster the girls shared.

"But are you sure, Miss Temple?" This from Henrietta, a gentle creature who appeared to be a female of rather too much sensibility. "I can sleep anywhere, and I do think you ought to be comfortable tonight."

Felicity refrained from retorting the impossibility of finding any comfort in her present predicament. "I could not possibly incommode you further. The truckle bed will suit me very well."

The more commanding Silvestre, who was shaking out a fresh cotton nightgown, tutted at her sister. "Hetty, you can't expect her to wish to sleep beside a stranger." She held out the garment. "I hope this will do, Miss Temple."

Having already shed her evening gown and under-petticoats at Henrietta's urging, Felicity was only too glad to take it, removing her shift and throwing on the voluminous nightgown instead. She emerged to find Henrietta presenting her with a hairbrush.

"Pray make use of this, Miss Temple. Oh, and I must fetch a shawl to you."

She fussed as she hunted in a large dresser, while Silvestre threw a quilt over the made-up makeshift bed. "You will be cold in the night without curtains."

"Thank you, but I'm used to a simple cot." Felicity sat down on the truckle bed and began to brush through her loosened hair. "We don't run to grand beds at the academy. One becomes inured to the cold."

Silvestre's eyes registered distress. "Gracious, is it so indeed? I am ashamed to think I have been bemoaning our need to retrench. At least we will not be reduced to having to seek employment."

Before Felicity had a chance to make any suitable response, Henrietta came to lay a warm Paisley shawl about her shoulders. "Well, you shan't be cold in this house, Miss Temple."

Sudden irritation seized her. "I wish you will call me Felicity. It seems ridiculous to be so formal under the circumstances. Besides, you make me feel as if I'm back at the academy with the girls — Miss Temple this and Miss Temple that all day long!"

Both girls instantly emphasised the impression by dissolving into giggles, which made them seem at once much younger and a great deal easier to like. Felicity's inner despair lightened. She smiled at the two of them, seated side by side on the big bed.

"Now you sound just like a pair of schoolgirls. How old are you?"

"We are eighteen," said Silvestre, sobering. "We came out last year and if only either one of us had become betrothed then, we should not be such a charge on poor Papa."

"Yes, indeed," chimed in her sister. "He does not say so, of course, and if he had only told us at Christmas, we would have foregone coming to town at all."

"If you ask me, Mama persuaded him in hopes we might secure husbands." Silvestre sighed. "It seems silly to say so, Miss — I mean, Felicity — but in a way I envy you. At least you are not obliged to dispose of yourself in matrimony."

Disregarding this, Felicity fastened upon the salient point. "You appear to be informed of the situation now. How did you find it out?"

Henrietta's pretty features fell. "By the veriest accident. I overheard Mama talking to Aunt Angelica — Mrs Summerhayes, you know."

"And she told me and I taxed Papa with it the first chance I got. He didn't want to reveal the truth, but I insisted and at last he told me."

Curiosity overtook Felicity. "Forgive me, but what is the truth? Don't feel obliged to tell me, if you had rather not."

Henrietta reached out to press her hand. "Oh, why not? Your situation is worse than ours, and I can't think you would betray us."

"Certainly not."

"Besides, Mrs Summerhayes is bound to tell you," said Silvestre in a practical spirit. "You see, Papa was heir to our great-uncle Silvester —"

"Yes, and Silve was even named after him because of it."

"— only the wretched man has gone and married again, and his wife bore him a son at the end of last year." Her tone took on exasperation. "He is called Horatio, of course."

"After our fallen hero. I think it is perfectly charming to have named the baby for Admiral Nelson, Silve."

"I dare say, but that does not alter the fact that this little Horatio has cut Papa out of the succession."

Henrietta's eyes swam and her voice became husky. "It wouldn't matter so much, only that great-uncle cut off his allowance as well."

"Yes, and I expect he would have taken back the little estate he made over to Papa if he could, but Papa says he can't for the lawyer told him the contract is binding."

"At least we have somewhere to live," said Henrietta, sniffing into a pocket handkerchief dug out of her sleeve, "but this must be our last season. Papa cannot afford another."

"That is why Aunt Angelica — she is our godmother, you must know — came up with the idea for the auction."

"Was it to raise funds?" asked Felicity, thankful for the diversion from her own miseries.

"Oh, no." Henrietta looked at her sister. "At least, was it? Aunt Angelica only told me she hoped it would bring us into better notice."

"I suspect she thinks it may cover some of the expenses of the party," her sister said. "It is not as if the bids were huge. It was only a game, after all."

The subject served to keep the twins engaged while they readied themselves for bed. But they did not neglect their guest, Henrietta insisting on sending down for a glass of hot milk and enquiring every so often if Felicity were comfortable.

The truckle bed was comfortable enough, if a trifle narrow, but the incessant chatter made her head ache and she longed for the freedom to become lost in her own dark thoughts. However, by the time the girls were tucked up and the candles snuffed, exhaustion took over and Felicity fell asleep to the muffled whispers coming from behind the curtained four-poster.

The door to Lord Lynchmere's Berkeley Square mansion was opened by the porter at the footman's knock. Raoul dismissed the servant and his coachman drove off towards the mews. He entered the marbled hall, his thoughts still maddeningly centred on the peculiar happenings of the evening, and handed his hat and coat to the porter.

"Thank you, Bullman. That will be all. Lock up and go to bed."

The fellow coughed. "Yes, my lord, but there is something, my lord."

What now? The tone was hesitant. In the light afforded by the two candelabra placed on tables either side of the hall, he was able to note an apologetic mien in the porter's face.

"Out with it. What has occurred?" Before Bullman could answer, the book room door opened and his secretary came out. "Are you still up, Jerram? What the deuce has been happening here?"

The porter fell back as the fresh-faced young man approached, obviously relieved not to be obliged to relate whatever ill news awaited. "It is nothing very serious, my lord, but I thought you would wish to be informed. An odd circumstance merely."

Impatience rose up. "Well, don't be so mysterious, man. I've had a night of it already, I thank you."

"Your pardon, my lord. Perhaps I had best show it to you." He indicated the open doorway to the book room.

Frowning now, Raoul strode purposefully in, Jerram close behind. The candles in the wall-sconces had been left alight, as well as those in the small candelabrum the secretary kept for his desk. Raoul's eye went directly to the alien object standing on the desk: a bulging valise.

A series of lightning notions chased one another through his head, connecting too many coincidences for his comfort. Damn it to hell, was that what he thought it was?

"How the devil did that get here?"

Jerram passed him and went to the desk, setting a hand on the objectionable piece of luggage. "It was not Bullman's fault, my lord. He opened the door to a knock and some fellow thrust the thing at him and fled."

Worse and worse. "Did he think to give chase?"

"I fear he was too bemused, my lord. But he had the sense to summon me and I took charge of it."

At last Raoul approached the desk, eyeing the thing with revulsion. "Have you looked inside?"

"Yes, my lord. It was not locked." Jerram's hand went to his neck-cloth and he cleared his throat, a sign of embarrassment Raoul recognised. "It — er — it obviously belongs to a lady, my lord. Would you care to look?"

"I will do no such thing, I thank you." Bad enough as it was. He was not going to pry into Miss Temple's belongings, if the wretched thing was indeed hers as he suspected. He bent to examine the valise, trying to find a monogram. "Was there anything inside to indicate the name of the owner?"

Jerram grimaced. "Well, I didn't rummage, my lord, once I realised what was in it."

There were no initials near the clasp, nor on the sides. Raoul picked up the valise, which was heavier than it looked, and checked underneath. "Nothing to indicate ownership." He was tempted to look inside despite his reluctance, but caution won as he pictured the girl's face should he be obliged to confess to having done so. "However, I think I know to whom it belongs."

A long sigh escaped his secretary. "In that case, I am glad I did not have it immediately thrown into the street, which I promise you I thought of."

"Yes, that would have been a mistake."

Jerram's countenance, which had a trifle of chubbiness that made him look younger than he was, took on diffident question. "Do you know the lady, my lord?"

Raoul raised one eyebrow. "She is not my mistress, if that is what you're thinking."

"Of course not, my lord." But the blush belied him.

Setting the object back on the desk, Raoul contemplated the thing with his thoughts winging to the Latimer house. No use going back. By now the little redhead would be tucked up in bed. He had gone to his club when he left the party, there to brood over a glass of brandy and exchange desultory greetings with one or two acquaintances. His meditations on the possible whereabouts of Miss Temple's errant guardian had not proceeded far by the time he was driven out by the arrival of a party of boisterous young men who had been at the Latimer event and appeared determined to live the auction all over again.

Little had he expected to be confronted, on seeking solitude and his bed, by this evidence of Maskery's skulduggery. What in Hades did the fellow mean by planting the girl's belongings on him? Clearly Miss Temple had indeed spotted the wretch looking in when she had become agitated at supper. He must have seen Raoul with her and made the not unreasonable assumption that he had won her company at this confounded auction and therefore dumped her luggage at his house, effectively saddling him with an unwanted charge.

Damn it, this was all Angie's fault! Now what was he to do? It was all very well the girl bleating on about returning to her wretched academy, and no doubt she could, but that would not ease his conscience. One did not, if one wished to retain the slightest claim to be called a gentleman, turn one's back on a lady who had been cruelly tricked and abandoned to a despicable fate. For only one construction could be placed upon Maskery's disgraceful actions. Unless he was all about in his head, he could not suppose Raoul would marry the girl. Nor, if that was the case, would Maskery have given her valise into his keeping. He meant, if Raoul did not miss his guess, to hand Miss Temple over in lieu of his debt, to become — just as Jerram had very obviously thought — his mistress.

The notion had an oddly jangling effect upon his senses. The sneaking thought he would not be averse to the implications rose up only to be firmly quashed. There was no going down that road.

"I suppose it is too much to hope there was any message given along with this thing?"

His secretary looked regretful. "No, my lord. I asked Bullman specifically, but he says the fellow said nothing at all."

Irritation rose again. "Did he at least get a look at him?"

"He thinks the man was a groom, my lord."

Grimness began to settle in Raoul. "No sign of a carriage nearby? He did not hear wheels or hooves?"

Jerram's gaze became troubled. "Nothing at all, my lord. Or if there was, Bullman did not hear it. I suspect he was too taken aback to pay close attention. The man's running feet is the best he could come up with."

"Curse the fellow!" He saw the startled look in his secretary's eyes and waved a dismissive hand. "Not Bullman, you fool. I'm talking of Lord Maskery."

Jerram's brows flew up. "Lord Maskery? Good God, sir, is that who —?" He broke off, clearing his throat. "I mean, have you reason to suppose...?"

Raoul raised a finger. "This is between you and me, Jerram. It is to go no further."

"Your lordship may rely upon me, as I hope you know. But I dare not suppose the occurrence will not be discussed in the servants' hall."

"Hell and the devil, you're right, of course! You'd best put it about that the valise is unknown to me and we think the man mistook the house."

"Very well, my lord, but what, if you will permit me to ask, is the truth of it?"

"I believe this belongs to a lady I met tonight." Raoul gave him a succinct account of the events of the evening, and the relevant facts. "Make enquiries, if you please. There is the Black Swan and Maskery's lodging, wherever that may be. He's badly dipped, I know that much. I hold his IOUs myself and I don't doubt there are others who have not been paid. I've a suspicion he may have taken off for the Continent."

"Not France, my lord," objected his secretary. "Not in these times."

"Holland, then. Or Spain."

Jerram rubbed his chin, seeming dubious. "I'll see what I can find out, my lord."

"Put forth your best endeavours." Raoul hefted the valise. "Meanwhile, I will take charge of this. I will return it to Miss Temple tomorrow."

He recalled her upset at the loss of her personal mementoes, and a rush of warmth came in at the thought he could at least relieve her of that particular distress. The notion was swiftly followed by one less welcome, and he cursed with some fluency.

It was too much to hope Miss Temple's keen intelligence would overlook the implications of the valise coming into Raoul's possession.

CHAPTER FOUR

Lord Lynchmere's dictum proved correct. The situation seemed indeed less desperate in the clear light of day. Unless Felicity's senses were merely dulled. She had slept like one dead, finding it hard to pull herself into wakefulness, as if she had been drugged. She was even moved to tackle Henrietta over the breakfast cups.

"You did not add laudanum to my milk last night, did you?"

The girl set down her tea and waved hands of horror. "Gracious, no! Why would I do such a thing?"

From across the table her twin looked up from buttering a warm roll and regarded Felicity with a knowing eye. "I see what it is. The aftermath of shock. I expect you feel as if you have been hit in the head with a brick."

Felicity had to laugh. "That is it exactly. How perceptive of you."

"That is Silve all over." Henrietta sipped her tea. "If you are not careful, she will start advising you on just what you should do."

"I can't help it if I think of these things, can I?"

"No, but there are older and wiser heads than yours."

"Well, none of them are here just at this moment, are they?"

Apart from a somewhat somnolent footman, the young ladies were breakfasting alone. Mrs Latimer had not yet risen, they had been told upon enquiry, and their father had eaten earlier and retired to his library, as was his custom.

"Papa can never bear our chatter in the morning," Henrietta had explained. "He insists upon his peace." She turned now to

Felicity with her apologetic air. "You had much better listen to Aunt Angelica. Silve is so impulsive."

Her sister gave her an unloving look and retired into her baked eggs. Feeling unequal to mediate between the two, Felicity confined her attention to consuming her portion of ham and trying to decide upon a sensible course of action.

Clothes were paramount. She was at this moment attired in a borrowed morning gown belonging to Henrietta. It was a trifle loose and had dragged on the ground until the twins' maid had pinned up the hem and tacked it. But at least it looked respectable. To have been obliged to go about in the evening gown would have been embarrassing, to say the least. However, it was not perhaps as bad as she had supposed. She had her cloak and might with propriety travel to Bath thus attired.

"Will it suit if I wear this gown to my destination, Henrietta? I will be obliged to post it back to you and that may take some days, I fear."

Henrietta made a hushing sound and indicated the sleepy footman waiting by the sideboard loaded with covered silver dishes. She leaned close to whisper. "We should not advertise your situation, Felicity, but of course you may. As it chances, I have not worn that gown for an age."

"No," chimed in her sister, "for it is last season's, but remember you will have to make this season's do for the future." She made no attempt to keep her voice at a level to be inaudible to the servant. Evidently she'd had no difficulty hearing her twin, who shushed at her in a frantic way.

"Do stop, Silve! You are just trying to drive me into losing my temper."

"I wish I might!"

Henrietta sighed. "You are as grumpy as Papa in the mornings, horrid creature!"

Her twin made an exasperated sound and then produced a bright smile as she glanced at Felicity. "You must be feeling very much at home by now, I should think."

Felicity had to laugh. "What, with the two of you scrapping like a couple of schoolgirls? Is it ever thus between you?"

"Yes!" they chorused. The two girls glared at each other for a moment and then fell into giggles at exactly the same time.

"Our poor nurse was used to despair of us," said Henrietta, still bubbling with mirth.

"Yes, and our governess gave up in the end and told Mama we were devils and she could not endure it, so Mama was obliged to teach us herself." Silvestre smiled at her sister as she added, "All my doing, of course, but Hetty got tarred with the same brush."

"I got spanked with the same brush," retorted her sister. "Though I must own I deserved it just as much as you did. Not that Mama resorted to such punishments, and Papa can still silence us with a look."

The affection between them was evident, despite the squabbling. Felicity could not but be grateful for the diversion from her difficult problem, but it reared its head again when the three of them finished breakfasting and were alone in the front parlour awaiting the arrival of Mrs Summerhayes.

"You expect to be permitted to go back to Bath, don't you?"

Silvestre's sudden question took Felicity aback. She looked across to the sofa opposite from where she was sitting in an armchair set to one side of the fireplace. The twins were seated side by side, Henrietta occupying herself with sketching in a book that appeared to be filled with patterns involving images of flowers.

"Permitted? I am my own mistress, Silvestre."

"True, but you don't know Aunt Angelica."

"She is not really our aunt, you must know," Henrietta chimed in, "but we call her so since we have known her forever."

"She is your godmother, I think you said? Though she seems a trifle young to be so."

"Well, she is younger than Mama," said Silvestre, "but not by many years. Only she was extremely particular and did not marry until she was almost upon the shelf."

"Whereas Mama was just seventeen when she and Papa wed," added her twin, "and Aunt Angelica was just old enough to become our sponsor."

"Not that I can recall her ever being other than managing and authoritative."

Felicity balked. "Well, she has no authority over me."

Silvestre snorted. "That won't stop her if she has made up her mind to befriend you. And since it is Lord Lynchmere who asked her, I imagine she will be doubly anxious to do so."

A faint ripple ran through Felicity's veins at mention of his lordship. Recalling instances of last night's events, she felt distinctly unsure about meeting him again. It came to her she had been half hoping to remove from the metropolis before he had a chance to catch up with her. She adopted a dismissive tone. "He told me they are cousins, and he seemed to think she would come up with a scheme to help me."

"Oh, Aunt Angelica is forever scheming," chimed in Henrietta. "She is so good-hearted."

"So interfering, you mean." Silvestre waved her sister down as she began to protest. "The thing is, she dotes on Lord Lynchmere and I am sure she will encourage you to do as he suggests."

Felicity almost unconsciously drew herself up. "I cannot think Lord Lynchmere is likely to concern himself with my future. Why should he? He was indeed chivalrous last night, but I am convinced he found the whole episode tedious."

Two pairs of eyes became trained upon her with identical expressions of disbelief.

"I am sure I don't know why you should look at me like that," Felicity said, flustered.

Silvestre's gaze became earnest. "I have never known Lynchmere to do as much for anyone."

"Exactly so." Henrietta looked apologetic again. "You see, he is in general such an aloof man. Even Aunt Angelica did not suppose he would actually bid on anyone."

"We were all perfectly astonished, if you want the truth." Silvestre smiled. "You must have made a hit with him."

Felicity's insides crawled with discomfort. "I did not. I am useless at small talk and I told him as much. Besides, it is irrelevant."

"Is it? When he told you he means to extract his money's worth for his twenty pounds?"

"He was jesting!" Recalling the warm look in Lord Lynchmere's eyes at that instant, Felicity experienced another flip in her veins. She suppressed it. "He was merely trying to comfort me. He knew I was upset, that is all."

Henrietta set her sketchbook down in her lap. "Well, all I can say is, I have never seen him behave so towards a female."

Felicity could not help the question. "Do you know him well, then?"

"Gracious, no! We only met him last year and he hardly ever attends parties."

"No, indeed. I am sure he only came last night because Aunt Angelica nagged him. She has been trying to marry him off for years, you must know."

"Not to one of us, I trust." Henrietta shuddered. She pointed her pencil at her twin. "You might cope with that horrid sarcastic manner of his, Silve. He frightens me into sounding like a complete ninny."

Silvestre laughed. "You goose, Hetty. He does it on purpose to put females off setting their caps at him. That's what Aunt Angelica says and she should know."

"Are they very close, then?" Despising herself for asking, Felicity could not ignore a thread of curiosity. "It did not seem so to me, I must say."

"That is the pragmatic Frenchness in him," said Silvestre. "She has it too."

"Frenchness?"

"They are both half French. He is called Raoul and Aunt Angelica is really Angelique. Their mothers were sisters."

Henrietta leaned forward with an air of sudden excitement. "They were not precisely émigrés, for they both married Englishmen before the Terror began, but it was a lucky escape for them all the same."

"Although Lady Lynchmere unfortunately died a few years after it all started."

"Her heart broke," said Henrietta, "when they lost members of their family. That's what Aunt Angelica says."

Silvestre gave her sister a pitying look. "You shouldn't believe her nonsense, Hetty. In fact, Lady Lynchmere died giving birth to her daughter."

"Lord Lynchmere has a sister?"

"Yes, but she is not yet out. Aunt Angelica will do the honours, I expect."

"Does the girl then live with Mrs Summerhayes?"

"Heavens, no! She is incarcerated at Ruscoe Hall in the care of a cousin or some such thing."

Henrietta tutted. "Really, Silve, you should not say such things. Incarcerated indeed!"

"Well, I should not care to have Lynchmere for a guardian." Silvestre pointed a finger at Felicity. "Mark my words, if he has any idea of interfering in your plans, you will be quite overborne."

The memory of his lordship's remarks upon her scheme of returning to Bath by the stage rose up in Felicity's mind. He had been a trifle autocratic, and he did have an abrupt and sarcastic way with him. On the other hand, he had been kind — when he was not looking decidedly bored. No, she could not flatter herself his interest would go further than assisting her in the present necessity as he did last night. Nevertheless, she confessed to being intrigued by this glimpse into his private life.

Mrs Summerhayes, arriving like a whirlwind, put all thought of Lord Lynchmere temporarily out of Felicity's head.

"I have it all planned, my dear, and you can stop worrying," she said the instant she set foot in the parlour. She waved at the twins. "Excellently done, my loves, for she looks a good deal restored. Is it one of your gowns, Hetty? Yes, it must be," she went on, answering her own question without giving either girl a chance to respond, "and a good choice too. But we will soon be able to give it back to you, for I mean to take the girl at once to *Cerisette* and have a few gowns made up."

Felicity blinked and Silvestre twinkled across at her. "What did I tell you? You may as well give in at once and be done with it."

Henrietta jumped up, catching at Mrs Summerhayes' arm. "But, dear ma'am, she does not mean to remain in Town, you know. And perhaps it will embarrass her to be taken to *Cerisette.*"

Mrs Summerhayes became even brisker. "That is just why I chose *Cerisette* and not *Pandora's*. Madame Cerisette may be relied upon to be discreet, and we won't meet anyone fashionable there. As to remaining in Town, there is no question of that. I am taking her with me to Barkham, but she must have something to wear."

"Taking her with you to Barkham?" echoed Silvestre in astonished accents. "What in the world for? What should she do there?"

"Do? Good heavens, child, I don't know! Whatever she wishes to do. She will play with the children, I expect."

"Oh, do you mean for her to become their governess, then?"

Mrs Summerhayes raised her brows at the other twin. "My dear Hetty, what are you talking about? Sally is far too young to need a governess, and Hugh insists the boys must go to school when they are a little older."

"Well, but —"

"Hetty is thinking of Felicity's plan to return to her academy, Aunt, and I must say I should suppose she will be anxious for employment of some kind."

Mrs Summerhayes threw up expressive hands. "Oh, I know all that, my dear Silve, but that is for the future. Nothing can be done until we discover what has become of her guardian."

She turned as she spoke to Felicity, who had made no attempt to stem the flow, too bemused by the give and take of words and Mrs Summerhayes' competent air to voice any objection. But at this, she rose swiftly to confront the matron.

"I have no wish to find my guardian, ma'am. I should never have allowed myself to be beguiled into taking this step, and the sooner I return to my former life the better."

Mrs Summerhayes grasped her hands, her face wreathing in a smile of such warmth that Felicity was taken aback. "You are bound to say so, my dear child, after the way he has behaved towards you. But I know Raoul, and if he has not already set in train a means of ferreting out the truth, you may call me a Dutchwoman."

Felicity's stomach clenched. "Lord Lynchmere? But why should he? I am persuaded he cannot wish to pursue the matter. He will be only too relieved to be rid of such a troublesome charge."

To her astonishment, the matron let out a snorting laugh as she released her. "Ah, you have his measure already. In general, I would agree with you. Raoul loathes anything that threatens to disrupt the tedium of his days. Would you believe it, he *likes* a dull life?"

This did not ring with Felicity's experience, for she strongly suspected Lord Lynchmere's attitude of boredom was carefully cultivated. But she refrained from saying so, merely reiterating her intention to return to Bath at the earliest possible moment.

"Whether Lord Lynchmere agrees to it is irrelevant. I am of age, and even Lord Maskery had no hold over me."

"Ah, but there's the rub, my dear Felicity — if I may?"

"Of course, but —"

"It is clear to me that you know very little of Maskery and his reputation. Hard living is the least of it. The plain fact of the matter is he has enormous gaming debts, and although my cousin would never mention it to me, I happen to know that Lynchmere is one of his creditors, to the tune of several thousand."

The intelligence that her guardian owed Lord Lynchmere a considerable sum of money set up a train of discomforting reflections in Felicity's head. So much so that she was too distracted to protest as strongly as she'd intended when Mrs Summerhayes insisted upon carting her off to the modiste of her choosing.

Several thousand, to one used to eking out a matter of guineas every quarter, was an impossible sum. Felicity's head felt cloudy from trying to imagine it. That a marquis could afford to gamble to the tune of thousands was perhaps understandable. Foolish and reckless, of course, when she dared say there were better uses for his substance. But that was no concern of hers, she reminded herself, trying to subdue a rise of indignation at the sheer waste of it all.

Lord Maskery, however, was another matter altogether. If he was so deeply in debt, what in the world induced him to drag his erstwhile ward from her secure employment to an uncertain future at his hands? Some reason he must have had. And not the impulse of kindness he had pretended.

A gut-wrenching apprehension floated at the back of her mind, making her abruptly glad to be doing something other than thinking when Mrs Summerhayes, in concert with the elderly Madame Cerisette, whose accent spoke her origins, began bundling her in and out of a variety of gowns, the like of which she had never before worn.

"I think the leaf green muslin with the lace trim, my dear, and the pale jonquil we liked so much with that blue riband around the neckline. Both complemented your hair so well."

Realising her hostess was bent upon making actual purchases, Felicity dragged her attention fully in. "Ma'am, if you insist upon doing this, let us leave it there, if you please. I cannot bear to be so beholden."

Mrs Summerhayes waved this away. "Nonsense, my dear. You can scarcely go about in Hetty's gown for days, now can you?"

"I will not be here for days."

"True, but we do not have a modiste anywhere close to Cherry Lodge whom I could trust to make up gowns. Barkham is merely a village, you must know. Petticoats and shifts may be had in Reading, but we must certainly do shoes and hats before we leave Town."

She then turned back to continue negotiating with the modiste. The scheme of returning to Bath receded further out of Felicity's reach. She felt too deeply enmeshed in the farce into which her guardian had thrown her to be able to extract herself easily. The simplicity of getting onto the stagecoach had been swept away by the dreadful realisation that she was somehow involved in Lord Maskery's debt-ridden state. An inkling of the truth made her writhe inside. She could not even take comfort in the notion she was not to blame. She had ignored her instinctive distrust and allowed her doubts to be overborne. Now here she was incurring indebtedness on her own account. Rebellion rose up.

Without ceremony, she interrupted the conference. "Excuse me, if you please, Mrs Summerhayes, but may I have a private word?"

The matron's brows flew up, but she cared nothing for the implied rebuke. Seizing the woman's arm, she pulled her to the far end of the little salon, which was thankfully free of any other persons beyond Madame Cerisette's assistant.

"Mrs Summerhayes," she began in a determined way.

"You may as well call me Angelica, my dear."

Felicity was in no mood to be interrupted with social niceties. "As you wish, ma'am, but pray pay attention!"

The brows, so like Lord Lynchmere's as it suddenly struck Felicity, rose up again. "Dear me. You sound just like a schoolmistress."

"Well, I am one," Felicity rejoined impatiently. "The thing is, I wish you will not purchase any more gowns for me. I concede the two, for I can see —"

"Oh, I am not going to pay for them, if that is what worries you. I shall charge them up to Raoul, never fear."

Horror swept through Felicity and she stared at the creature. "Charge them up to Raoul?"

"Of course. He asked me to help you, so I am sure he will expect to stand the nonsense. He can well afford it, you know."

Afford it? No doubt! "I must beg you will do no such thing, ma'am. I cannot possibly accept clothes at Lord Lynchmere's expense."

"In the ordinary way, no. It would be quite ineligible. But the circumstances are far from ordinary, are they not?"

"Yes, they are, but still —"

"No one will ever know. Madame Cerisette is the soul of discretion and is besides a family friend. She was used to make clothes for our mothers when they were girls and still in France."

This piece of information, while it was an intriguing glimpse of her hostess's history, did nothing to quieten Felicity's dismay. "Nevertheless, I cannot allow —"

Mrs Summerhayes smiled suddenly, capturing Felicity into a convulsive hug. "You poor dear! It is all too overwhelming, I expect. Now, do not be making difficulties over a very simple matter and let me contrive with Madame."

With which, she swept off, leaving Felicity without a word to say and considerably troubled. The situation was getting out of hand, and the lurking question of these appalling gaming debts could not but cast a pall of gloom over her spirits.

She made no further attempt to prevent Mrs Summerhayes from dragging her to a hat shop, where a pretty confection was acquired, consisting of a cap of worked muslin with a double trimming of lace and a wreath of flowers tied around the crown, as well as a small-brimmed straw hat with green ribbon threaded through. A shoe shop came next, from which she came away with a pair of fawn-coloured pumps and a sturdier shoe for walking.

"You'll need it in the country, and we can always get sandals in Reading. I think that will do for now. Madame Cerisette has promised to deliver your gowns within three days, which suits with my present arrangements."

Felicity had no need to ask what these were because Mrs Summerhayes proceeded to lay out her plan for retiring to the country within the week.

"I must first ensure that Gawcott calls in all the money for the bids and then I may be easy about dear Margaret's difficulties, poor love. One can only hope the girls receive offers before their situation becomes generally known."

Felicity listened with only half an ear as the matron beguiled the short journey to her home with much in the same vein. Her thoughts remained obstinately with what she was going to find to say to Lord Lynchmere. She must thank him. Yet she was not nearly as confident as Mrs Summerhayes that he would be happy to pay for her attire. She could only be glad the assumption was none of hers, and that she would make abundantly clear.

It was with a good deal of reluctance that Raoul presented himself in Angelica's modest house in George Street. Not least of the difficulties that plagued him was the wretched valise he was carrying. He should have taken a hackney instead of walking round to his cousin's. Already two acquaintances he'd met along the way had given the offending article questioning looks.

Not that he had the slightest intention of explaining away the battered, bulging object. Let them make of it what they would. Yet the incongruity of it against his customarily suave appearance was bound to strike a discordant note. Which was, now he thought of it, perfectly in keeping with the whole affair.

In the cold light of day, the hideous truth could not be avoided. Maskery, the unmitigated scoundrel, had thrust him into a situation likely to plunge the lot of them into a decidedly unpleasant scandal. For which Angelica's ill-judged insistence upon his attending her wretched auction was palpably to blame. Having reached this conclusion, he knocked on her door with an unpleasant feeling of entering upon an inescapable doom.

The butler admitted him, offering the unwelcome news that his cousin and the young lady were awaiting him in the Yellow Parlour above stairs. Raoul nodded, giving up his hat and cane into the fellow's hands.

"May I take the valise, my lord?"

"No, you may not. At least, you may hold it for a moment while I remove my coat."

He gave it up into Maunder's keeping, stripping off his gloves and shrugging himself out of his overcoat. He moved to check his appearance in the oval mirror set above an ormolu table to one side of the narrow hall, flicking his hair back and deftly smoothing a crease in the sleeve of his mulberry coat. He reset his quizzing glass into place and held out his hand for the valise, shutting the uncomfortable reflections out of his head.

"You need not announce me. I know my way."

But this did not suit with the butler, who insisted on leading him up the stairs and across the gallery to the pretty front room his cousin reserved for informal occasions.

"Lord Lynchmere, madam."

Raoul set his teeth and walked into the parlour, his fingers tightening on the handle of the valise. His glance went directly to the red-headed figure seated at the bureau with her head turned towards the door. He had evidently disturbed Miss Temple in the act of writing. He met her eyes briefly. Was it consternation in them?

There was no time to determine, for Angelica's voice cut across his thoughts. "I thought it was you. What an age you have been!"

She was hovering by the window and Raoul curled his lip at her. "Have you been keeping watch, then?"

"Well, of course." She moved out into the room, her eyes going to the object he carried. "What have you there?"

A small cry escaped from Miss Temple. "My valise!"

She sprang up and came quickly to meet him as he hefted it higher for her to see. "It is yours, then?"

She fairly grabbed it out of his hold, clutching the thing to her as if it was a long lost child. Her clear gaze came up to meet his. "I thought I had lost it forever. Thank you! Where was it? Did you go back to the Black Swan?"

Raoul hesitated, for once thankful for his cousin's garrulity as she joined them.

"Gracious, what a relief! Now you need not replenish all those little items so indispensable to a female. I am sure you must have all kinds of things in there which are precious to you."

"Indeed, yes." To Raoul's intense dismay, Miss Temple's eyes grew bright and luminous. "Small mementoes I have treasured for years. I've been trying to tell myself I could live without them."

"Now you don't have to. Splendid. You are quite a genius, Raoul. How in the world did you find it after all?"

Confronted by two expectant faces, Raoul could prevaricate no longer. He drew a breath and plunged in. "It was by no action of mine. The valise was brought to my house last night by a servant, who thrust it into my footman's hands and ran away."

Angelica's comely countenance exhibited her astonishment. "How singular!"

But Raoul's gaze was drawn to Miss Temple's as the glow slowly died out of her eyes.

"Your house?" Her tone was hushed. "But that means…"

He saw realisation dawn and cursed inwardly. Had he not known how it would be? He tried to avert disaster. "Don't jump to conclusions, Miss Temple."

Her grip on the valise loosened and her voice became hard. "What other conclusion can there be? I saw him, did I not? He was there. I did not imagine it."

"Good gracious, Felicity, what in the world are you talking of? Who was where?"

"She is talking of Maskery, Angelica."

"What? Where was he?"

Miss Temple took the question, moving to set the valise down on the chair she had vacated. "I saw him look into the supper room last night. Your cousin went to see, but he had disappeared."

"But what has he to do with the valise —? Oh!" Consternation leapt in Angelica's eyes and she hurried to Miss Temple's side. "My dear girl, do not be making a mountain out of a molehill. I am sure there is a perfectly rational explanation."

Raoul took a hand. "Rational perhaps, but not, I venture to suggest, as necessarily vengeful as I suspect Miss Temple supposes." He hardly knew why he was trying to lessen the impact. He knew as well as the girl just how damaging Maskery's actions were. To the both of them.

To her credit, she neither broke out in despair nor lost her temper. Only her limbs, peculiarly rigid, gave away her inner agitation as she walked across to the mantel and gripped its edge. Avoiding Angelica's sympathy?

Angelica turned to Raoul. "What does he mean by it then, Raoul?"

"One can only conjecture, but it seems clear he returned to the party to ascertain just who had won Miss Temple's company."

"Then chose to plant the valise on you? Was there no message? No note or explanation?"

"Nothing at all. Though that is not to say a letter will not arrive in due course."

"There was none delivered this morning, I take it?"

He shook his head, his gaze fixed upon Miss Temple's unresponsive back. Angelica lowered her voice.

"What do you mean to do?"

"Return Miss Temple's property to her, which is what I have done."

At that, she turned, her eyes afire. "You may as well have handed me a live coal, my lord. I am as surely damned."

His lip twisted. "You mean you may burn in hell? I doubt it, Miss Temple. I imagine that fate is reserved for your guardian. You are an innocent victim in this, I believe."

Her chin went up. "Not so innocent, sir, as I told you last night. I should have followed my instinct and refused to be tempted by the promise of a different kind of life." A note of cynicism worthy of his own efforts entered her voice. "Not that I had in mind the sort of life my guardian evidently intended."

Predictably, Angelica threw up horrified hands. "I will not have you talk so, Felicity! Whatever Maskery meant by this, you cannot suppose —"

"That Lord Lynchmere will snap up the opportunity?" Her tone was harsh, her eyes fierce as they met his. "I acquit him of any such intention. But there is no denying he could. I have been neatly sold into your hands, my lord. In payment, I presume, for whatever vast sum my guardian lost to you at the gaming tables."

"Felicity!" Angelica threw Raoul an anguished glance. "I told her in confidence, Raoul. I never thought…"

He waved her down, crossing to where the girl stood. She met his eyes boldly.

"Defiant and proud to the last, Miss Temple?"

She did not flinch. "Yes, when the alternative is abject humiliation."

A shaft of sheer admiration ran through Raoul and he could not help the smile. He gentled his tone. "That you will never be. Sheathe your sword, if you please. We have both been duped. Let us not allow Maskery's sordid scheme to win the day."

For a moment the glare held. Then a long sigh escaped her and she dropped her gaze from his. "You are right, sir. It is unfair to lay the fault at your door. Especially after your chivalry last night. I beg your pardon."

He put out a finger and raised her chin, forcing her to look at him. "Don't. It's not your fault either." Releasing her, he indicated the chair to one side of the fireplace. "Let us all sit down and consider this affair calmly."

She nodded, moving to drop into the chair indicated. Angelica hurried up, taking her place on the sofa opposite. "Yes, indeed. There is nothing to be gained by falling into a distempered freak, my dear Felicity. Not that I blame you for that. I should be in hysterics myself in a like case."

Raoul laughed as he took his seat beside her. "No, you wouldn't, Angie. You're not one of these pathetic swooning females, I'll give you that."

"I never was. Though I must say, poor Felicity is perfectly entitled to a good swoon if she feels like it."

For the first time since his entrance into the room, Miss Temple's lips curved a little and she seemed to relax slightly. "I never had time to swoon. When one is forever handling the stresses and strains of youthful maidens, one learns to be robust."

Angelica laughed. "I can well imagine it. My Sarah is but five, yet she promises to cause no end of trouble to us all, imperious little madam. Unlike your dutiful Lucille, Raoul. Mind you, the poor child likely does not dare to cross you, so strict as you are."

Raoul threw up his eyes. "I am not nearly strict enough, as it happens, and if you were better informed of Lucille's character, you would know she is a minx who has long since learned how to twist me around her little finger."

70

A tiny smile curved Miss Temple's lips. "Your sister, sir? Silvestre mentioned you were her guardian."

"An unenviable role, I promise you."

"I can imagine."

He was both touched and gratified. Most women, like Angelica, assumed he paid only lip service to his guardianship of his little sister, taking no hand in her upbringing. It was true he left her largely in the care of Miss Wimbush, but he had made a point of spending time with the chit ever since their father's demise despite the greater calls on his time for having come into the responsibilities of the title.

"Never mind that now," said Angelica, calling the meeting to order. "What do you propose to do about Maskery?"

The shadows returned to Miss Temple's eyes and Raoul was conscious of annoyance. Was the girl to be allowed no respite? She spoke before he could answer.

"How much does he owe you, my lord?"

Taken aback, he sought refuge in prevarication. "Why do you ask? It is a matter between him and me."

A spasm crossed her face. "No longer, sir, when he has clearly thrown me at your head as payment in kind. I should like to know what I am considered to be worth, if you please."

"Felicity, for heaven's sake!"

He ignored his cousin's interjection. "As far as I am concerned, Miss Temple, you are worth twenty guineas, remember? Maskery's dealings with me have nothing to do with you."

She struck her hands together. "How can you say that? Do you expect me to disdain the insult of it?"

"I do, yes. You may choose to take it so, or you may, like the sensible woman I believe you to be, refuse to allow a selfish man's desperate throw to wound you unnecessarily."

71

"Unnecessarily? Good heavens, Lord Lynchmere, but you are a cold fish indeed!"

Raoul flinched inwardly, though he gave no sign. Why the accusation should feel like a slap in the face he could not imagine. It had been said of him often enough.

To his chagrin, Angelica chose to add her mite, leaning towards the girl in a confidential fashion. "My dear, you have gauged him exactly. It is useless to expect Raoul to enter into your sentiments. He has no proper feeling at all."

"I thank you, Angelica. Don't hesitate to vilify my character any time it suits you to do so."

"I won't. You are quite horrid, and Felicity will be wise to know it at the outset."

Miss Temple's freckles danced as she went into an unexpected peal of laughter. "Oh, I know it, ma'am. He was at pains to demonstrate the worst of his character to me last night." Her features softened as she looked across at him. "Except that you are not uniformly unsympathetic, as I have good reason to know."

His ruffled feathers subsided, yet it galled him to think he could be in the least dismayed by her ill opinion of him. He summoned his habitual pose of bored indifference. "I dare say we will do better to turn our minds to what may be done to discover Maskery's whereabouts."

A crease appeared between her brows. "Can they be discovered?"

"Readily, I imagine. I have put my secretary on to it. The fellow cannot have disappeared without trace."

Angelica snorted. "He would not be the first gamester to flee the country to escape his creditors."

Miss Temple's frown deepened as she regarded Raoul. "Is that what you suppose? He has gone abroad?"

"I think it probable."

"But not France, Raoul."

"Holland, more likely. From there he may find his way to Prussia, or eventually Italy. Out of reach, in any event."

"Leaving everyone who won from him out of pocket, including you, Raoul."

He shrugged. "It's the risk of gaming." He found himself under the beam of Miss Temple's direct gaze. Was there disapproval in it? He raised his quizzing glass and surveyed her through it. "What, ma'am? You look as if you have a ready lecture under your tongue."

She made a faint moue of disgust. "I should have thought a marquis might have a better use for his money than to squander it in such a wasteful fashion."

Angelica's shocked intake of breath echoed a streak of fury in his breast. It was short-lived. He gave a rueful laugh, dropping his glass. "Your society, Miss Temple, is nothing if not chastening. How right you are."

A faint colour overlaid her freckles for a moment, and then receded. "I ought to take it back, I dare say, but I won't. When one must count every penny, the very thought of such shocking extravagance is anathema."

He cocked an eyebrow. "Do you include your guardian in this wholesale condemnation?"

"Of course. More indeed, since he clearly could not afford it. Talk of playing with fire. I only wish he might have refrained from involving me in the business."

He was glad of Angelica's intervention, which saved his having to answer the unanswerable.

"That is past praying for, my dear Felicity." She returned to her usual briskness. "It appears there is nothing further to be done until your fellow Jerram has found out anything he can.

73

We will repair to Cherry Lodge in a day or so and you may send to us there, Raoul, when you know something."

Miss Temple said nothing, instead regarding the clasped hands in her lap. Had she acquiesced in this scheme, then? He recalled she had been writing at the bureau when he entered the room.

"Have you a scheme of your own in mind, Miss Temple?"

She looked up and Raoul noted strain in her eyes. "I had been swayed by your cousin's persuasions, but now…"

"Now, Felicity, don't say you have changed your mind. Merely because of Lynchmere's news? Raoul, speak to her!"

"If Miss Temple has decided otherwise, I cannot think any words of mine will alter her determination."

"No, they won't." She was sounding defiant again. Then she seemed to soften, turning to Angelica. "Don't think me ungrateful. I am tempted beyond endurance, if you wish to know the truth."

"Excellent." Angelica beamed. "Then there is nothing more to be said."

"Yes, there is." Her gaze returned to Raoul's. "You had better know your cousin insisted on buying me clothes which she says you will pay for. That was all very well before I knew of this dreadful debt Lord Maskery owes you, but —"

"Good heavens, child, that is nothing to the purpose! As Raoul says, and I agree, the debt is not your concern. Moreover, the clothes are a bagatelle, are they not, Raoul?"

He held up a hand. "Enough, Angie. You are oppressing Miss Temple." Bypassing the whole matter of the clothes, which were indeed a bagatelle as far as he was concerned, he addressed another point. "To whom were you writing? Your employer at the academy?"

She nodded. "I must ask her at once if she will have me back, or she will fill the vacancy and there will be no place for me."

"In which case, you may remain with me," said Angelica brightly.

"To do what, ma'am? I must earn my keep. I cannot batten upon you for the rest of my days."

"Who said anything about the rest of your days? If nothing else, you may take it as a holiday from your horrid academy. If you insist upon it, I dare say I can find you more congenial employment."

An eager look animated Miss Temple's countenance. "Could you indeed? I am very well equipped to take up a post as governess."

Angelica waved nonchalant hands. "I don't doubt it, and I could certainly enquire among my friends."

Raoul felt compelled to nip this in the bud. "Yes, well, let us at once dismiss this flight of fancy. You will do no such thing, Angie."

"Why ever not, Raoul? It seems to me a perfect solution."

"A woman of your experience, my dear cousin, ought to know better. Miss Temple cannot appear at this ghastly auction of yours one day and be touting among the same people for a post as governess the next. Especially since I am known to have bid on the wench and won."

Angelica's face fell. "Oh, dear, that is very true. I had not thought." She threw an apologetic glance at the girl. "Your reputation will be quite ruined, my dear. As it is, I dare say there is a good deal of speculation, for no one knows who you are."

"Nor how she gained entrance to the Latimer party," added Raoul on a dry note, "since she was not seen in Maskery's company."

"Well, what a good thing that is. No one need know Felicity has any connection to the wretched creature."

"It won't fadge, Angelica, and you know it. You can't take a nameless girl under your wing without the whole world wanting to know why and who she is. And thanks to your machinations, I am inextricably involved."

CHAPTER FIVE

Felicity paid no heed as Mrs Summerhayes broke out in voluble protestations. The truth of his lordship's words could not be denied. Like a magician pulling a rabbit out of a hat, Lord Maskery had thrown her into public display and then vanished himself, leaving the rabbit to its certain fate.

"He chose that party deliberately. He must have planned for whoever might bid upon me to be saddled with me." Only half aware of speaking aloud and thus attracting the attention of the cousins, she frowned down at her restless fingers. "But it makes no sense. He cannot be in debt to all." She looked up and met Lord Lynchmere's eyes. "What if some other had won? If you had not topped their bids, sir, there were two gentlemen arguing over who had won me."

"Finglesham and Abinger, as I recall."

"Was it indeed?" Mrs Summerhayes tapped her fan on her knee. "They are both rather wild, but I should doubt of either being able to afford to play against a hardened gamester like Maskery."

Puzzled, Felicity returned her gaze to Lord Lynchmere's face. "How then could it serve him? He could not have known you would win."

"Of course not. That proved sheer luck for Maskery, I imagine."

"She's right, Raoul. Have we misread his intentions? Is it possible he means mischief in some other fashion?"

His lordship's expression gave him away. "You have already thought of this." Felicity stiffened her spine. "Do not spare me, sir. I had rather know the worst."

What did it matter after all? A resolve was already forming in her mind. The rabbit had every intention of finding its way back into the safety of the hat. An ignominious retreat, but at least she could lick her wounds in private. She could not remain, an embarrassment to all. With her meagre hoard of coins once more in her possession, she need not rely upon anyone else for the means to travel to Bath.

Lord Lynchmere's lip curled in the wry look he had worn before. "I suspect your guardian had it in mind to extract whatever monies he could."

"By what means, Raoul?"

He shrugged. "There are several possibilities. As long as Miss Temple, finding herself destitute, was obliged to beg help, some sort of compromising situation was likely to arise."

Mrs Summerhayes snorted. "What you mean is, a lesser man might have taken advantage."

"Quite so." He did not look at his cousin, and Felicity felt burned by his forthright gaze. "I imagine Maskery's plans were flexible. I should think my return to my house, alone, was noted. Had Miss Temple been with me, I dare say Maskery would have been standing on my doorstep this morning in righteous indignation, demanding reparation for his ward's loss of reputation."

"You mean he was instead obliged to fall back upon leaving her to you in compensation for the debt? But it's monstrous!"

"Desperate men take desperate measures. A more honourable man might have disposed of himself rather than his ward, but Maskery is not of that persuasion."

"Then I wonder at your playing cards with him at all," snapped Felicity, goaded.

"One does not measure honour when one is flirting with the throw of the cards, ma'am. The excitement lies in the heady game of risk."

"Then you are no better than he!"

It did not need Mrs Summerhayes' sharp intake of breath to bring Felicity to shame. Lord Lynchmere flinched only slightly, but his expression remained imperturbable. She put her fingers to her brow, pressing against the pain that had been imperceptibly growing there.

"I did not mean that. It is untrue. Unpardonable of me to say it."

Dismayed to hear the huskiness in her own voice, Felicity kept her eyes closed, unwilling to face the cynical gleam that had been in Lynchmere's gaze as he spoke.

She was rescued from the scourge of her own ill-thought words by the sound of someone entering the room. Felicity straightened, opening her eyes. But it was only the butler, armed with a tray which he set down upon the inlaid table near the window.

"Madeira, madam. And Ratafia, should miss prefer it."

"Thank you, Maunder, but leave it. His lordship will serve us."

The butler bowed and withdrew, and Felicity's eyes were drawn to Lord Lynchmere's tall figure as he rose to do the honours.

"I will take a drop of the Madeira, Raoul."

He nodded, not troubling to look round. So cool, so unmoved he was. An irrational urge to prick him into something more attacked Felicity. She fought it. His unruffled air, while she was so wound up, annoyed her.

He looked across at her. "Ratafia or Madeira, Miss Temple?"

"Neither, I thank you." She would kill for a cup of coffee! She struggled with the tempest rising in her bosom.

Lord Lynchmere poured two glasses from a decanter and returned to hand one to his cousin before retaking his seat and sipping at his own glass. He seemed utterly undisturbed, despite having a stray female thrown at his head.

The stray female, like an infuriated cat, wanted to scratch at him with her claws. Come, this would not do!

Felicity rose abruptly, crossing to the bureau. She picked up her valise, resisting the urge to throw it across the room with some violence, and set it down on the floor. Without a word, she sat down and picked up the pen, dipping it into the inkpot in the marbled stand. Then she sat, staring at the half-written sheet, reading the words but taking in nothing of their meaning.

She became aware of murmurs behind her. Then Mrs Summerhayes called out.

"You are not asking for your post back, are you?"

Yes, she was. At least, it was what she meant to do. She felt incapable of doing anything. Her determination to be gone notwithstanding, she was gripped with a frenzy of conflicting emotions that left her paralysed.

She half turned, glancing at her hostess. "I don't know. I must — I must at least let Mrs Jeavons know what has happened. She will be thinking... Oh, I have no notion!" She set down the pen, spraying ink across the sheet. Giving way to the turmoil inside, she set her elbows on the writing slope and dropped her head in her hands.

"Good heavens, Raoul, the poor girl is in despair! I'll ring for brandy. Or no, I will get my smelling salts."

A rustle of skirts was followed by the opening and closing of the door. Felicity heard it only in the background of her mind as the pain in her head began to rise in concert with the churning in her breast.

A floorboard creaked, and then a warm pair of hands was set upon her shoulders, kneading gently. The sensation both soothed and made her conscious. She pushed herself upright but the hands continued to massage. It felt good. Her tense muscles began to relax and she sighed out a low-voiced "Thank you."

Released, she opened her eyes and twisted on the chair, looking up into Lord Lynchmere's countenance. For once there was no trace of cynicism there.

"How did you learn to do that?"

His lip curved. "A trick that works with my little sister when she threatens a tantrum."

A rueful laugh escaped her. "You guessed I was about to throw a fit?"

He sank back a little, regarding her with a lurking twinkle. She had not seen that before. "I imagine your emotions at this point defy description."

Felicity had to laugh. "They do. I confess I could readily have thrown something at your head for remaining so infuriatingly unmoved."

The cynical gleam appeared. "A knack I have perfected. You should cultivate it, Miss Temple. You will find it endlessly useful."

"I thank you, but I have had practice enough at concealing my annoyances. Only this —!" She broke off, letting out an overwrought breath.

"This is a situation of which you can have had no previous experience. It is unsurprising you are overset."

The understanding words were balm, despite the faint irritation engendered by his continued calm tone. Felicity gave in to impulse. "If you don't desire to be pummelled into reaction, my lord, I wish you will ring for coffee."

His brows shot up. "Coffee? Why did you not ask for it before?"

"Because I did not wish to appear forward and demanding. Also because I was too cross to think of it."

He laughed as he moved to the bell-pull. "That is one way of putting it."

"Well, agitated then."

"Why coffee?"

"It is my preferred solace and it is plentiful. Tea works even better, but it is expensive." She fell silent, glancing at the ruined letter. "What a mess!" She set the pen back in its holder, picked up the sheet and scrunched it up. The sensation relieved some of her feelings and she kept going, mutilating the paper into an unrecognizable ball.

"If you throw that at me, Miss Temple, I warn you there will be consequences."

Felicity could not help laughing as she turned to look at him. "I should dearly love to, but I will refrain."

His lips twisted. "Excellent. I dislike being forced into retaliation."

"Or into anything," Felicity said before she could guard her tongue.

An eyebrow lifted. "Am I that transparent?"

She eyed him. "Not at all. You are admirably veiled. Aloof, Henrietta said, and I think it describes you precisely."

He said nothing, his countenance as enigmatic as ever. Felicity felt unaccountably distanced and was glad when the door opened and Mrs Summerhayes hurried in, the butler behind her.

"You are too late, Angelica. Miss Temple is much recovered, but she would be glad of a cup of coffee. No doubt Maunder is capable of producing one."

The habitual pose of indifference was back. Was it a pose? She had glimpsed a very different side to him here and there. Felicity could not but admit to being intrigued by the wretched man, in spite of all.

Mrs Summerhayes was in busy discussion with the butler, but when he departed on his errand, she came to the bureau and looked closely into Felicity's face. "You still look peaky, my dear child. Are you all right?"

Felicity forced a smile. "I have a trifle of the headache, ma'am, that is all."

"I am not surprised. Mind you, I cannot think coffee will help. A tisane would be better. Perhaps you should go and lie down?"

Felicity waved the suggestion away. "Presently, ma'am. I must write this letter first, for it occurs to me that I might ask his lordship for a frank and I dare say he has had enough of me for one day."

A choking sound from the vicinity of the sofa arrested her attention and she found Lord Lynchmere standing behind it, his glass in his hand, coughing with evidence of some discomfort.

"His lordship is in agreement," he said, his voice a trifle strained. "Especially if you mean to make him laugh just when he is sipping Madeira."

Felicity's heart lightened as she chuckled. "I beg your pardon. Such was not my intention."

He lifted the glass. "I acquit you. Write your letter. You may have a frank, but revenge will follow in due course."

Felicity laughed, but as she turned back to the bureau she became aware of Mrs Summerhayes' expression, compound of astonishment and — satisfaction, was it? Surely not. Unless she was merely glad of Felicity's better mood?

Her hostess left her to her letter and went back to the sofa. "Where did I leave my glass? Oh, there it is. Raoul, will you pass it to me?"

Felicity pulled a fresh sheet of paper towards her and once again dipped her pen into the inkpot. In as few words as possible, she put Mrs Jeavons in possession of the facts and begged the headmistress to allow her to retake her post, if she had not yet found a replacement. She ended with her direction, asking for a reply by return as otherwise she would be whisked away from the metropolis by the kind lady who had offered her shelter. She said nothing of Mrs Summerhayes' schemes on her behalf. If Mrs Jeavons wrote positively, she would lose no time in hastening off to Bath.

It only remained to seal the letter and have Lord Lynchmere frank it. That done, she could unpack her things with a clear conscience. At least she would have done everything she could to secure her future — and remove her embarrassing presence from his lordship's life.

As Raoul leaned over the bureau to apply his signature to Miss Temple's folded letter, a riffle disturbed his veins. She had pulled back in her chair to allow him access. He could wish she had stood up instead.

The flourish with which he always signed complete, he set down the pen and straightened, glad to be able to move away. Her nearness disturbed him. When he'd massaged her shoulders, he had detected a subtle but recognisable scent that lingered in his senses from the moments he'd had her in his arms in his carriage. At the time, wishing only to offer comfort, its draw eluded him. Today it was producing an unwelcome effect. He took refuge in his habitual manner as she thanked him.

"A mere nothing, ma'am."

She smiled faintly. "It is not nothing to me, sir." She blew on the fresh ink to dry it as she rose. "If you will forgive me, I must see to its despatch at once."

"Maunder will do that, my dear," came from Angelica. "Ring the bell again, Raoul."

But as he crossed the room, the butler entered, bearing a loaded tray. "Ah, your coffee, I apprehend, Miss Temple."

"Set it down, Maunder, and take —"

But Miss Temple cut Angelica short. "Would it be too much to ask to have the coffee in my chamber? Do you mind if I retire, ma'am?"

"Dear child, not in the least. You ought to rest. Maunder, have someone take the tray to Miss Temple's room. Oh, and see to it that her letter is despatched forthwith."

As a footman was called in to take the tray, Raoul found Miss Temple coming towards him, valise in hand. His attention fastened on the piece of luggage. Incongruous and inappropriate. She ought not to be obliged to carry it herself. An unpalatable reminder of her poverty. He took it from her and held it towards the butler.

"Maunder will take that for you, ma'am."

She blinked in a confused way. "I am capable of carrying a valise, you know."

"I dare say." He handed the thing to the butler, who had immediately moved to take it.

"Send a maid to assist Miss Temple, Maunder."

The girl's frown intensified as she turned to Angelica. "Truly, ma'am, there is no need to bother one of the maids. I can manage."

Angelica waved an airy hand. "I expect you can."

But she did not rescind the order, to Raoul's satisfaction. He waited until the servants had left the room. "Try not to advertise your situation to the whole world, Miss Temple."

Her mouth fell open and her eyes flashed. Raoul felt a prick of conscience, but ignored it.

"Is that said to provoke me, sir?"

"Not at all. Servants gossip. You would do well to remember it."

Miss Temple's eyes narrowed. "Is it my situation you despise, my lord, or merely my refusal to engage in pretence?"

He was a trifle taken aback, but did not show it. "Neither. I was thinking rather of Angelica's position in this."

She looked conscious, colouring a trifle. "I beg your pardon, ma'am. Have I embarrassed you too?"

Angelica disclaimed, rising to catch the girl about the shoulders. "Dear child, pay no heed to Raoul. Maunder is discretion itself. If visitors were present, it would be another matter." She turned her head as she spoke, throwing Raoul a concealed look which contained an unmistakeable message to desist. "Off you go, my dear, and have that coffee and then I suggest you lie down upon your bed. It has been a horrid time for you, and I am sure a rest will do you the world of good."

Miss Temple allowed herself to be ushered towards the door, but with obvious reluctance. The moment Angelica released her, she turned. "One moment, if you please, ma'am. I cannot rest unless I say something first to his lordship."

Her gaze slammed into his and Raoul found himself bracing. What now? He summoned his blandest tone. "Yes, Miss Temple?"

Her bosom was rising and falling in a manner that demonstrated the extreme nature of her emotions. What in the world was coming?

"My guardian may have thrown me at your head, sir, and I do you the justice to own you have behaved in a gentlemanly fashion over it, for which I am obliged to thank you." The calmness, with its husky undertone, changed. "But do not imagine for one moment that I will tolerate your autocratic manner. I am not your property!"

With which, she turned her back on him and wrenched open the door, closing it behind her with a decided snap.

Raoul did not know whether to laugh or give way to a flicker of rage. He was saved from having to make the choice as Angelica turned upon him with a face of unholy glee.

"There's for you, Raoul!"

He opted for bewilderment that took him unawares. "What in heaven's name brought that on?"

"Don't ask me, but I must say I am delighted to see you confounded for once." Angelica retook her seat and waved him to another. "We need to talk, Raoul."

"Yes, I dare say, but I still want to know what I've done to incur the chit's wrath."

"She's not a chit. She's mature beyond her years and very much her own mistress."

"So it would seem." He was annoyed to realise he was smarting still from the unprovoked attack. "Anyone would suppose I had staked a claim of some kind, instead of which..." He faded out, appalled to realise what he was about to say. To boast of voluntarily giving up thousands of pounds of debt rather than taking the girl in lieu was scarcely a worthy sentiment. He was surprised to find that it rankled. Miss Temple was not to blame for it, but he nevertheless felt deprived. Had he unconsciously assumed rights over her? It was what she supposed.

"Raoul, are you paying attention?"

He came out of his thoughts to the realisation his cousin had been speaking and he had not heard a word. "No, I am not." He dropped into the chair the girl had originally occupied and was instantly reminded of that damned scent. He tried to ignore it. "What were you talking about?"

"Felicity, of course. I am saying we must decide how we are going to play the game in public after last night's fiasco."

"We?"

"Of course we. Do you mean to abandon the child?"

"I thought you said she was a mature woman."

Angelica made an exasperated sound. "That is nothing to the purpose. I have been thinking and I believe I know how we may proceed."

Raoul suppressed a groan. Angie thinking invariably ended in some plan he was bound to dislike. Was he not already embroiled enough? "Say on."

She gave him one of her mischievous looks. "I intend to. You need not fret. It is nothing untoward. On the contrary, it ought to mitigate any harmful effect, although you will be obliged to participate."

He sighed. "Don't spare me."

"As if I would." Her characteristic business-like manner returned. "Our difficulty, as I see it, is the inevitable speculation about Felicity's background."

Raoul frowned. "Yes, about that. Has she told you anything of it?"

"I have not yet asked her, but I will worm it all out of her, never fear." She pointed her fan at him. "Don't interrupt me or I shall lose the thread."

"I can guess what you are going to say. No one could cavil at Maskery's antecedents, despite his excesses. Thus you suppose her parentage to be at least acceptable."

"Not necessarily."

The words damped Raoul. Miss Temple had been well educated, but was that her deceased father's doing, or Maskery's? Highly unlikely. "If you are thinking a reprobate like Maskery put the girl through school out of the goodness of his heart, I beg to differ."

"I am not thinking it. But whether Felicity's father is a gentleman or not is beside the point. We must make him one. If I say, as I plan to do, that she is a young acquaintance of mine, everyone will automatically assume it. Moreover, it will account for you bidding on her. We will put it about that I have taken her under my wing and chose to introduce her at the Latimers' party."

Raoul inspected the scheme and found a flaw. "Why then did you not present her to some of your acquaintance before this wretched auction of yours began?"

Angelica gave him an indignant look. "It was not wretched. It was eminently successful and will be talked of for the rest of the Season."

He refrained from saying that the party had fizzled out once supper was over. Besides, his interest did not lie with the Latimers. "That does not answer my question."

She threw up exasperated hands. "You are impossible, Raoul! Can't you think of anything for yourself? I was busy. I had no time to be doing the pretty with the wench. Use your imagination! Are you going to help me do this, or are you not?"

Under normal circumstances, he would have given an unequivocal negative. But his involvement prevented that response. "What is it you wish me to do?"

"I've told you. When you are twitted about bidding on Felicity, as you no doubt will be, simply say what I've outlined."

"And if I am further questioned?"

"You don't know anything, of course. No one will be surprised at that. It's not as if I haven't thrown dozens of girls in your way only to have you ignore them."

An instinct of danger rose up. Raoul eyed his cousin with burgeoning suspicion. "What are you up to, Angelica?"

She showed him an innocent face. "But I have told you."

"Indeed? I've an idea there is more to it." A thought occurred and he frowned. "In any event, it won't fadge. She was in my company for some time. None will believe I know nothing about her."

His cousin's brows rose. "Well, what did you talk of?"

"The fact that her duenna and Maskery had both disappeared." The memory of his first moments with Miss Temple passed through his mind. "She was not forthcoming. Except to tell me she had no social arts. She did speak of the academy and being a schoolmistress, but that was all I could get out of her."

"Well, don't go telling people that, for heaven's sake! In fact, you need say no more than what will place her with me. Any other question you may treat as an impertinence."

He knew he was famed for his set-downs. They provided a useful shield against gossiping tongues. "To tell you the truth, Angie, people are unlikely to ask me anything about it at all."

"All to the good. But I believe you are too sanguine. Silve and Hetty both overheard the business mentioned, and separately at that. If you were not in general so disobliging, Raoul, it would not matter. But you behaved so out of character, it is bound to be remarked upon."

He cursed aloud. "I wish to heaven I never had bid on the creature!"

"It is too late now." Angelica gave him a speculative look. "Moreover, I rather think she intrigues you more than somewhat. Am I right?"

She was, but he was damned if he was going to admit as much. "My interest, if any, has been forced upon me. I may find it inconvenient and galling, but I am not so callous as to leave Miss Temple to bear the burden of her guardian's iniquity. At the least, it behoves me to see her safely returned to her former life — if that is what she wants."

"At best, then?"

The gleam in his cousin's eye revived the snake of suspicion in his breast. What the devil was Angelica planning?

Once she reached the comfortable chamber her hostess had shown her into earlier in the day, Felicity lost no time in getting rid of the various servants. Still seething, she nevertheless managed to assume the required air of confident authority. She had not been a schoolmistress for nothing.

A word of thanks despatched both the footman who had brought the coffee and the butler with her valise. The latter bowed himself out, assuring her upon enquiry that the missive entrusted to his care would be taken immediately to catch the earliest post. The moment the door closed, Felicity let her breath go in a whoosh and plonked down on the chair next to a small octagonal table where the tray had been set. She lifted the silver pot and poured, dismayed to find her hand shaking.

The devil take that man! How dared he belittle her? So high in the instep as he was himself, did he expect her to behave in the same arrogant fashion? Don't advertise her situation to the world indeed! No, it was *try not to* advertise it, was it not? Insufferable. Patronising, top-lofty, infuriating man! Just when she had been warming to him too.

She added cream and a lump of sugar to her cup, grumbling as her jerky movements made the liquid slop into the saucer. Lifting the cup with scrupulous care, she wiped beneath it with a finger and sipped. The hot brew soothed and her temper began to cool, bringing the inevitable stirring of regret.

She should not have allowed herself to be provoked into unbecoming conduct. Yet she might be pardoned for it, Lord Lynchmere's remarks coming as they did so closely upon the discovery of her guardian's outrageous act. He ought to be grateful she had not thrown herself to the carpet, screaming and drumming her heels. But, no. He must needs draw unnecessary attention to the wide disparity existing between a marquis and her parlous condition.

Oh, dear me, Miss Temple, we cannot have you carrying your own valise like the nonentity you are. Not in this house. At least try to pretend to a right to call yourself a lady. Faugh!

A knock at the door interrupted her inward tirade. Instinct bade her get up to answer it, but the consciousness that in this house she ought not, stayed her.

"Come in."

The door opened and a capped head peeped around it. "I'm Peg, miss. Mr Maunder said to wait on you."

Felicity sighed. "Well, come in then."

The girl did as she was bid and closed the door, bobbing a curtsy, and glancing around the room. She was a pretty wench, scarcely older than some of the girls in Felicity's care at the academy.

Spotting the valise, Peg picked it up. "I'll put your clothes away, miss."

Without further ado, she went to the dresser to one side of the room, setting the valise down on a chair. Unused to being waited on, Felicity hesitated. But when the girl opened the thing and gasped, staring within, she could no longer be still.

Half-empty cup in hand, she rose. "What is the matter?"

The girl glanced at her. "Begging your pardon, miss, it's all a-jumble."

"Is it?" The marquis's admonishment loomed large in her mind. She could hardly say she had not packed it herself. She fumbled for an excuse. "Yes, I dare say it is. I packed in a hurry."

Drawn by the whole sorry reminder of last night's fiasco, she moved to look. It was indeed a jumble. Whoever had stuffed her belongings inside — Mrs Sprake? — had made no attempt to fold anything, evidently shoving things in pell-mell without regard to order or logic.

Dismayed by this fresh evidence of her guardian's flight, Felicity forgot to be careful of her tongue. "Great heavens, but they were in a hurry indeed!"

The maid blinked at her in obvious surprise, but was clearly too well-trained to express it. Instead, she lifted a bundle of clothes out of the valise and took it to the bed. "I'll soon sort it out for you, miss, never fear."

For a moment, Felicity watched in a resurgence of distress as Peg began sifting through her crumpled garments. Her old brown muslin showed creases, her worn shift was scrunched up and her heavy black shoes had been shoved in among the linen. Finding her cup in her hand, she drank the rest of the coffee and went to the table to put it down. Her headache, which had begun to recede, returned to plague her. Felicity set her hands on the back of her chair and gripped it, closing her eyes against the pain and the turmoil of her mind.

All very well for her to snipe at Lord Lynchmere, but if not for his aid where would she be? Moreover, he had been open with her all along, making no attempt to conceal her guardian's clear intent. She had been unfair. Ought she to apologise? Well, if he came again, she would have to. Would he, though? He had discharged his errand in bringing her valise to her. But he had left her in Mrs Summerhayes' care, and she intended a visit to her home. There was no necessity, as far as she could see, why his lordship should involve himself any further.

"It's only the top bit as is all a-jumble, miss. The rest don't look as bad."

Felicity let go of the chair back and turned, recalling the state of the valise when she had last seen it. "I had not unpacked it all."

"I'll do it now, shall I, miss?"

"Wait!"

She crossed to look into the valise. The remainder, after the mess had been cleared, was not as neat as she had left it. Had it been disturbed? There were creases and gaps where the contents looked as if they'd been pulled apart by a hand searching within.

Apprehension filtered through her veins. Aware of Peg's gaze, she dug deep into the recesses of the valise, feeling for the hard edges that would reveal her hidden coins. She could not find them. The flitter deepened into the beginnings of panic. Without hesitation, she began to pull items out of the valise.

"Take these!"

The maid obeyed, grabbing the articles shoved at her and tossing them onto the bed as Felicity dragged out her jean boots, her folded chemise and a spare nightgown. Papa's journal, thank heavens, was still tucked in among her under-petticoats and she set it aside. She lifted the small box containing her precious mementoes and opened it. A splatter of relief took off a modicum of the panic. These at least were safe. But the coins?

She handed the box to Peg. "Be careful with this." Then she paid no heed as the maid placed it on top of the dresser, too busy scrabbling at the oddments still left in her meagre piece of luggage as she hunted for the careful packages stowed among the articles at the base of her valise. Of her old glove there was no sign. The stockings did not materialise either.

Bereft, Felicity ceased her frantic search, staring into the empty valise in stunned disbelief. Had Lord Maskery stooped so low as to rob his own ward? Or was it Mrs Sprake who had seized Felicity's last hope of independence?

Whichever of them had taken them, her coins were gone. Now she was destitute indeed.

CHAPTER SIX

The club's upper room was desultory with the aftermath of a good dinner. Wisps of pipe smoke mingled with the haze of burning candles and the lingering aromas of beefsteak and cheese. Raoul sipped the fine port, enjoying the distraction from the previous night's events. It was not total. Images of dancing freckles and red hair hovered in the back of his mind with irritating and obstinate persistence.

He was reluctant when Jerram reminded him of the engagement and had considered crying off. But as president of the Leisureman's Club he could scarcely fail to make an appearance at this season's dinner. Besides, he had personally initiated its beginnings in a spirit of irony towards the energetic Corinthians of the Four-Horse Club. It amused him when the notion attracted a coterie of like-minded members, mostly men of maturity and sense, good company for a conversable evening.

He was not best pleased to find Nalderwood, who had chaired the auction last night, to be his immediate neighbour at the table. But as Guineaford sat on his other side, he was able to engage the latter in a discussion of the hostilities with France. Though, like most of society, he cordially disliked the man's wife, Guineaford was popular with his peers. Raoul found him astute and knowledgeable, and was inclined to enjoy his occasionally acidic wit.

The talk veered from the complicated arrangements to preserve Nelson's body for the lying-in-state and then its burial in January to the potential for peace in Europe after Austerlitz. Guineaford gave it as his opinion that Britain had not seen the last of Napoleon, but as he expounded his theories, Raoul's mind gave in to a tendency to rove over his more pressing personal concerns.

He had not neglected to check on his secretary's progress.

"I had no more success than you, my lord, at the Black Swan. However, I repaired to Lord Maskery's lodging —"

"Good man! How came I to forget that?"

"Perhaps because you knew him to be staying at the inn, my lord. In any event, I drew blank there. It seems he gave the place up more than a week since."

"Had he been staying at the Black Swan all the time, then?"

"I will ascertain tomorrow, my lord. I also have the intention of checking at any livery stables within a reasonable distance, since his lordship must have had a vehicle to bring the lady back from Bath."

"To take him on to the Continent as well, perhaps. Admirable, my dear fellow. Advise me the moment you find out anything of value."

Jerram bowed. "Naturally I will do so, my lord. I am sanguine, for he cannot have disappeared without trace."

True enough. Someone was bound to know something. Raoul began to entertain some hope of unravelling the mess.

"By the by, Lynchmere, who's the filly Maskery brought to the Latimer do?"

Startled back to the present, Raoul regarded Guineaford through narrowed eyes. How the devil had he slipped from the activities of the lately crowned Emperor of the French to this objectionable subject? "You saw him with her?"

"In the hall, yes. I was late myself." Guineaford gave him a shrewd look. "Surprised me to see you make that bid, I'll admit."

Raoul curled his lip. "I dare say you are not the only one."

"Because you never indulge in follies of the kind? No, no, my dear boy, that's not it. Your cousin no doubt persuaded you."

Which was true enough. Were Angelica's machinations common knowledge, then? Or was it Guineaford's peculiar ability to read between the lines? Just what had he specifically noticed to make him bring it up?

"What are you getting at, sir?"

Guineaford pursed his lips and picked up his glass. "It's none of my affair, of course, my dear boy, and I confess I was in two minds about speaking out."

"Cut line, Guineaford. We are well enough acquainted, and I know you don't indulge in futile gossip."

The man sipped and inclined his head in acknowledgement. He sat up and set his elbows on the table, leaning in and lowering his voice. "The word is Maskery is all to pieces."

Raoul threw up his eyes. "Tell me something new."

"I've a riddle for you instead. Why would a fellow who hasn't a feather to fly with show up at a fashionable event with a strange girl and his own doxy?"

It hit with some force. The Sprake woman was Maskery's mistress? And he'd used her as a duenna for his ward. Lord above, was there no end to the fellow's effrontery?

"Do you know this for a fact?"

Guineaford nodded, wafting away a stray drift of smoke from one of the nearby pipes. "Most certainly. I've seen him with her before, and not where you'd take a lady."

Small wonder she'd made herself scarce as soon as she could. The insult to Miss Temple rankled, but was superseded by the immediate danger if this got out.

"Is it generally known?"

"I doubt it. Maskery is lax, but he has some scruples."

"Not many." The bitter note slipped out and he caught Guineaford's faintly raised brow. "Don't ask."

"Wouldn't dream of it. I see I have already spoken out of turn."

Raoul hesitated. But Guineaford's discretion was to be relied upon. Miss Temple's reputation must be protected. "I am more deeply enmeshed in this business than it appears, Guineaford. Not, I hasten to add, by my desire. I must beg you will refrain from mentioning what you have told me to anyone else."

Guineaford raised his glass in silent acknowledgement and Raoul was satisfied. But he reckoned without Nalderwood, who ended a laughing conversation with another and turned at that moment.

"Been meaning to ask you, Lynchmere. Where in the world did the Latimers dig up the little redhead?"

Aware of the ironic twist of Guineaford's smile, Raoul took refuge in Angelica's version of events. "Miss Temple? She's an acquaintance of my cousin's."

"Ah, that explains it. I wondered what maggot got into your head to be making that bid." For once Raoul was glad of Angelica's propensity for running other people's lives. It proved insufficient to cover everything, however. "Who is she? Does Mrs Summerhayes realise she caused something of a stir?"

"It is my cousin's habit, as I am sure you know," said Raoul, sacrificing Angie without a moment's hesitation. "Nothing delights her more than to spring a surprise."

Nalderwood laughed. "Ha! She gave you the office, I dare say."

"To bid on Miss Temple? To some purpose."

Come, this was better than he could have hoped for. As long as Nalderwood kept to banter.

"Does Mrs Summerhayes mean to satisfy everyone's curiosity?"

Raoul shrugged. "I have no notion." He hoped he was giving the impression he did not care either. "The girl is staying with her, that's all I know."

"It can't be all, old fellow. You were talking with her long enough. Must have found out something about her."

Damnation! He summoned his habitual tone of boredom. "We cannot be said to have talked of very much at all. A desultory conversation at best."

Nalderwood slapped the tablecloth. "You're a dull dog, Lynchmere. Good grief, man! A ripe plum falls into your lap and you spurn it."

Raoul winced inwardly. It was truer than the fellow knew. With what Guineaford had told him of Sprake, he could no longer doubt Maskery's intention. But the assumption was convenient. He produced his most cynical sneer. "I am immune to my cousin's wiles, Nalderwood. I chose not to gratify her with a show of interest."

The other laughed. "Still trying to get you to church, is she? That's females all over. Well, she'd hardly fob you off with the wrong sort of female, so this Miss Temple of hers must be respectable."

Raoul said nothing, devoutly hoping her connection to Maskery would remain safely buried. Had it occurred to Angelica that she was perpetrating a fraud upon Society? God help her if the worst should come to light!

"How much was there, if you don't object to my asking?"

Felicity gave her hostess the sum, still smarting from the loss. She had not intended at first to say anything about the vanished guineas, but two circumstances changed her mind. For one thing, Mrs Summerhayes was as shrewd as they come and would likely notice her abstraction and demand an explanation. For another, there was no point in concealment when the maid Peg had been present to see her dismay. It would be all over the house within hours, if not sooner. She had not dealt with young girls for years without learning it was futile to expect them to keep secrets. If she was any judge, Peg would be eager to relay the story of the jumbled clothes in her valise as well.

Wasting no time, Felicity put her hostess in possession of the facts over dinner, no longer paying lip service to Lord Lynchmere's admonition to keep her situation undetected. What, in any event, were the servants to make of a guest who arrived with nothing and was handed a valise by the marquis upon the following day? It could not have escaped their knowledge either that Mrs Summerhayes had purchased clothes on her behalf.

"I dare say it is a paltry amount to you, ma'am, but it meant a great deal to me."

Her hostess signed to the butler to remove the remains of the ragout and the roasted fowl, with their accompanying dishes of green beans, peas and a savoury omelette. "Also, Maunder, do, for heaven's sake, refrain from passing on anything you have heard in this room."

In the act of removing two silver dishes from the table, the butler bowed. "Your ladyship may rely upon my discretion. I sent Matthew out of the room the moment Miss Temple began to speak of the matter."

Felicity sighed. "Of what use to do so when Peg already knows?"

"You may leave Peg to me, miss. She will not speak of it."

As Maunder departed with a full tray, Mrs Summerhayes leaned in, lowering her voice. "She will, of course, but it can't be helped. Maunder will see to it that none of the servants gossip outside of our own."

"It makes no matter to me, ma'am. Though no doubt your cousin will object."

Mrs Summerhayes waved this away. "Oh, we won't regard Raoul. I have set him to put it about you are an acquaintance of mine, by the by."

"Thank you, but I hope you may not be obliged to concoct excuses for me for long."

"Not for the Town busybodies, in any event. However, we had best have something of your real background at our fingertips for the local gentry round about Barkham."

Dismay swamped Felicity. "I beg you will not hold by that scheme, ma'am. I am determined to return to the academy forthwith, if you will be kind enough to lend me the necessary fare."

"Certainly not." Her hostess twinkled. "Don't look so dismayed. Of course I will lend you whatever you need, but I hope you will think better of going back there."

Felicity eyed her in some degree of dismay. "But why, ma'am? You cannot wish for such a scandal as is likely to break if the truth were to become known."

"Oh, pish! How is anyone to find it out?"

"Very easily, I should think. Can you not see how my guardian's actions show him to be utterly unscrupulous? There is no saying what he may do. I will not be the cause of bringing shame upon anyone, however unwitting."

Mrs Summerhayes wagged a finger. "You need not be concerned for Raoul. It is about time he was shaken up a trifle. He is far too set in his ways."

"I am not concerned for Raoul — I mean, for his wretched lordship!" Aware she was snapping, Felicity reined in her escaping temper. "I beg your pardon, ma'am, but he has an unhappy knack of rubbing me up the wrong way."

Her hostess giggled like a girl. "I noticed. Highly delightful it is too. I wish you may drive him to distraction."

A disturbing snake of suspicion crept through Felicity, but she paid it little heed, anxious to win her point. "Pray don't think I am not grateful, Mrs Summerhayes, but —"

"I thought we had agreed on Angelica?"

"Angelica then, but —"

"I don't wish to hear any buts. My dear, at the very least it will give you a respite, which I am sure is very much needed."

Felicity began to despair of making any impression on the creature. "You don't understand, Angelica. How should you indeed? I cannot drift along in such a way without securing my future. Mrs Jeavons needs the post filled. If I don't seize it now, I will be obliged to seek one elsewhere and I had much rather go where I am known and valued."

She was obliged to break off as the butler re-entered with a full tray. Despite her conviction that all was already known, she found herself reluctant to talk of her true occupation in this milieu.

As the butler set out a selection of sweetmeats, fruit and succulent tarts, Felicity could not but reflect on the huge disparity between this meal — which her hostess had described as simple — and the frugal fare she must return to at the academy. Not that her appetite was able to do justice to it. She was too wound up to partake of much more than a few mouthfuls of each dish.

"A little more wine, Maunder, and then you may leave us to serve ourselves." The butler refilled each of the glasses and withdrew, what time her hostess gave Felicity a sympathetic smile. "I do understand, my dear child, and if you are set upon this course, I shall not stand in your way."

"Thank you." Relief warred with a trifle of disappointment, but Felicity shook it off. "I did ask if my post was still vacant in the letter I sent."

"Well then, you may at least wait for a reply, don't you think?"

"I can scarcely do other, ma'am. I would not embarrass poor Mrs Jeavons for the world."

Angelica had no response to this, except to draw Felicity's attention to the various dishes on offer. She loaded her own plate with a variety of sweetmeats and a few grapes.

To please her, Felicity took a slice of damson tart, toying with it as an unaccountable weight of depression threatened to engulf her. She had won her point. She ought to be relieved and glad. Instead she found herself wondering if she would ever see Lord Lynchmere again.

Not that she wanted to, but she did owe him an apology. She would also like an opportunity to thank him properly for all he had done for her. Infuriating he might be, with his caustic way, but he had been chivalrous. Kind, too. A distressing urge to weep overtook her as she recalled the way he had pulled her into a hug when she had been overcome with shock. Felicity fought it down, forking a morsel of tart into her mouth and chewing with determined attention.

"A penny for them?"

Felicity started, her glance shifting to her hostess. Angelica was regarding her with a lurking expression of amusement. "Oh, nothing very much." She shook off her abstraction. "I was thinking that I have been a little unfair on your cousin. He behaved with remarkable forbearance towards me and I have been rather grudging, I feel."

"Don't waste your regrets on Raoul, I beg. He is perfectly provoking and I'll wager he prefers your bite."

A reminiscent laugh escaped Felicity. "He does. He said so."

"There you are, then. Don't go thinking you owe him any sort of apology. Indeed, we will be much better employed in talking of you. Tell me, what was your father about to be naming a man like Maskery for your guardian?"

Felicity winced. "I cannot think Papa can have known his true character. Or perhaps he had not then fallen into a gaming habit. It was all so long ago."

"But had your father any particular reason for trusting him?"

Angelica's persistence both grated and gratified. Reticent about talking of her origins, Felicity was yet conscious of feeling pleased someone was interested enough to ask. It made her feel something more than a nonentity. The question, however, was an impossible one.

"To be truthful, I don't know. I was not privy to the particular relationship between Papa and Lord Maskery. I did not even know him except as the shadowy figure who arranged for my schooling. Until he died, you see, Papa attended to my education himself."

Angelica's brows flew up. "Singular. Was he a scholar?"

Felicity was betrayed into laughter. "Far from it." The long-buried images sprang to life. "He was too fond of a joke to be a scholar. I remember him as laughing and rather what one might call devil-may-care. He taught me more by precept than application. Also adventure, as he called it. We moved around a great deal."

"Was he a military man?"

"Oh, no." Felicity frowned over a circumstance that had ever puzzled. "As far as I know, he had no occupation, but we managed somehow. I believe there was an allowance. I really don't know how he contrived. However it was, it all vanished with his death." She saw Angelica hesitate and guessed at the question hovering on her tongue. With a little difficulty, Felicity broached the discomforting subject. "You are thinking he was a gamester like Lord Maskery. Don't imagine it had not occurred to me."

Her hostess fiddled with a grape. "But you don't wish to think it. That I can understand."

Felicity pushed away her plate and set her elbows on the table, steepling her restless fingers to still them. "It is not that. At least, of course I don't wish to believe my father was a man of Maskery's stamp, but I truly do not think he was. For one thing, I doubt he could afford to gamble. He sold stories sometimes, but he was never assiduous in trying to make a living at it. When he wrote it was largely for pleasure, I believe. Papa was insouciant and carefree. But also responsible, at least where I was concerned. He used to talk of making do until the quarter, and of settling down soon so that I might have a home and a governess. He said he had expectations, though what that meant I never discovered." The familiar pang twisted in her gut. "He was killed before I was old enough to learn these things."

"Good heavens, you poor child! What happened?"

Felicity could talk of it now without distress. It was almost as if the dreadful event had happened to someone else. "An accident. He was knocked down. I don't know the exact details, but I understood it was a team of horses, driven fast."

Angelica's hand went to her mouth and she gasped. "But how terrible!"

"Yes, it was. I didn't see it, thank the Lord. Our landlady told me. Nan? Yes, that is it. Nan. I called her *Nanny*. She looked after me until my guardian appeared, and he packed me off to school in Bath."

"Where you have been ever since?"

Felicity had to smile. "Don't look so horrified. Mrs Jeavons is a very motherly woman. She took me to her bosom, so to speak. Without her, I should have been miserable indeed."

"Ah, I begin to see why you feel you had rather return to her than find yourself obliged to seek a post elsewhere."

If she was truthful, Felicity would eminently prefer to do neither. These few short days of freedom from the drudgery of her former life could not but beckon, despite the hideous quandary into which they had thrown her. But there was no choosing that path. Return she must. To be wholly dependent upon the generosity of others was to put oneself at a disadvantage. Papa had said it often enough.

"Never allow another to control your destiny, Flissie, my love. Always go your own way. Independence, that's the thing."

He had spoken of it often, with many sayings of the kind. Felicity guessed it irked him to be waiting on the quarterly allowance. But he had nevertheless endured with a gaiety she tried to emulate.

"Don't let the slings and arrows get you down, Flissie. A glad heart and laughter will carry you through the worst life may throw at you."

It had been hard to find that glad heart when he was gone and her life changed so dramatically. But Felicity had not forgotten and she did her best to live up to Papa's dictum. It helped that she had inherited his sense of humour, and she never lost the lack of pretension he had early instilled with his light-hearted banter and irreverent approach to his fellow man.

"But, Felicity, had you no other family?"

The question kicked at a point that had ever niggled. "Not that I know of. I must suppose there are relations somewhere, but I have never heard of any."

Angelica's expression became fierce. "But it's monstrous! Why did not Maskery tell you these things?"

Felicity shrugged. "I never saw him."

"You mean he dumped you at this academy of yours and vanished, never to be seen again?"

"Until he came to fetch me." She frowned, caught by a memory as she absently reached for a sugared almond. "No, wait. He did come once. Or it may have been twice. I recall being sent for to Mrs Jeavons' parlour. There was a gentleman there, whom I supposed was my guardian."

"Did not you recognise him? When he came this time, I mean."

For the first time, Felicity tried to fit the face she now knew to the one she had earlier seen. She drummed her fingers lightly on the table, staring at them as she contemplated the older image. "Do you know, I cannot tell. I was so shocked, I think, by his proposal, all my faculties became blunted. It must have been he earlier, for I should not think anyone else has ever heard of me, much less known where to find me. No, no, it is absurd, Angelica."

"What, to be thinking perhaps another sought you out? Why should they not? Your father's death must have been reported. It sounds to be exactly the sort of event the journals delight in printing. The newspapers are full of such reports."

Felicity had to agree, despite the train of speculation set up in her mind. Perhaps there might be a way to learn something? She did not mention the nebulous thought.

"If such a report reached your father's family," pursued Angelica, "it is conceivable they made enquiries and found out what had happened to you."

Felicity remained sceptical. "Well, if anyone did, they did not see fit to make any sort of change. For which I must be thankful. I could expect nothing but to have been a drudge of a poor relation and once again dependent upon others for my livelihood." She shuddered. "No, no, Angelica. I had far rather receive a wage for my services. And if I had not been so foolish as to fall into Lord Maskery's trap —"

"That will do, Felicity! You are not to blame. The villain dangled an irresistible carrot before your face."

The image this conjured up could not but make Felicity laugh. "Let us admit I was dazzled, Angelica, and leave it at that. It is pointless to dispute about it."

"That is all very well, but you have intrigued me, Felicity." A positively fanatical light came into Angelica's eyes. "For my part, I think we should do all we can to discover your relations. It cannot be difficult. There are not many families bearing the name of Temple."

"To what end, Angelica? Do you suppose I am going to force them to recognise me? I had rather not know, to be truthful."

It was plain this view of the matter did not sit well with Mrs Summerhayes, but she thankfully dropped the subject, becoming brisk. "Time enough to be thinking of all that. Now, what would you like to do tomorrow? I must follow up with Margaret Latimer and make sure Gawcott is doing his part. You may come with me, if you choose. Unless you would prefer to see some of the sights? Peg can accompany you and I will put one of my carriages at your disposal."

Felicity blinked at this programme. "See the sights? What sights?"

"Good heavens, child, London is full of remarkable things! The Tower where you may see the wild beasts, or the British Museum — do you like antiquities? Oh, and at present it is *de rigueur* to visit Nelson's tomb at Westminster Abbey. Yes, and you must not miss The Whispering Gallery at St Paul's. Not that in general one has time for these things, but you are at leisure, so you may do as you please."

"Thank you, ma'am," Felicity said when she was finally able to edge in a word, "but I would infinitely prefer to remain quietly here. I need to sort out the shambles made of my things, and —"

"And sit brooding on your situation. I won't have it, Felicity." Angelica nodded with finality and rose. "We will take tea in the private parlour and retire early. You will accompany me tomorrow and if you don't choose to see the sights, I shall leave you in the care of Hetty and Silve."

While she could not but be amused by Angelica's managing way, she was equally irked. A half-formed intention of an early departure began to dissipate. If she asked for a loan, Angelica would guess what she meant to do. Besides which, she really ought to wait for Mrs Jeavons to answer her letter. Yet the urge to be gone was an unrelenting itch. Had it been thus with Papa? Was that why he shifted ground so often?

The niggle set up in her brain by Angelica's questions returned. She had never before had reason to wonder about Papa's antecedents. It occurred to her for the first time that if his allowance had stopped, someone must have known of his death.

CHAPTER SEVEN

The letter, franked with an illegible scrawl, was awaiting Raoul at the breakfast table. Since Jerram always sifted through his correspondence, its presence, at the top of a neat pile of invitations, signalled a question. His secretary clearly judged it as needing Raoul's personal attention. Jerram had breakfasted and gone by the time his employer came down and was likely already off about his investigations.

"Has Jerram left the house?"

The butler was proffering a silver dish. "An hour since, my lord."

Raoul grunted, regarding the letter with disfavour as Oakley served him with his usual preference of ham and eggs. Anything untoward at this point was suspect. Was the direction written in Maskery's hand? After what he'd learned last night, Raoul had no desire to have any communication with the man.

He ate in frowning silence, mulling over the consequences of Angelica's ill-fated auction. Instinct bade him wash his hands of the whole affair. It was not as if Miss Temple wished for his intervention. He had never met a more independently-minded female.

The simplest thing would be to send her back to this infernal academy. Not by the stagecoach, of course. He could at least have her conveyed in his travelling carriage. An image of the girl arriving in Bath in his private coach with a crest on the panel leapt into his head. No, that would not do. He would have to hire a chaise. The vision of the lone redhead therein proved equally unpalatable.

Hell and the devil, that would not do either! The girl could not jaunter about the country unaccompanied. As well put her on the stage after all. He would have to send a maid with her. Angelica could provide one.

At which point his entire scheme came apart. His cousin would never consent.

"Ale, my lord? Or coffee?"

He came out of his reverie. "Coffee." He had slept off last night's potations but he needed to think.

What maggot had got into Angelica's head? He had asked her to provide the girl with a roof for the night. But, no. His cousin insisted on an elaborate plan to drag Miss Temple off to Cherry Lodge. If his first suspicion had any foundation, any such scheme was unlikely to hold when Angelica heard that Maskery had provided Miss Temple with a so-called duenna in the person of his mistress. The ramifications were too scandalous to be contemplated. Even Angie must see the ineligibility of thrusting the girl onto the *Ton* after such an introduction.

He downed his coffee and found the letter still staring him in the face. He set it aside and checked through the invitations. His presence was requested at a number of the balls, soirées and musical evenings that proliferated at this time of year. Ha! With all this palaver going on, he'd be lucky to have time to attend any of them. Not that he wanted to. After the fiasco of the auction, he would much prefer to abandon the metropolis in favour of his home. Lucille at least would be delighted.

He tossed the invitations aside. The obnoxious letter remained. There was nothing for it. He would have to broach the thing.

Rising, he took it up. "I will be in the library, Oakley."

Ensconced in his favourite leather-bound chair by the fire, Raoul at last broke the seal and spread open the closely-written sheet. At least the lines were not crossed. He glanced at the signature.

Damn it to hell, it was Maskery! Had he not known it? With deep misgiving, he lifted his glass to the page and began to read.

A tense hour of speculation while the twins argued, poring over Mr Latimer's copy of the Peerage, did Felicity no good at all. She began to wish she had not been drawn into revealing the circumstances of her father's death.

"The trouble is," said Silvestre, raising her head from the tome, "we do not know if Temple is a family name for one of the peers, or merely a remote connection."

The two girls were seated side by side at a card table in the upstairs parlour, whither Henrietta had dragged Felicity while Silvestre went off to the library to dig out the required book.

"No one will disturb us here," said the gentler creature. "Although I don't doubt Aunt Angelica and Mama will be engaged for some time with Mr Gawcott."

Silvestre soon joined them in the cosy apartment reserved only for family use with its faded sofa, untidy work table dotted with sewing silks, parchments and a tambour frame, a small bureau near the wall and a variety of ill-matched chairs. She plonked the heavy book down on the table and settled into a chair, pushing aside an open box of dominoes.

"Papa has gone off to his club, thank goodness, so I did not have to account for why I wanted his Peerage. Now then, let us see what we can find."

A prolonged search, with Hetty arguing for a systematic method while Silve flipped the pages back and forth, yielded nothing but a plethora of family names utterly remote from Temple.

"Can you not remember anything that may help us, Felicity?"

"I wish I could. I was only a child and Papa was all the family I knew."

Silvestre flipped pages again. "What about friends? Your papa, I mean. Did you meet any of them?"

"Not that I recall. I suppose he had them. He used to go out sometimes, leaving me with a maid or the landlady sometimes. We had no settled home, you see."

Henrietta looked shocked, but Silvestre's eyes sparkled. "It sounds a very gypsy life. I've often wished I might live so. I'd like to follow the drum, I think. Such adventure!"

Hetty shuddered. "Don't, Silve! I can think of nothing more unpleasant."

Her sister struck the open tome. "This is useless. We could go through the whole book and find nothing."

"I fear you are right." Felicity smiled. "But thank you for trying."

Silvestre set the book aside. "Letters! Papers! That is where we should be looking."

"But I have none!"

"Impossible. You must have something."

"Oh, hush, Silve!" Henrietta threw an apologetic look across the table. "Don't heed her, Felicity. She means well."

"Do be quiet, Hetty. This is important. There must be something, Felicity. What happened to your papa's effects? Someone must have taken care of all that. A person does not die without leaving a whole —"

"Silve!"

Felicity gave a rueful smile. "It's all right, Hetty. It does not hurt to talk of it. And Silve is right."

115

The other twin grinned. "I'm as blunt as Aunt Angelica. But I am right, aren't I? There would have been clothes, letters, papers. All kinds of possessions must have remained, even if you were living out of a portmanteau, as it appears you may have been."

Images coursed through Felicity's mind. The tumbled disorder of the room in which they'd slept, she invariably in a cot or truckle bed, out of which she'd crept many a night to slip in beside Papa's sleeping form. He'd never minded. Once or twice there had been a separate room, but mostly they'd shared. Clothes? Yes, a plethora of garments strewn pell-mell on chairs or the dresser or the bed in the day. His boots discarded on the floor until he remembered to set them outside for polishing. His shirts, neck-cloths and other mangled articles flung in a pile awaiting the attentions of a laundress. The parlour, when they'd had one, which was not all the time, with his books piled higgledy-piggledy on the tables, the sideboards, everywhere a surface offered. Papa had swept them aside for her lessons, picking up any he needed to illustrate some point he made.

"Books," she said aloud. "He had a lot of books. I have no idea what happened to them."

"But papers, Felicity. Think!"

Thus exhorted, she swept her mind for an appropriate image, and found none. If there were papers she had no memory of any, other than the ink-spattered sheets covered in her laborious copperplate as she transcribed at his dictation, or copied a passage he designated to be done while he was out. Also her childish attempts at sketching, which Papa was apt to overpraise and display with prominence wherever he could find a space.

"I don't remember any papers. Only his journal, which I have preserved." Her mind jumped. Papa's journal! She'd thought it lost to her forever, but Lord Lynchmere had restored it to her, along with her valise.

"The very thing! There must be a clue in a journal. Come now, Felicity. You cannot have had it all this time without reading it."

"Don't be silly, Silve. She probably knows it by heart."

"I don't." Catching a little of Silvestre's enthusiasm, Felicity lit with hope. "I have read it, of course, but as for recalling anything pertinent…"

"What do you remember from it, Felicity?"

Henrietta's hesitant query amused her, what with Silvestre's positively gimlet gaze boring into her with unmistakeable demand.

"In the main, it is an account of the places where we stayed, and what we did there. Or what Papa did there, though I cannot say it made much impression upon me. I was more inclined to dwell on his references to my progress, where he wrote that Flissie's writing was improving or praised a particular drawing. I was used to skip the rest."

"Who shall blame you?" Henrietta's eyes were swimming. "You poor thing! So tragic. I should think any such mention was balm."

"Oh, for heaven's sake, Hetty! Must you turn into a watering pot?" Silvestre cast an exasperated look at Felicity. "I apologise for my sister's ridiculous sensibility."

"Can I help it if I am soft-hearted?"

"You ought to. Do you see Felicity crying over it? It was a long time ago. Besides, it is not in the least helpful to be falling into the dismals."

"I am not in the dismals! I am merely sympathising with poor Felicity's plight."

"If you sympathised with her present plight, it would be more to the point."

"I do, but —"

"Pray stop, the both of you!" Felicity shook her head at them. "Really, I don't know whether to laugh or to ring a peal over you."

A rueful look came into Silvestre's countenance and she put her arm about her twin in a quick hug. "I'm a beast, Hetty. Don't heed me. There!"

Henrietta sniffed. "Well, I won't. I am just as anxious as you to help Felicity, if you wish to know."

"Very well, but let us concentrate on the journal. I think you should read it again, Felicity."

"In the hope of finding mention of Papa's family? Frankly, I very much doubt I will. If he never spoke of them to me, and I am sure he did not, I cannot see why he would write about them."

Henrietta looked daunted, but Silvestre was clearly made of sterner stuff.

"You don't know that. You said yourself you don't recall what was written in it besides what he said about you."

"Very true." Although Felicity was not sure she wished to find out. But she did not speak of her reluctance. One aspect did beckon, however. "What may be of use, perhaps, are his entries about where we were. The journal ends abruptly. I never thought to look at the name of the place where he died. If it is there."

Silvestre's gaze brightened. "The very thing! It may jog your memory about his effects. Moreover, I have been thinking about this allowance you mentioned."

"What of it?"

"Well, did it stop? And who was providing it? You might find a clue to that in the journal, perhaps?"

Even Henrietta began to look more interested. "Gracious, Felicity! By rights, it should have come to you!"

"Well done, Hetty! Yes, indeed. Who paid for your schooling?"

Felicity frowned, feeling all at once uncomfortable. "I must suppose it was my guardian."

"Lord Maskery? But he never has a feather to fly with!"

Henrietta's eyes grew intense. "Felicity, do you suppose he used the allowance?"

"What, for my schooling? Perhaps. I don't know. I have been earning my keep for so long, I had not thought about it."

"Well, think now," said Silvestre, looking dissatisfied. "I must say, I find it most odd you seem to have had no curiosity at all about all this, Felicity."

She had to smile. "When you have to earn your living, there is little leisure to indulge in curiosity. A schoolmistress is rarely off duty, you know. Most of our girls board, which means one may be needed night and day to supervise, or to sort out a problem. Or if one of the girls is ill, perhaps."

Now she came to think about it, she had not opened the journal for years. It was a keepsake, like Mama's locket, representing Papa, a substitute in his absence. Its contents were precious for being written in his hand, almost as if the journal thus contained something of his essence. Bereft, she had held it dear all this time, never thinking to search its pages for a past that had become little more than a cloudy and distant memory.

"To tell you the truth," she said aloud into a thoughtful silence, "until my guardian came to Bath with his proposition, I never questioned my destiny. It was fixed."

Silvestre's brows drew together. "You never wondered about your father's family?"

"I'm afraid not. Or if I did, it was but a fleeting interest."

"What of your mother, dear Felicity?" Henrietta sounded hopefully anxious.

"I hardly remember her. I don't even know what she died of, just that she was ill."

"But her family?" Thus Silvestre, still delving. "Perhaps this journal may contain a clue to that?"

"I doubt it. I'm not sure it goes that far back. Papa may not have set up the habit of writing it while she was alive."

"Or there may be earlier versions."

Henrietta tutted. "It is no use saying that, Silve, when she has only the one."

"True. It is odd, though, that all your papa's things have disappeared without trace."

"Perhaps Lord Maskery dealt with it all," Henrietta suggested. "He came to get you, Felicity. And he was your guardian."

"Yes, and someone must have arranged for the funeral. Did you attend, Felicity?"

A remembered pain sent a pang through Felicity's breast as a series of pictures flitted through her mind. "Our landlady was with me. There was a church. I don't know who was there. Not many. We stood around the grave. Nanny clutched my hand throughout, I remember." She gave a tiny laugh. "I think she was more distressed than I. It was not very real to me at the time. Afterwards…"

She faded out, recalling the emptiness of a world without Papa's merry laughter and the warm hug of his arms when he lifted her up.

A sudden remembrance of the other night, caught in Lord Lynchmere's arms, caused a flush of warmth within. She had not been held like that since she'd lost Papa. Not by a man. It had been like, and yet unlike.

She came to herself to find Henrietta weeping again, her twin patting her on the back in a resigned way. Although there was a suspicious brightness to Silvestre's eyes too. Felicity pulled herself together.

"I do beg both your pardons. I had no wish to make a parade of my sorrows."

Henrietta at once disclaimed in a somewhat watery tone, but Silvestre became bracing, rising and crossing to the bell-pull. "What we need is a cup of tea to cheer us all up. Or would you prefer coffee, Felicity?"

Opting for the latter, Felicity heaved a sigh of relief. The whole exercise was depressing in the extreme. She wished with some fervour that her guardian had never come to Bath with his preposterous and false proposal. He had turned her world upside-down to no purpose. Or rather, to an evil purpose which had cast into doubt everything she previously knew or thought about her existence.

"Is he even my guardian?"

She had spoken aloud unthinkingly. The reaction was almost laughable. Henrietta gasped, her mouth dropping open. Silvestre, in the act of returning to the table, halted abruptly.

"Good heavens! Do you think Maskery may have lied about that too?"

Felicity felt warmth rising in her cheeks. "I don't know. It just seems everything is suspect now."

"But you never had occasion to doubt him before," said Henrietta, finding her tongue again. "Would not your Mrs —? I forget her name."

"Mrs Jeavons."

"Would not she have known? She cannot have taken you in without being assured of him being who he said he was."

Silvestre came to the table, standing over her sister. "Why not? Why should she think otherwise?"

"No reason, I suppose, but —"

"I spoke a random thought aloud," Felicity cut in before another argument could develop. "Pray don't make an issue of it. I dare say it is nonsense."

But this would not do for Silvestre. "All the more reason to discover what you can about your papa's family. I wish you will consult this journal as soon as possible."

Felicity had every intention of so doing, but she would infinitely prefer to keep the matter private. The twins meant well, but Silvestre was showing signs of wishing to delve into the mystery of it and Felicity could not persuade herself that any answers she might find were likely to be palatable.

By the time her hostess was ready to return home, Felicity felt more battered than enthusiastic. The Latimer twins were exhausting, not least because of their tendency to interlard every discussion with little squabbles, thus losing the point and going off into unimportant side issues.

Felicity had been glad to be interrupted by the two matrons, who lost no time in changing the direction of the conversation. She was able to retire into her own thoughts while the more positive effects of the auction became the topic of the day. Not that she was permitted to sit quietly throughout, being constantly appealed to by one or other of the two girls to support their ideas.

It was too much like the academy, and she was dismayed to realise how much she was dreading a return after this brief respite. Had she been merely enduring all these years? Had this sense of suppressed frustration always been a part of her life? Or had the talk of Papa merely dredged up too much comparison with a time when she was happy?

The recognition that her life had been uniformly unhappy ever since could not but dismay her. Surely it was not so?

There had been shared laughter, with the girls sometimes, with other teachers and Mrs Jeavons on occasion. Little flashes of colour in the grey painting of her existence. Not dull, no. Never that. One could not be dull with a plethora of lively girls needing attention. Tedious. Demanding. Tiring. With then that thread of dissatisfaction that ran, unheeded, through everything.

Was that why she had fallen victim to Lord Maskery's promised land? Felicity was both shamed and distressed by these reflections. They came tardily, unwelcome when she had determined on going back. How in the world would she settle again after this?

Somewhat subdued, she felt relieved when Angelica failed to notice, being still engrossed in the results of the auction even as the carriage drove them back to George Street.

"I must say I did not expect the thing to come off in quite so spectacular a fashion. When Gawcott told me the sum of his collections I felt quite stunned. Besides which, not all have as yet honoured their pledges. I hoped it would cause a stir, and so it has. But poor dear Margaret is so grateful for the money. She may buy the girls a new gown or two, which she hopes will hide the fact they are now purse-pinched. Not that she intends to squander the takings. Indeed, I advised her to hoard them against a rainy day."

She continued in this strain until the carriage came to a standstill and she was obliged to desist to get down. Felicity was looking forward to a period of quiet, but this hope was shattered by the first words the butler spoke to his mistress.

"Lord Lynchmere is awaiting you in the Yellow Parlour, madam."

"Good heavens! How long has he been here?"

"A good hour, madam. I did venture to suggest a return at a later time, madam, but his lordship insisted." Maunder coughed. "I should perhaps advise you, madam, that he appeared a trifle put out."

Felicity's heart sank. What now? Angelica appeared no less dismayed. She threw a comical glance of question at Felicity.

"What in the world ails him, I wonder?" She gave up her cloak to her waiting maid and untied the ribbons of her bonnet. "Take this, Warden. Come, Felicity."

Handing her cloak to the footman, Felicity followed as her hostess took the stairs at a smart pace and sailed into the family parlour. She stopped short and Felicity caught sight of Lord Lynchmere pacing away from the mantel.

"Raoul?"

He broke stride and turned hard eyes in a set countenance towards the door. "What an age you have been, cousin!" His gaze passed over Angelica and met with Felicity's. His tone was clipped. "I will not say well met, Miss Temple, since the tidings I bring are scarce likely to please you."

The fleeting remembrance of their last meeting, with its adjoining discomfort at the way she had spoken to him, vanished at once. Felicity hardly heard Angelica's strident demand to know what had happened for the abrupt tattoo pattering in her breast.

"What is it, my lord?"

Barely had she got the words out than he fished into an inner pocket and flourished the folded paper thus extracted. "This!"

Instant comprehension. The tattoo redoubled. "From him?"

"Your surmise is correct, ma'am. It is indeed another Maskery abomination."

Mrs Summerhayes threw up her hands as she marched into the room. "Good heavens, Raoul, must you be so dramatic? What does he say?"

Lord Lynchmere's lip curled. "A hypocritical accusation, coming from you, Angelica. In this instance, I believe I am entitled to indulge in a modicum of histrionics."

"Well, don't keep us in suspense!"

His gaze veered to Felicity, an unkind light within it. Harsh. Even cruel, as she felt it, her stomach dropping along with the heavy beat of her heart. What fresh horror was this?

"You look as if you are ready to swoon at last, Miss Temple, but you need no longer maintain the act. The murder is out."

Incomprehension blanketed her mind. "I beg your pardon?"

"You may well. You have been less than truthful with me, have you not?"

"Raoul, what in the world are you talking of?"

He turned eyes suddenly blazing on his cousin. "For once in your life, be quiet, Angelica! This is between Miss Temple and me."

"Gracious heaven, what can you mean?" But her tone had changed. Less demanding than bewildered.

A spark of indignation overlaid Felicity's violent apprehension. She looked from Lord Lynchmere's hard and angry countenance to the letter in his hand. "He has suborned you too. Of what am I deemed guilty, pray?"

He took a pace towards her, the letter rising in his fingers, held accusingly before her face. "A trustee, Miss Temple? I am to expect trouble from a trustee, am I?"

125

Utter confusion wreathed her brain. Overwhelming enough to subdue the rising anger. "What trustee?"

"Yours, I understand."

She looked from the letter to his lordship's steely gaze, meeting it now without flinching. "What has he said? I know nothing of any trustee."

His mouth twisted. "Oh, very good, Miss Temple. You are all too plausible. But you have chosen the wrong man for your tricks."

The spark of hovering anger flared, vanquishing every precept of proper behaviour. Felicity struck him, a cracking blow to the cheek. His head flinched to one side, but he held his ground. Her tongue threw words at him, deep and guttural. "Go to hell!"

She heard Angelica gasp, but the pent-up agonies of the past few days had burst forth and would no longer be contained.

"I don't care what he wrote! I don't care what you think of me, do you understand? I don't need you, or anyone! I have looked after myself all these years, and I can do so again. Go! Take his cursed letter and may you choke to death on it!"

But it was she, choking on sobs, who tried to leave. Turning, she made for the door, her legs so unsteady under her she stumbled and went to catch at the nearest object. Through the blurring at her eyes she saw the arm. Tried to evade it, swatting it away.

But it caught her, dragged her back. Then she was prisoner in a hold of iron, her sobs stifled against the roughness of fabric, a faint aroma of maleness in her nostrils, and a soothing voice, rumbling in the chest against which she was held.

"Hush, now… Forgive me… I had to be sure."

Felicity was beyond thought. She struggled to contain the burden of weeping trying to escape her breast. In a vague way

126

she understood she had been tested and found good. But the accusation rankled, dragging her back to its cause.

With violence she pulled out of his embrace, shifting away. She dragged the back of her hand across her face, heedless of the moistures there, intent on the necessity to speak.

"How dared you do that? You had to be sure? What, that I am not a lying schemer on a par with my guardian? I would have to be fifty kinds of a fool to put myself in a situation fraught with danger. And for what? To catch myself a keeper? I am not a whore, sir!"

"Felicity!"

She spared no glance for her hostess, her glare upon Lord Lynchmere. He appeared unmoved by her words, merely holding out a pocket handkerchief.

"Pray make use of this, Miss Temple. Then we will talk."

She snatched it from his hand, throwing him a look of loathing. "I have no wish to talk. I want to go home!"

"Who shall blame you?" Angelica was up, coming to put an arm about her. "Raoul, how could you? That was cruel, whatever the provocation of that letter."

"To be frank, I didn't intend it. I was furious with Maskery, and became convinced I had been duped."

Still fuming, Felicity wanted to shake off her hostess's arm, but she endured as she wiped away the tearstains and blew her nose. Without thinking, she tucked the handkerchief away in her sleeve and confronted his lordship. "Duped by me? I thank you, my lord. I had not realised the extent of my acting abilities."

He threw up a hand. "Oh, be quiet, woman! I've made my regrets."

"And that makes up for it?"

"It should. Tit for tat, Miss Temple. I have not forgotten your previous attack." A wry smile came. "It is rather like handling a wild cat. She seems tame enough when you stroke her, but beware her claws and the spitting hiss."

Despite herself, amusement bubbled up. "I hate you, my lord, I hope you realise that."

He laughed. "I rather got that impression, yes."

Felicity became aware of Angelica looking from one to the other, her brows flying. "From one extreme to the other! Really, I don't know what to make of either of you."

Felicity sighed and plonked down into the nearest chair. "You had best let me read this ghastly letter, sir."

He fished it out again. Presumably he had re-pocketed it during the late contretemps. "I'm not sure you ought to read it. I can give you the relevant points."

"And censor it to suit? I had rather see it for myself, I thank you."

He held it back. "It does not make for pleasant reading."

"That, my lord, is patent. Let me see it."

Angelica had re-seated herself on the sofa. "Give it to her, Raoul. She is entitled to know what that wretched creature has said."

Nevertheless, when the close-written sheet was put into her hand, Felicity took a moment before she brought it near enough to read. To have prompted the marquis to such fury, it must contain matters too vile for consumption. She glanced up from it to find his lordship's intent gaze upon her as well as Angelica's anxious one. Lord Lynchmere's cheek bore still the imprint of the blow she had dealt him and Felicity's conscience awoke.

"I should not have behaved in so unladylike a fashion, my lord."

His shoulders shifted as if in dismissal and he jerked his head towards the letter. "Would you wish me to read it to you after all?"

She drew in a breath, her eyes on his. "You will have none of my apology, then?"

His brows rose. "Was that what it was?"

Angelica huffed. "Raoul, do stop being so provoking! Read the letter, Felicity. Aloud, if you please."

But this she could not consent to do. Not before she had seen whatever obnoxious contents had driven the marquis into a frenzy. His words flipped back into her head. Trustee? Without conscious decision, she dropped her eyes to the sheet, reading with a startled mind.

My lord — I write in haste, forced to it by this unexpected outcome. To have a lesser man take the bait would have better served my purpose, but I dare not hope your lordship will take a route to the altar as another would have done at my instigation.

"He meant to force a man to marry me? How might he do that?" She glanced up again.

"Easily, once you had spent a night under the fellow's roof." The tone was dry, impersonal, just as if the mischief was not aimed at him.

"Gracious heaven! Thank goodness she fell into your hands, Raoul."

"That, Angelica, remains to be seen. Read on, Miss Temple."

Felicity felt a little sick, but she bent her eyes once more to the letter.

Thus it behoves me to give you warning of a difficulty you may face should you choose, as with confidence I anticipate, to use the party now in your possession —

"In your possession!" She flung a flashing glance at the marquis. "That, sir, I am not!"

A wry smile curved his mouth. "I make no claim beyond my twenty guineas, Miss Temple, as you know."

"You have had your value of that, Raoul. Now be quiet and let her read."

— the party now in your possession in lieu of a certain transaction that lies between us.

"Such veiled terms he uses! Does he mean the money he owes you? Yes, he must mean that."

"I wish you will not be so cryptic! What does he say?"

Felicity's glance strayed to her hostess's impatient face. "He misjudges your cousin, ma'am, supposing he would have taken me for his mistress to make up for the debt — just as you surmised, sir."

"Read on," was all the response she got from his lordship.

She bent her eyes to the letter and caught the word that had begun this painful scene. "Here it is — the trustee." She continued aloud, "*The expectation of trouble, if it comes, will emanate from a trustee of sorts. Therefore, my best advice is for discretion in your dealings with a certain party.* He means me? Yes, he must do. *Bandying a name* — What, mine? Temple? — *Bandying a name may bring the devil out of the woodwork, since an interest exists of which such party may or may not be ignorant.* So that is why you accused me!" Frowning now, she stared across at the marquis.

130

"Ignorant? But he knows I am ignorant! Did he mean to make you suspicious of me? To what end?"

Angelica was clucking, but the marquis waved her to silence. "He may not be certain of your ignorance."

"Of the existence of a trustee? Of course he is certain. He knows very well I have had dealings only with Mrs Jeavons and himself as my guardian."

"A trustee of sorts, he says," cut in her hostess. "What does that mean?"

Lord Lynchmere was looking thoughtful. He leaned forward, holding out an imperative hand. "Give me the letter."

Felicity glanced at it. "Wait. There is more. *If the history be opened, let the record show I did then and have here done what I might to make amends. I am, sir, your lordship's obedient...* Oh, etcetera!" Without will, she looked up, directing her puzzlement at the marquis. "Amends? What amends? Of what is he talking?"

Lord Lynchmere held out his hand again. "Give it to me."

Felicity passed it across, distracted now, and watched the marquis look it over, his quizzing glass held over the sheet. He dropped the glass, striking the letter with the back of his hand as he looked up. "An interest. He does not specifically say you may be ignorant of the trustee, but of this interest."

"Whatever that may mean," said Angelica in a frustrated sort of tone. "It is too provoking of the man." Then she brightened. "Your family, Felicity! What a pity you made no headway today with the girls. But it must mean that, must it not? Trustee? Interest? What else could it be but your father's family?"

Felicity ignored this, her mind dwelling obstinately on the introduction of the last part. "History? What history? What does he mean he made amends? Amends for what?"

Angelica had seized the letter and was busy devouring its contents for herself. Lord Lynchmere's brows were drawn together.

"By issuing this warning, is how I took it, but I grant you that does not altogether fit, now I have leisure to think of it."

The fleeting thought he had been too angry at the notion she had deceived him to look closely at the rest passed through Felicity's mind. But the puzzle held her attention. She became engulfed by an urgent wish to confront her guardian and demand an explanation.

"When did he write that? From where? Is it possible we can find him?"

Lord Lynchmere's customary manner was back. His voice held all the usual blandness. "Impossible, I fear. I have not yet had an opportunity to tell you, but my secretary made the rounds of livery stables within the vicinity of the Black Swan. Maskery hired a chaise for that same night to take him to Harwich. By this time, I have no doubt he has crossed to Holland."

"He wrote to you from Harwich?"

"It seems likely. There is no direction on the letter. It was delivered this morning."

"Then he is out of reach." Balked, Felicity found her temper rising again. "He might at least have said who is this trustee. What does he mean by leaving me with this horrid mystery? It is all of piece!"

"With his using you?" The marquis curled his lip. "I doubt he had any expectation you might see the letter. The warning is for me, man to man, to ensure my discretion in my dealings with you."

Angelica leapt in. "Be quiet, Raoul! If you mean what I think you mean, you ought not to speak of such things before Felicity. Or me, come to that."

Beyond understanding the implications of this, Felicity directed a look of enquiry at his lordship.

He met it with a lift of an eyebrow. "You favour candour, Miss Temple. A man may flaunt a kept mistress in public and display her to his friends. Angelica and her ilk will of course ignore the existence of such females."

"Raoul! Not but what it is perfectly true."

He paid no heed to his cousin's intervention. "Or he may keep her close, visiting her at his leisure and ensuring his attentions are unknown to the world at large. It is this latter course Maskery is exhorting me to pursue."

"What, after he deliberately threw her into the public eye at the Latimer party? Ridiculous."

The burn of humiliation in Felicity's bosom was accompanied by a most unwelcome sliver of a different sort of heat, engendered by the notion of what such discreet visits must entail. She was not so ignorant she did not understand the implications. The urge to fidget under that steady gaze was strong, but she suppressed it. She would not give him the satisfaction of seeing her humbled by the indignities her guardian had heaped upon her. She forced her tone to calm.

"I see. Well for you, sir, that you had no desire to make the choice."

He made no reply to this. "I have instructed Jerram to make further enquiries at Maskery's last known lodging. He has no other home. It is common knowledge he gambled away his inheritance long since, and sold off his estates."

"But to what end, Raoul? If he has left the country, we must suppose his debts are too numerous to be met. He will be obliged to live abroad."

"True. However, we may glean something if there is a valet or other servant who may testify as to his movements before he fetched Miss Temple."

Felicity, still smarting, could not immediately see his reasoning. "What will you be at, sir?"

His brows flew up. "Don't you wish to unravel this mystery?"

"Indeed I do, but I cannot trespass upon your time. Nor, under the circumstances, upon Angelica's generosity." She ignored that lady's indignant protest. "To tell you the truth, I am only awaiting a letter from Mrs Jeavons and then I had it in mind to beg your cousin for a small loan so that I might travel back to Bath."

"That you won't!"

"But I must, Angelica. After that —" she gestured towards the letter still in her hostess's hand — "it becomes imperative."

"Nonsense! The man is gone. We need not regard anything he says. It is all to do with a different outcome than the one that has transpired. You are now an acquaintance of mine and I have taken you under my wing. There can be no difficulty."

Felicity warmed with gratitude, but it would not do. "Yes, there can. You are very kind, Angelica, but I am a fraud. These hints from my guardian make it worse. Who knows what sort of secrets may emerge? It is far better for me to disappear."

"Better for whom?" The question came from Lord Lynchmere, a half-smile softening his face. "Is it pride that makes you look a gift horse in the mouth? Do you want to be a drudge for the rest of your life?"

"Of course I don't, but —"

"Then allow Angelica to support you for a space."

Felicity gave a groan. "You don't understand! I cannot bear to be a charge on anyone. You know perfectly well you would much prefer to wash your hands of this whole affair."

The wry look appeared. "I should, infinitely. Sadly, I am plagued by a demon of curiosity. A rare thing, which promises to break the intolerable tedium of my life. You are not who you seem to be, Miss Temple, and that intrigues me."

CHAPTER EIGHT

Alone in the parlour, Felicity felt relieved Angelica had been obliged to attend an evening engagement. She could not have endured to read Papa's journal in company. Or at all. But after the revelation of Lord Maskery's letter, it was imperative to find out anything she could to throw light on his cryptic hints.

"Try for names, places and dates," Lord Lynchmere had advised. "We need a starting point."

It was odd indeed to be scheming with him and her hostess. She ought rather to be securing her future. Although, according to Angelica's airy notion, to discover her antecedents would do just that. Felicity remained unconvinced. If it was not for the question concerning Papa's allowance and what had happened to it, she must have dismissed the possibility of family interest. But her guardian…

The thoughts faded. That word had become anathema, sitting awkwardly on her tongue. Almost unconsciously, as she read, she realised she was looking for his name in the pages of the journal. Surely Papa must have mentioned him? If they were friends, acquaintances even, or related by associated interests, it would be natural for his name to appear. But so far she had not found anything to indicate the presence of Lord Maskery in Papa's life.

Reading his journal was throwing up a plethora of memories, more and more forgotten images coming to life. Little scenes of rare domesticity, with here and there a puzzle at the time which now made sense to her adult mind.

Must take more care. Flissie woke tonight. Found her curled up in the chair in the parlour. Too distracted, too much liquor, and the creature I'd brought home was with me.

Felicity recalled the incident. She had woken as Papa lifted her, seen the painted face of a female and heard a cooing sort of voice — "oh, poor little lamb, she must be cold —" as he carried her to bed. He had murmured and petted and she had sunk back into slumber, disturbed again by odd noises and laughter coming from the room next door. By morning, however, it was forgotten. The significance was clear, and perhaps telling. She did not think Papa had again brought a female back to their lodging, no doubt careful of his small daughter asking questions impossible for him to answer.

For the most part, his entries were cryptic and irregular. He had written intermittently, with here and there a burst of description: a fall of countryside, a grotto he thought mystical, a stormy sea in a bay where a wrecked ship drew a crowd hopeful of plunder. A vague recollection of a piratical story Papa invented for her benefit surfaced. One of the fairy tales with which he had entertained her, and then written down. Or had the writing come first? From time to time he had come home flourishing a bank draft.

"We are rich again, my little sweetheart! A treat is in order, don't you think? What would you like? Shall we have an adventure?"

An adventure often meant a change of residence, but Felicity recalled theatres, colourful markets, a waxworks once, or merely the luxury of a tea shop with buns or ices. Papa had not recorded these, but the mention of a sold story in one entry brought it all back.

We shall hie us to Middenhall after this. Mrs Kimble was ever accommodating. She may know of an apartment. High time we settled for Flissie's sake. We liked the area and she enjoyed adventures in Savernake Forest. Far enough from the Beast. Near enough to Rusper if I should need to beard the old nipcheese.

Something clicked in Felicity's mind. Nanny Kimble! The landlady who had seen her through the tragedy. Then it must have been in Middenhall that Papa died.

Urgent questions leapt in her head as her reading sped up. She held the letter closer to the candle she had set upon the occasional table next to her chair to facilitate reading.

Was this now Middenhall? She flicked through the entries following Papa saying they would hie there, looking for dates: November; January; then January again and one in February. He had died in February, on the last day. She was going on ten at the time, so it had to be '94. Was it then the October of the previous year he decided to go to Middenhall? Had they been there throughout?

Flipping to the final entry, she looked for a date and found none. However, it must have been written within a few days of his death. The one before was in February. She worked backwards through the last entries of the journal, hunting for the names that had now taken on significance.

There! Yes, here it was. Middenhall. And a date in late November. Then they had been there about three months or so. The name of Rusper caught her eye.

Shall hie me to Rusper. The old nipcheese will be glad to hear I plan on taking a proper apartment. If only the Beast can be persuaded to disgorge a trifle more.

138

But had he been so persuaded? She read from that point on, feeling feverish with anxiety. No further mention of the plan. No word of this Rusper, or of hearing anything in return. Had Papa actually gone to *the old nipcheese*? Or had he delayed, in his inimitable careless style, until it was too late?

Left Flissie with Mrs Kimble. This sentence occurred several times, showing they had remained in Middenhall.

Had Papa been absent a great deal? Felicity could not remember, those last days blurred by the subsequent cataclysm of his loss. Even Mrs Kimble had slipped out of her head, despite having been her refuge in the first hideous aftermath. Later, with the subsequent change in her circumstances, there had been too much to take in, too much heartbreak. Small wonder her mind had chosen forgetfulness.

But here were the clues. Here was the starting point Lord Lynchmere requested: a place, a date, and names.

Felicity's heart shied away from the possibilities inherent in discovery, but equally she knew there would be no rest now, no peace of mind, without it.

Angelica was predictably scandalised. "Jaunter about the countryside together? Without the vestige of a chaperon? Raoul, have you run mad?"

Within an ace of replying in the affirmative, Raoul clicked an impatient tongue. "What difference does it make? The whole affair reeks of scandal already, and Miss Temple has no intention of attempting a further assault upon Society."

His cousin threw up agitated hands. "That is just why, Raoul. If you are determined upon behaving in this disgraceful fashion, she won't have a prayer of doing so. You will ruin the poor girl, and for what?"

He threw a glance at the girl in question, looking perfectly composed where she sat on the sofa, her father's journal held between the fingers in her lap. Or were they gripping the thing? He was conscious the journey to investigate her past might well change her mind about her social prospects. He had made the offer upon learning of her discoveries, without even thinking about it. The suspicion he had indeed taken leave of his senses could not but hover in the recesses of his brain, yet there was no going back. The eager flare in Miss Temple's eyes might have dulled, but that first instant reaction told him how vital to her was the prospect of finding out, and he would not willingly disappoint her. Or was she regretful now?

"Are you afraid, Miss Temple? Do you wish to cry off?"

A tense look came into her face. "I can't." Her gaze turned to Angelica. "But I can go alone, if his lordship will lend me the funds."

Angelica snorted. "Even worse! A lone female may be subjected to every sort of annoyance. No, no, if you must go, you must be escorted."

"Exactly so. Moreover, she will find it a great deal easier to institute enquiries under my aegis."

"That I won't deny." Angelica's eyes brightened. "I have it! You may go yourself and leave Felicity with me in the meanwhile."

"No!" This from Miss Temple, chin up and clearly determined. "Grateful as I am to his lordship, I will not be excluded. This is my quest."

"Yes, I know. But this scheme won't do, Felicity, believe me."

Raoul sighed. "There is little point in my going without her, Angelica. I may be able to open doors, but only Miss Temple knows the pertinent questions to ask. I could be stumped by an answer, whereas she is likely to have it trigger a memory, just as she found, as she says, in reading the journal."

Angelica's expression was changing as she looked from him to the girl and back again. Raoul groaned in spirit. He could practically read her mind.

"Then there is only one thing for it. I shall have to accompany you."

Raoul said nothing for a moment, beset by a plethora of rising objections. They would be obliged to go in a coach, which would slow them down. He had meant to drive his curricle, affording both speed and a modicum of respectability to the venture. Adding his cousin would add also to the expense. Not that he cared for that. It came to him, with a sense of shock, that his chief objection was the introduction of a gooseberry between himself and Miss Temple. The realisation threw him into speech.

"I thought you were obliged to go home."

Angelica gave him one of her more astute looks. Had she divined his real reason? "They can very well manage without me for a little longer."

Raoul cast about in his mind for some legitimate excuse to exclude her, but Miss Temple forestalled him.

"I could not reconcile it with my conscience to incommode you so far, Angelica. You have already done so much."

"But, my dear girl, you have no notion how your reputation will suffer if it becomes known you have been in Raoul's company."

"More than if it becomes known Lord Maskery introduced me under the aegis of his mistress?"

Raoul winced. He had withheld that tale from her ears. "Did you have to tell her that, Angelica?"

His cousin went a trifle pink, but did not buckle. "She had to know, Raoul. Besides, you are perfectly aware Felicity prefers to be told the truth."

"Yes, I do, ma'am, and I am glad you told me. It has given me just the spur I needed to quit this sphere and return to my proper place."

Angelica looked aghast. "You are not planning upon returning to that wretched academy? Was that the letter you received this morning?"

Raoul's attention snapped to this new fetch. "What letter? Not from Maskery?"

Miss Temple flicked him a faintly amused look. "No, thank heavens. I hope I may never hear from him again. It was from Mrs Jeavons." Her face closed. Had she not said yesterday she was expecting a letter from her erstwhile headmistress?

"And?"

"And what, sir?"

Angelica huffed. "What did she say, for heaven's sake?"

Miss Temple's gaze dropped to the journal in her lap. Why was she reticent? The reason leapt to mind.

"Your place is taken, is that it?"

Her eyes flew up, meeting his with a fleeting expression of anguish. Her voice was flurried. "She has appointed one of the pupils. A girl like me, in need of a future. Mrs Jeavons believes I could not wish her to undo an advantage from which I also benefitted."

"Well, I am glad of it," said Angelica stoutly. "This means you must accept my invitation."

Miss Temple did not look happy. "Yes, that is what Mrs Jeavons suggested. At least, she supposed from my direction that I am in good hands."

"Which indeed you are, my dear child." Swooping upon her, Angelica hugged the girl.

It appeared to Raoul that she endured rather than enjoyed this attention. The desire to remove her from his cousin's suffocating affections invaded his breast. Really, Angelica's presence would drive them both into a frenzy. He made up his mind.

"All the more reason to be discovering what the devil Maskery meant by this *interest* and some shadowy trustee."

He spoke in a bracing tone and was rewarded by light coming into Miss Temple's features as Angelica released her. She rose from the sofa and confronted him.

"My lord, I will be glad of your escort, but pray let us go in your curricle as planned." She turned to Angelica. "Before you say it all again, hear me out."

"Oh, go on then. But I won't be talked out of coming along."

Miss Temple caught her hands. "Truly, there is no need for it. You are leaving Town in any event. If any even remember me, they will suppose I have gone with you. You may so inform the Latimers at least."

"Well, yes, I could, I suppose."

"Besides which," she added, releasing Angelica, "I am not so ignorant as you suppose. Remember I have had to do with young girls for years. In an open carriage, with a groom up behind, there is no impropriety."

"True, but you will be obliged to stay at an inn together." Angelica's gaze flicked to Raoul and then back again. "You cannot say there is no impropriety in that."

"It will scarcely matter at Middenhall. Who is to know me?"

Angelica gave one of her indelicate snorts. "They may not know you, but Lynchmere is a very well-known figure. It only

143

needs for one sighting to be reported and the fat will be in the fire."

Raoul took a hand. "There is no need for all these heart-burnings. If necessary, I can instead take her to Ruscoe Hall, where she will be chaperoned by Miss Wimbush."

Angelica opened her eyes at him. "To your home?"

"Why not? If I am to judge by Savernake Forest, the place is well within reach of the Hall."

"A good fifty miles or more. You will scarcely manage it within the day."

"Nonsense. It is nowhere near that distance to Lambourn, and the Hall is a few miles beyond that. A couple of hours' journey only." He read a retort in his cousin's eye and continued smoothly, "If we must needs stay on the road, we will find an obscure village inn."

His cousin snorted. "That is no guarantee. You'll be on the main Bath road."

Raoul sighed. "Very well, but you've said it yourself, Angelica. No one will know Miss Temple, even if they recognise me. Therefore they will have no reason to question her presence in my company."

"Except to suppose she is something less than respectable." She threw up her hands. "Well, do as you wish, then. But don't blame me if you are compelled into an unlooked-for path by the consequences."

Raoul had no difficulty in interpreting this cryptic utterance. He ignored it, hoping Miss Temple might not catch the significance. "Then it is settled. Can you be ready to leave at an early hour tomorrow morning, Miss Temple?"

Buoyed for the first couple of stages by a sense of excited anticipation, Felicity soon found doubts creeping in. Was this wise? Ought she rather to leave well alone? Although had she a choice, now that her former life was closed to her? She huddled into her cloak, forcing her attention back to the passing countryside and the gloved hands holding the reins.

"Are you cold, Miss Temple?"

She looked round at his lordship's profile. "No, indeed. I am quite comfortable."

"There is a thick travelling cloak under there if you should need it." Without taking his eyes from the road, he dipped his chin towards the seat below them.

"Thank you, but the rug will suffice for the moment. My cloak is warm enough."

She made no mention of the stuff gown she was wearing beneath it. One of her old school gowns, of a dull brown, made unfashionably high to the throat, but of kerseymere and thus warmer than any other she had. She had donned it as more suitable for the journey, in preference to those Angelica had purchased on her behalf. Or rather, Lord Lynchmere had, he having been billed for them. Both the new gowns had fortuitously arrived just before dinner last evening. Angelica had insisted on providing her with a portmanteau to replace the battered valise, despite her protests.

"Good heavens, child, we must have a dozen of them in the box room. Take it. I never wish to see it again."

All her worldly goods were now disposed inside, including the new clothes, with the exception of Henrietta's gown, which she had begged her hostess to return with thanks. She would not be more beholden than she need. She had bidden Angelica a somewhat tearful farewell and been chided for it.

"What, are you weeping? For heaven's sake, why? It is not as if we will not meet again. I made Raoul promise to bring you to me at Cherry Lodge when you are done with this quest of yours."

"But, ma'am, I cannot trespass upon your kindness any further."

A snort had greeted this. "Indeed? Where do you propose to live until you have found another place? I shall expect you within a matter of days."

Felicity had said no more. It would be useless. Who knew where this adventure might end? In the restless night watches, she had formulated half a dozen plans and discarded them. But one had potential, if Mrs Kimble could be found. Also, if Lord Lynchmere was prepared to let her go her own way. Although even that path was rocky. Without funds, she was at risk. Her anger with her guardian revived.

"That was a stab too far."

"I beg your pardon?"

She had not realised she said it aloud. Turning her head, she caught his lordship's puzzled glance. "Did I not say?" It came to her there had not been an opportunity to impart the worst. She threw a look over her shoulder at the groom on his perch behind and lowered her voice. "He stole my money."

His brows drew together and he flicked her another quick look. "Maskery?"

"I had it secreted within garments at the bottom of my valise. It was but a few guineas, but he took it all."

Lord Lynchmere made no comment at once. He appeared to ruminate. "How do you know it was he?"

"It must have been. He took my valise, did he not? Everything I had unpacked was jumbled up inside, but the rest had been disturbed as by a rummaging hand."

He nodded, evidently turning it over in his mind. Felicity watched him, surprised to note how the set to his mouth and jaw, even in profile, indicated the trend of his thoughts.

She echoed them. "It was deliberate. Or so I think."

"You mean he meant to prevent you doing anything other than seeking my protection? No doubt. Though I should suppose he would seize upon any chance to augment his funds, however meagre."

"To the extent of robbing his own ward? Really, I wish I had known with what a scoundrel I had to deal. I should never have left the academy."

He looked round, a wry note entering his voice. "And never have found out the truth of your origins."

The purpose of this exercise came back full force. "There is no saying I shall find out anything. Nor am I so sure I wish to."

"Cold feet, Miss Temple?"

"Positively freezing."

He laughed. "Inevitable, I fear. Stiffen your spine, my girl. There is no going back now."

This bracing treatment had a curiously warming effect. A rush of gratitude swept through her and she turned to him again. "I can't thank you enough, sir. I don't know why you are doing this for me, but let me say at least once — before you again manage to provoke me as I have no doubt you will — how extremely grateful I am."

His smile was twisted. "Do you know, Miss Temple, I much prefer your bark to having you lick my hand. I shall take care to keep you provoked."

She had to laugh. "I don't suppose you will need to try very hard."

"*Touché!*"

She fell silent again, allowing her mind to wander with her gaze as the miles flashed by. She had leisure to observe with what skill her escort managed his team, threading a careful path through heavy traffic in the towns and letting the horses have their heads when the road was clear.

"You would never drive at speed through a busy thoroughfare, I'll be bound."

He turned his head briefly. "I learned that lesson young. My father had a salutary method of dealing with any such foolhardy conduct."

Felicity eyed his profile once more. He was an odd mixture. The world-weary air that characterised him had disappeared. Temporarily? There was no saying when he might resume the pose. Was it a pose? For a man who professed to be irked by the responsibility forced upon him, he was going to an inordinate amount of trouble on her behalf. Why?

He could have bowed out of this near farcical situation at any time in these last hectic days. Yet here he was, enmeshing himself in her affairs when he could as easily have left her to her own devices, or to Angelica's mercies, or indeed despatched her to Bath. Incomprehensible for a man of his stamp. Not to mention rank.

"What is it, Miss Temple? Have I a smut on my cheek?"

Warmth rose to her face but Felicity could not prevent a gurgle of mirth escaping. It did not occur to her to withhold her thoughts. "You intrigue me, sir."

He flashed her a look, one eyebrow flying. "So? In what way?"

"I was trying to fathom your reason for doing this when you need not."

"I thought I had made that clear at the outset."

148

Felicity waved one gloved hand. "Oh, you pretended an interest in my origins, but I do not believe that was it."

"Why not? As I recall, I used the very same word. You intrigue me too."

"That is nonsense. I have been nothing but a trouble to you from the outset. You need not deny it, for you said it yourself."

"I have no intention of denying it. You are a confounded nuisance. But that does not preclude my finding your history a puzzle worthy of being unravelled." Felicity emitted a sound of disbelief, tossing her head. "That snort was worthy of Angelica. Do you in general reserve it for your pupils?"

Again she was unable to refrain from laughing, but she threw him an irritated look nevertheless. Wasted, since he had his eyes on the road. "I wish you won't attempt to turn it off with a jest, my lord."

"Turn what off?"

"You know very well. Why are you doing this? It is of no use to say you feel responsible for me due to my guardian's machinations —"

"I was not going to."

"— because there is no reason why you should be."

"Then we are of one mind. You may say, if you insist upon making more of it than is there, that it suits me to escape from Town for a space. However, I really cannot see why you must needs hunt for more than the simple truth of the matter. Typical female, of course. You will never accept that we men are simple creatures. We don't delve into the deep waters that occupy the feminine mind."

Felicity regarded him in some dudgeon. "Now you are being deliberately provocative."

He looked round, flashing a sudden grin. "I make a habit of it, had you not noticed?"

"Yes!" She gave a reluctant laugh. "I notice also that you are prevaricating, but I shall refrain from plaguing you on the matter."

"Thank God for that! You've saved me from the intolerable boredom of my existence. Don't spoil it by becoming tediously inquisitive."

Thrown back into instant annoyance, Felicity held her tongue with difficulty upon a sharp retort. There was no sense in pursuing the subject if he was determined to evade her. Not for a moment did she accept his assertions. Some cogent reason he must have. Was it sympathy? Fellow feeling? No, for he had no concept of her condition, as pampered as his life must be. Chivalry? At the start, perhaps. But not now.

With a small sigh, she let it go. Why it should bother her she did not know. Except that she felt altogether beholden, anathema to her. Lord Lynchmere clearly did not realise how galling it was to her to lose control of her own life, to be wholly dependent upon his charity. To be obliged to swallow her pride and accept his help without being able to make any sort of exchange was difficult for her. However, there was nothing to be done about it at the present time.

The curricle was slowing, catching her attention. She saw a sign protruding from a building set a little off the roadside. "Are we stopping for another change already?"

The last had been at Colnbrook and Lord Lynchmere had said his horses were capable of sixteen miles at a stretch. His lordship did not look round, engaged in directing his team into the yard of an inn, its swinging sign designating the head of a boar.

"I sent a team ahead to Reading last night. We'll change there and then again at Newbury, where I have horses permanently stabled. This team may rest here while we take refreshment. I dare say the Boar's Head can produce acceptable fare."

"Where are we now?"

"Twyford."

Light dawned. "You've chosen an out of the way place. To avoid recognition."

The groom jumped down as the equipage came to a standstill and ran to the horses' heads.

"Never let it be said that I don't take my cousin's strictures to heart."

"I wish I may see it!"

He raised his brows. "You are seeing it."

"Oh, nonsense. Do you take me for an idiot? You would have done so without her warning."

He merely smiled in that enigmatic way he had and, releasing his hold on the reins, leapt down. In a moment, he had come around to her side and held up a hand to help her descend. Gathering her skirts Felicity climbed down, glad of the strong grip. She half stumbled as she reached terra firma and an arm clamped about her shoulders, steadying her.

She looked up. "Thank you."

He did not immediately let her go, looking down into her face, still with the odd twist to his lips. Felicity was conscious of a thread of heat snaking through her veins. Her voice became trapped in her throat.

Lord Lynchmere spoke, a soft murmur. "I'm glad we dissuaded Angelica."

Then his arm dropped and he moved away to address his groom, leaving Felicity breathless and utterly confused.

By the time she had relieved herself, removed her cloak and hat and been installed in a small coffee room, which was all the privacy the wayside inn boasted, Felicity had recovered sufficiently to be able to approve his lordship's suggestions.

"There is not a deal of choice, but they can provide sliced beef with bread or a piece of egg and ham pie, if you prefer."

Suddenly conscious of gnawing hunger, Felicity opted for the beef. "I was afraid to swallow too much at breakfast, for I have never been a good traveller. But your vehicle is well sprung."

He nodded, as if this was a matter of course. "An open carriage is usually better for anyone who struggles with the motion."

"True. My father was used to hire a gig for our wanderings to avoid having me sick on his hands."

The twisted smile appeared. "Another very good reason we were not obliged to take my coach. Will you drink ale or lemonade?"

"Water, if you please. But coffee would be welcome too, if they have it hot."

He relayed her request to the waiting servant and left the door partially open. Discarding his hat and coat, he threw both onto a convenient chair near the wall and came across to take a seat at the table, already laid with a white cloth and a little tray of condiments in silver dishes.

Felicity, reminded of her earlier discomfort by his words about the coach, hurried into speech. "How long do you think it will take us to reach Middenhall?"

"We are nearly halfway there. All being well, another three hours or so should do it, if you can last that long."

"I? Why should I not? More to the point, can you endure the driving?"

"You said you don't travel well."

"True, but —" She broke off, staring at him across the table. "You knew all along we would have to stay on the road."

His brows rose. "Of course. You need not look so accusing. It is upwards of sixty miles from London to our destination. We would undoubtedly break the journey if we were travelling by coach at this time of year. However, I am happy to make Middenhall today, if you are, but we will hardly have time to locate your Mrs Kimble."

Recalling his placatory words to Angelica, Felicity was once more assailed with a sense of deep-seated suspicion. The fleeting thought passed through her mind that he meant after all to take advantage of her guardian's machinations. She dismissed it at once. He had no need to take this elaborate route if he had that intention. Yet she could not account for his evident satisfaction in being unencumbered by a chaperon.

"Delving into deep waters again, Miss Temple?"

The amused look in his eye was not to be borne. "I am trying to fathom why you are so pleased to have dispensed with your cousin's presence on the journey."

An eyebrow quirked. "Are not you?"

"Well, yes."

"Then what is the difficulty?"

"It is just…" She faded out, for once unwilling to spell out what was after all a nebulous apprehension.

His manner reverted to the habitual pose of boredom. "Try to use what common sense you possess, Miss Temple." Quick annoyance flared but he went on before she could retort. "Figure to yourself the utter inconvenience of a third in these investigations, that third being my esteemed cousin Angelica, who may be relied upon to thrust her oar in at every opportunity. Could you seriously have endured to have your every move subjected to a dissertation upon the rights and wrongs of it? And don't say she means well."

"You know she does, but I was not going to say so." Felicity could not but appreciate this point of view. However, she could not in conscience allow his words to pass. "But I will not sit here and have you abuse her to my face. She has been inordinately kind to me and I am wholly indebted to her."

A wry look entered his features. "You are wholly indebted to me, but you don't hesitate to abuse me to my face."

"That is another matter."

"It would be."

"You keep saying you prefer my bark, and I find it quite impossible to go on being grateful to you when you behave like a perfect boor."

His brows rose. "In what light then do you describe your own conduct, Miss Temple? I count myself lucky to still have my eyes and no raking tracks of your claws down my cheeks."

Caught between fury and laughter, Felicity shook her clenched fists. "I wish you will stop! And for heaven's sake leave off that ghastly pose of world-weary boredom! It does not impress me in the least."

"Would it surprise you to know that I have no desire to impress you?"

Felicity let out a frustrated mewl. "Oh, to perdition with you! You really are the most irritating, provoking —"

She broke off as the door was thrust open with a foot and the servant staggered in with a loaded tray. He dumped it on the table and proceeded to lay out a collection of dishes, plates and cutlery.

Felicity cast a fulminating glance at Lord Lynchmere and found him regarding her with a lurking twinkle. With a resurgence of feeling, she realised he had been deliberately driving her into a frenzy. Was it to put her off delving into deep waters as he called it? Or did he enjoy pricking at her only to amuse himself at her expense?

Well, she would not give him the satisfaction. Summoning the old smooth front she had ever employed at the academy, she surveyed the various viands now spread across the table. As well as the sliced beef revealed beneath the cover lifted by the servant, there was a loaf of bread, a dish of butter, a platter of fruit and another of tartlets, as well as a crumbly cheese set on a board. Her hunger returned, superseding all else and she accepted a serving of beef at the hands of his annoying lordship.

"May I cut you some bread, ma'am?"

The over-polite note made her look up from an inspection of her plate. He was wearing an expression of exaggerated subservience, one hand on the bread loaf, the other poised with a knife ready to slice it through.

Felicity broke into giggles. "You are ridiculous."

His mouth quirked. "One slice or two?"

"Two, if you please, *my lord.*"

He smiled at the emphasis, but said nothing more as he sawed through the loaf. He handed her a slice on the knife and cut another. Felicity buttered the bread as he cut slices for himself. With a flourish, he laid several pieces of beef on his bread, spread mustard over it and enclosed it with another slice.

"Behold! We are indebted to Lord Sandwich for this convenience, did you know?"

Following suit, she took his lead, determined to keep to light discussion for the duration of the meal. But she was so hungry, she had no leisure for talk, saying nothing at all as she finished partaking of her bread and meat and began upon a small plate of dainties.

Lord Lynchmere, having disposed of a couple of thick beef sandwiches, drained a tankard and set it down with a thump. "The deuce! Something I meant to tell you."

Felicity looked up, the remains of a tartlet in her fingers. A flitter of apprehension attacked her. "Something bad?"

"Unpleasant, rather." He reached for the platter of fruit and brought it closer to him. "Maskery's intention was set, it appears. My secretary Jerram found out that he had dismissed his servants and left without paying his shot at his lodgings."

"Before he came for me in Bath?"

"Just so. The landlord was disgruntled, as well he might be, but glad to be rid of an unreliable tenant. Jerram located Maskery's valet at a tavern he was used to frequent."

"Had he anything to add?"

His lordship's lip curled as he cut a piece off the cheese to add to the fruit he had selected. "To some purpose. Maskery despatched the bulk of his belongings by carrier to an address in Hanover."

The sense of betrayal resurfaced. "Then he never intended anything of what he pretended to me."

"I believe you represented a last-ditch attempt to recoup something from the wreck. This valet had not been paid all his wage, though he had been given a recommendation. Much good that will do him once Maskery's departure is generally known."

"Did he know of the plan to fetch me from Bath?"

Lord Lynchmere did not pause in his task of peeling an apple. "It seems unlikely. His part ended when he had despatched his master's effects. He returned to find Maskery gone, and a few guineas and the letter of recommendation left with the landlord."

Curiously, Felicity found this lessened to a degree her feeling of ill-usage. "I am not then the only sufferer."

He was quartering his apple, but glanced across, the twist to his lip pronounced. "By no means. A number of gentlemen besides myself stand to lose thousands, remember?"

Quick fury flared. "You count that a loss? You set your own thousands at risk to gain his. It is a hypothetical loss at best. This valet had worked for his wage, as had I for my few guineas. Those are real losses, sir." She paused, her breath shortened, realising she was being treated to his enigmatic look.

He set down his knife. "I stand corrected."

A slight twitch at his lip sent Felicity up into the boughs again. "You find it amusing?"

"Not in the least, ma'am." He picked up the coffee pot. "May I pour you a cup? The beverage often has a soothing effect, you know."

Felicity surveyed him, torn between dudgeon and a burgeoning desire to laugh. "You really are perfectly provoking, my lord."

That did produce the wry smile. "So you have frequently informed me. Consider me chastened."

Felicity emitted an unladylike sound of disbelief. But she kept her tongue as she received the filled cup from him. It was futile to argue the point. She added cream and sugar, stirring the brown liquid. But his bland manner goaded her at length. "Does nothing pierce your armour?"

He raised an eyebrow. "I have learned better than to tangle with an angry cat."

It was of no use. The giggle would not be suppressed. His answering smile warmed her. "A little more, sir, and you may well receive hot coffee in the face!"

"I don't advise you to try it."

She eyed him. "A threat?"

He lifted a warning finger. "Behave, Miss Temple."

A demon she did not know she possessed tempted her to push for more, but common sense prevailed. What in the world was she doing? And she called him provoking!

She drank her coffee in silence, reflecting that such moments did much to turn her thoughts from the dark apprehensions of this journey. Which brought her full circle to remembrance of those faint suspicions as to his real reason for taking all this trouble on her behalf.

Somehow it seemed less important than the realisation she enjoyed sparring with him and found him, in the main, agreeable company. A dangerous drift. She must not become accustomed. Once this quest was over, Lord Lynchmere would pass out of her life.

CHAPTER NINE

Contrary to Raoul's expectation, Miss Temple favoured pressing on the last ten miles after the change at Newbury and they reached Middenhall at dusk. Having consulted a map beforehand, using Savernake Forest as his guide, he had been able to plan his route beyond Hungerford, using the upper road from Newbury, and knew they must run into Middenhall about three miles short of Marlborough.

Warned that they were approaching their goal, his companion had sat up straighter these last few miles, looking about her as if she hoped for recognition of some landmark. As the horses trotted into what appeared to be a substantial village, Miss Temple's alertness increased.

"Is it familiar to you?"

She seemed distrait. "I don't know. Yes, I think. There ought to be a green and a church. Yes, there!"

The road had suddenly opened out, dividing into two lanes passing either side of a patch of common ground. A signpost indicated the one leading on to Marlborough. Spotting a tavern, Raoul took the other lane and brought his team to a halt within a short distance of the turn into its yard. At a word, his groom leapt down and went to the horses' heads.

There was no one about. In the way of villages at this hour, the place appeared asleep. Workers must still be about their labours and the business of the evening had not yet begun.

"The church was ... there, on the corner."

Raoul followed Miss Temple's glance as she looked along a row of houses from the tavern to a church spire at one end of the lane and a lych-gate leading in from the edge of the green.

Across the way was a cluster of cottages, with hedges browned by dust from traffic on the through road.

"It is smaller than I remember."

Raoul looked round. "That is a trick of aging. You were a child when you saw it last."

She did not answer, her gaze still travelling about. How much of it was as she recalled? A child's view was necessarily circumscribed.

"Has it changed much, do you think?"

"I cannot tell. There used to be a village shop. Mr Dog's."

"You jest."

A tiny laugh escaped her. "No, it was so. I don't think it was his proper name — Dog-something? — but everyone called him Mr Dog." She leaned towards the row of houses that flanked the tavern as she spoke. "Oh, it is still there! See: that one next door to the barber's pole, a little beyond the tavern. I wonder if Mr Dog is still the owner? He was a dear, forever slipping me a confection when Papa was otherwise engaged. But he was old. Or he seemed old to me then."

Raoul intervened before she could become lost in reminiscence. "Let me go and investigate this tavern. It does not look to me like a suitable place for you, but we shall see." He prepared to alight, but Miss Temple grasped his arm. Raoul paused, looking a question.

"Can you ask after Mrs Kimble?"

"I shall do so, of course, but if there is no proper accommodation here, we may have to go on to Marlborough."

Her grip did not relax. "It makes no matter to me. Anything will do. I would like to stay here."

She sounded tense. Raoul found himself melting. He laid a hand over hers and squeezed. "I'll see what I can do."

Then he released himself and descended from the curricle, heading directly for the Plough. Entering an unprepossessing hall, he followed a smoky trail to a large but rather dingy taproom. Was this the general meeting place for the village males?

A couple of elderly fellows were ensconced by an inglenook, smoking long clay pipes, tankards at their elbows. Three yokels were seated around a table near the window, and a beefy man of middle years, coatless and with an apron over his waistcoat, stood behind the bar, engaged in wiping down its surface. One glance served to inform Raoul this was no place for Miss Temple.

In the way of country people, every eye became trained upon the stranger and held. Well used to such stares, he paid no heed but moved to accost the landlord.

"A word, if I may?"

The fellow dropped his cloth and straightened, becoming servile. "How may I serve yer honour?"

"I am seeking accommodation for the night for myself and a lady."

The fellow looked dubious. "A leddy? Well, I'd be right happy and my rib'd be glad to serve a leddy. I've only the one room free, yer honour, and it ain't my best. Got two travellers already. Artists they call theirselves, off paintin' landscapes and the like."

"Thank you, but one room won't do. Where else may we find rooms? Is this the only inn here in Middenhall?"

The man sucked his teeth. "Properly speaking it is. Leastways, there's the Cat and Fiddle up the lane. Small place it is, and Mrs Dadford don't cater much these days. Getting on, she is."

One of the elderly men by the fire spoke up. "Don't talk daft, Jem. Ain't got no more years in her dish than I do, Mrs Dadford. Don't you pay no mind, yer honour. Much better place for the likes of you is the Cat. 'Cepting if it's a coach you come in, she don't have no place fer it."

Raoul thanked him, and turned back to the man Jem. "If I send my fellow Broome back here with my team, can you stable them and give him a bed for the night?"

The landlord brightened. "Four of 'em, is it, yer honour? Aye, we can do that all right. Stables ain't big, but we've only the old cob in there now 'sides the gig."

"I hope there is room for my curricle, then?"

Jem rubbed his hands, evidently pleased that at least a share of what promised to be lucrative custom was coming his way. "Aye, yer honour. There's the barn at need and it's weathertight and all."

This solution did not recommend itself to Raoul, but he could trust Broome to see all right. "Good. I'll send my man back when we've settled our accommodation." He nodded to the rest of the company and was about to withdraw when he remembered Miss Temple's request. He turned back. "One thing more. Do you know a Mrs Kimble hereabouts?" He once more found himself the recipient of a battery of stares. Jem's brows lowered.

"If you was wishful of taking a lodging with her, yer honour, she don't do it no more."

Raoul ignored this. "Then she is still living here?"

"Aye, just about."

"What do you mean, just about?"

"A widder she is, yer honour, and all but crippled now with the arthritics."

162

But she was alive. Quick interest kindled. "Give me her direction, if you will."

Armed with the necessary information, he left the inn and walked swiftly back to the curricle, looking up into Miss Temple's anxious features. "Mrs Kimble is still here. She lives up the lane, at some little distance beyond the church, I am told."

Miss Temple's gaze flicked to what was visible of the church, and both face and tone were eager. "May we go there now?" He hesitated, beset with unwillingness to dampen her enthusiasm. Her gaze came back to him, brows drawing together. "What is it, sir?"

He shook off the odd feeling, climbed into the vehicle and stepped across her to his place, gathering up the reins. "We won't go there now. We must first see if this Mrs Dadford up the road can put us up. Let them go, Broome." As he urged the horses to a walk, he became aware of Miss Temple's frowning gaze fixed upon him. He glanced round.

"You are keeping something from me."

He gave a rueful laugh. "Nothing of great note. It appears this Mrs Kimble of yours is a widow now."

The frown intensified. "She was then, as far as I know. That was why she took in lodgers."

"I see. Well, she does not do so now. Apparently she suffers badly with arthritis."

Miss Temple's face changed, swift compassion entering her eyes. "Oh, poor thing! That is a vile complaint."

"Indeed. However, there is at least hope her memory is not affected."

He expected her to dwell upon the matter, but it was clear her attention was caught by her surroundings as he turned the corner and took the curricle along what appeared to be a

163

lengthy lane bordered by intermittent dwellings nestling in cosy gardens. The second inn hove into sight and she exclaimed aloud.

"Oh, the Cat and Fiddle! I remember that. I used to love the sign and recited the nursery rhyme every time we passed the place. Are we to stay there?"

"If Mrs Dadford can put us up."

"Dadford? It rings a vague bell, but I don't think... Stay! Was she Minnie? Oh, I wish I had kept track of these things."

"You could scarcely have done so," Raoul soothed, "burdened with your occupation." He turned his head to address the groom behind. "I am led to believe there is no place for the horses here, Broome. I have arranged for you to take them back to the Plough. You'll stay there yourself."

"Very good, my lord."

Raoul turned in to the drive and brought the equipage to a halt in front of the swinging sign. Broome was already at the horses' heads as he prepared to alight. "Let us hope we may find a welcome here. I imagine you will be glad of the respite from being jolted."

A faint smile came his way, although Miss Temple seemed to have scant attention to spare for anything but the sign and the façade of the little inn. Even in the gathering darkness, it was seen to be a pretty house, with ivy climbing the walls and a wooden porch over the front door. As he approached this, Raoul could see the upper windows were partially open and candlelight twinkled through.

"Let me come in with you this time."

Since the place was clearly a good deal more genteel than the Plough, he made no objection, returning to the curricle to hand her down. By the time he had done so, the front door opened, and an elderly little dame peered through, candlelight showing behind her.

"Mrs Dadford?"

She looked from Raoul to the equipage and then to Miss Temple, her eyes widening. "Oh! Is it rooms you're wanting?"

Raoul led his companion forward. "Just so, ma'am. I understand you may be able to accommodate us. We require two rooms."

The little woman looked from one to the other. "Well, I don't have much call for it these days, but I can set young Margie to making all ready."

Raoul was about to respond suitably when Miss Temple forestalled him.

"I beg your pardon, but are you Minnie?"

Surprise flickered in the woman's gaze. "How did you know that, ma'am? I don't go by that name except to a favoured few."

"It is what Mrs Kimble called you."

"You know Nan Kimble?"

"I used to, a long time ago. I am Felicity Temple."

For a moment there was no reaction. Raoul watched the woman's features crease into puzzlement, and was again assailed with the odd frisson that deprecated Miss Temple's disappointment. Then astonishment lit up Mrs Dadford's countenance.

"Little Flissie Temple? Who was whisked away and never seen again? You never are!"

"I am indeed." Miss Temple's voice cracked. "I did not dare to hope anyone but Mrs Kimble would remember."

Two hands came out and seized hers. "As if we could forget! Bless me, I'm thrown all to pieces! Come in, come in, dearie, do! And you, sir."

Pulling Miss Temple along, she bustled into the house. With a brief instruction to his groom to wait, Raoul followed into a square hall, neat and clean and brightly lit by candles in two wall sconces and a candelabrum on a table, with a staircase to one side and several doors leading off. Still blessing herself, Mrs Dadford seized up the candelabrum and opened one of the doors, ushering Miss Temple into a comfortable parlour, rather overstuffed with furniture for its size, but with a cosy air.

"Sit you down, dearie, and I'll just go and give Margie the nod. Oh, and I'd best warn Cook. I'm sure you'll be glad of a meal to warm your insides, dearie, won't you?"

She set the candelabrum on the mantel and as she came bustling to the door almost walked into Raoul, who had remained just inside the room, amused to be wholly forgotten in the little creature's excitement at rediscovering the child she had known in Miss Temple.

"Oh, I beg your pardon, sir. Do you sit yourself down, too, if you would. Little Flissie Temple!"

Shaking her head over it, she bustled out and Raoul lifted an eyebrow at Miss Temple. She was still standing by the mantel, looking about in a bemused fashion, as if again searching her mind for past images.

"Has she gone off to kill the fatted calf, do you think?"

The freckles danced as she broke into laughter and warmth spread through Raoul's chest as he watched the procession of ants across her cheeks.

"I had no recollection of her at all."

"Is it coming back to you?"

She shifted her shoulders. "Vaguely. I don't recall this room. I think it is her own parlour. I wonder how well she knew Papa?"

"You will have ample time to ask." She sat down abruptly, consternation replacing the merriment. It struck him her laughter had held a note of hysteria. "Are you regretting having come so far?"

"No! Yes! I don't know." She covered her face with her hands briefly and showed him a countenance redolent with discomfort. "No, I don't regret it. I'm afraid of raking it all up, of feeling his loss all over again. I had it safely buried, or so I thought."

Raoul came to the fire and leaned an elbow on the mantel. "It cannot be as painful as it was at this distance in time, even if you do feel a resurgence of grief."

She dropped her hands into her lap and began to pull off her gloves. "You are right. I am being foolish. This is already luckier than I had hoped for."

"To be remembered? Perhaps Mrs Dadford can answer your questions."

"Some of them, perhaps. But she will scarcely know of Papa's financial arrangements."

"Nor, I suspect, will your Mrs Kimble."

"But she may know where we can find this Mr Rusper. Or if not that, at least where Papa went when he sought him out."

Raoul regarded her in silence for a moment. She was wholly absorbed, her countenance reflecting thoughts chasing one another through her head. Odd he could see it. Or was that a trick of her personality? She had not learned the art of putting up an artificial front to be interesting in the way of young females of the *Ton*. Yes, she had a way of clamping down on her emotions, no doubt a necessary part of her profession. But no pretence. No artifice. Was that what he found so refreshing?

She looked up abruptly. "Yes?"

167

Thrown, he blinked. "Yes, what?"

"I thought you were waiting for an answer. Didn't you speak?"

"I did not." He moved towards the door. "I'll see to our baggage and send Broome off."

Again he almost collided with Mrs Dadford as she came hurrying in.

"Oh! I do beg your pardon, sir."

He fell back to give her room. "I was just off to see about our baggage."

"My lad'll see to that, sir." The little creature hesitated, putting up a hand to her face and glancing from him to Miss Temple. "It was *two* rooms you were wanting, was it?"

Amused, Raoul glanced across at his now blushing travelling companion. "Yes, precisely. I am merely escorting Miss Temple."

She spoke up, her voice flurried. "This is Lord Lynchmere, Mrs Dadford. I should have said so at once."

The landlady's mouth dropped open, her eyes widening. "A lord! Bless me, sir! Oh! I should say *my lord*."

"Don't trouble. I must see my groom, if you will forgive me."

Consternation entered Mrs Dadford's features. "Gracious me! I've not got room in the stables for —"

"Don't disturb yourself, Mrs Dadford. I have arranged for the whole to be accommodated at the Plough."

"Oh, that's a mercy, sir — my lord, I mean."

Suspecting this could go on for some time, Raoul made good his escape. But not in time to miss Mrs Dadford exclaiming to Miss Temple.

"You should've said, Miss Flissie. Bless me if I can guess why you'd be going about with a lord! What'll Nan say to that? He's not your betrothed, is he?"

Raoul cursed as he opened the front door. Damn Angelica for being right as usual! Was Miss Temple's mind cool enough to think up a valid excuse?

Flurried, Felicity made haste to turn the little landlady off the topic. "Nothing of the kind, Mrs Dadford. I am greatly indebted to his lordship, but it is a long story and I am rather tired as we have travelled from London today."

The creature clapped her hands together, distress entering in. "Goodness, I should think you must be, dearie. You'll be wishful of a wash and such, or shall I fetch you a cup of something? I've the tea under lock and key, but seeing as it's you —"

"Tea would be very welcome," Felicity cut in, stemming the flow. "Indeed I should be glad of a chance to tidy myself presently. But pray first will you tell me what has happened to Mrs Kimble? They said at the Plough that she has arthritis."

Mrs Dadford's features crumpled and she shook her head, perching on a chair opposite. "Such a tragedy, poor Nan. She got worse and worse and she never said, dragging herself about after her lodgers for far too long. But in the end, she couldn't manage. She's tied to a chair these days and has to have Cissy help her to bed."

"Who is Cissy?"

"Nan's granddaughter. Does everything for her, does young Cissy. I go in to keep her company when I can and take her a little something, for she's struggling to make ends meet, poor Nan."

Felicity's half-formed scheme for her own relief vanished at a stroke, but her disappointment was overborne by intense fellow feeling. "How perfectly dreadful. Has she no means now she cannot take in lodgers?"

Mrs Dadford sighed. "I've a notion she'd a small nest egg saved, but likely most of that's gone now. Mr Dog was used to slip extras into her shopping, but he's gone now too, and —"

"Mr Dog has died? Oh, no!"

Mrs Dadford shook a vigorous head. "No, no, dearie. He sold the shop and went off to live with his brother's boy in Marlborough. It got too much for him, poor Mr Dogsmerfield."

"Dogsmerfield! I could not recall his proper name. In fact, I am not sure I ever knew it."

"Well, no one ever called him that, so I'm not surprised, dearie." The door opened and she jumped up. "But here's his lordship and I've not shown you to your room. Come along, dearie. I'll make the tea while you freshen up."

Within a half hour, refreshed, with her outer garments discarded, Felicity was again seated in the parlour, sipping the promised tea. Lord Lynchmere had been shown to his chamber and not yet reappeared and Mrs Dadford had gone off to supervise the preparations for dinner, twittering with anxiety.

"I've none of the fripperies his lordship must be used to, dearie. I only hope he won't despise a plain dinner."

She did not appear to be comforted by Felicity's reassurances, lamenting the shortcomings of her cook and debating whether to set her "lad" to dig up some spears of asparagus despite the difficulty of locating them in the dark.

Her mind far too beset with question to dwell on gastronomic possibilities, Felicity was glad to be left alone to ponder her fresh problem. How in the world was she to avoid falling in with Angelica's scheme now? Her admittedly vague idea of working out an exchange with Mrs Kimble while she sought a post was out of count. She could not impose upon an invalid. She would be nothing but a burden in the poor woman's present circumstances. Even if she had been able, Mrs Kimble evidently could hardly afford to feed herself and her granddaughter, never mind a penniless lodger.

Felicity was again wholly dependent upon the charity of Lord Lynchmere and his cousin. Could she make a bargain with Mrs Dadford? No, impossible. How explain her dilemma when she had arrived escorted by a marquis? The little creature would be bound to exclaim and question, and Felicity could not possibly expose her guardian's shocking machinations to the elderly dame.

Her ruminations were interrupted by the entrance of Lord Lynchmere, sporting a fresh neck-cloth and seemingly as energetic as ever despite having driven over sixty miles. He came to lean an elbow on the mantel and gave her a slight smile.

"Hungry?"

She eyed him. "Why, aren't you?"

One eyebrow lifted. "I wasn't being cryptic. In fact, I am devilishly hungry."

"I suppose I am, now you mention it. I had not thought about it."

His eye became keen. "You've found something out?"

He was acute, she had to admit. The worry returned. "About Mrs Kimble." She relayed what Mrs Dadford had said, omitting any mention of her defunct scheme to take refuge with her old landlady.

"You did not ask about your father?"

"I have not yet had a chance. Mrs Dadford was too exercised about serving you an adequate dinner. I told her not to get into a pother about it, but it was no manner of use. I could not compete with the virtues or otherwise of asparagus."

Lord Lynchmere sighed, sitting on the chair opposite. "I should be content with a hedgehog, providing it was served immediately."

"Somehow I doubt informing her of your preference would move things along any quicker."

He burst into laughter. "No, and on second thoughts, I should much dislike my tongue being pricked by spines."

"I believe pickled spines are a delicacy in some cultures."

"Are they indeed, Miss Schoolmistress? Is this the kind of science you see fit to impart to your pupils?"

She opened her eyes at him. "Good heavens, had you not heard of it? Surely a man of your wide experience must be familiar with interesting tidbits of the like?"

He held up a hand. "Desist, you little fiend! You are ruining my appetite."

She smiled, feeling her mood lifting. "Well, you have pulled me out of the doldrums at least."

His enigmatic look appeared. "Have I? For how long, I wonder?"

She was not obliged to answer this for Mrs Dadford entered to announce dinner, twittering as she led them to the dining parlour opposite where the table was laid with covers for two. A number of covered dishes were set upon the sideboard and a breathless maid, goggling at his lordship, stood waiting to serve.

Felicity interrupted their hostess's catalogue of the viands on offer. "Are you not going to join us, Mrs Dadford?"

She looked horrified. "Gracious no, dearie! Me, sit down to dinner with a lord? No, no. I'll take mine on a tray in my little back parlour as I always do."

"I was hoping to ask you about my father and — and certain other matters." Felicity cast an imploring look at Lord Lynchmere.

He smiled as he held the chair at one side for her. "Sit down with us, Mrs Dadford. You need not stand on ceremony with me." The little creature hesitated as Felicity took her seat and he went to one at the head of the table, gesturing to the other side. "Come, ma'am. Have your girl lay a cover for you. We should much prefer to have your company. Miss Temple ought to be chaperoned, don't you think?"

That did the trick. Mrs Dadford clicked her tongue. "Goodness, I had not thought! Well, I will say it's not what I'm used to, sir, but I take it kind in you to condescend so far."

With which, she bustled off to the sideboard and produced a cover and cutlery, setting a place for herself as she urged on the maid. "Start, Margie, there's a dear. We can't have the lady and gentlemen waiting for their dinner, now, can we?"

But it was she who insisted upon plying the guests with the proffered dishes, serving up portions while the maid held them to the plates and talking all the time.

"Now it's a good piece of beef, sir, for we had a cut off the joint yesterday, and these steaks should be tender as lamb... I've had Cook cut just the tips off this asparagus so it won't be stringy —"

At which point, Felicity met Lord Lynchmere's ironic eye and had to bite back a giggle. He accepted a serving of the tips, along with potatoes steeped in gravy, but held up a hand when Mrs Dadford tried to ply him with a stew of cucumber.

"I am content, ma'am. Pray serve yourself and we may begin upon this excellent repast."

"I beg you won't wait for me, my lord. You want to eat it while it's hot."

Felicity, a more modest collection on her own plate, picked up her knife and fork. "Then let us begin. The aromas are making me hungry."

She nodded at Lord Lynchmere and he followed her lead. She was obliged to admit he had charm when it suited him. She was tempted to comment upon it, but refrained. It would not do to let Mrs Dadford see how free and easy they had become with one another. No, had been from the first. The realisation struck her with some force and she cast a surreptitious glance at Lord Lynchmere, who had begun to eat with a gusto that bore out his assertion of the extent of his hunger.

Mrs Dadford could not sit down to her own meal without first filling their glasses with wine. "I sent my lad down to the Plough for it. I do hope it's fitted for your palate, my lord."

It was evident Felicity's tastes were immaterial. Not that she minded. It was both amusing and irritating to see how the creature toadied to his lordship's rank. A good thing she did not know he was a marquis. She would become perfectly overwhelmed. As it was, she came to the table at last with a substantial plate on her own account and sat down to eat. Lord Lynchmere insisted on her joining them in the wine, and a very few sips served to make her relax a little.

Felicity at once took advantage of it, asking after the inhabitants of the village, which set off the loquacious Mrs Dadford for quite some time. But at length Felicity was able to turn the conversation to the subject closest to her heart.

"How well did you know my papa, Mrs Dadford?"

"Oh, poor dear Mr Temple!" The creature's eyes were instantly clouded. She swallowed the food in her mouth and leaned in. "Dreadful, it was! None of us could believe it. Such a vivacious young man, was Mr Temple. So full of life and always ready with a jolly word. Everyone hereabouts adored him, dearie, that I can swear to."

It was both balm and frustration. No surprise to hear Papa was universally popular, but Felicity yearned for detail. She tried again. "I remember him like that too, but I wonder do you know what he did? In the way of business, I mean. Where did he go? Did you hear of a Mr Rusper?"

"Business? Gracious me, dearie, whatever next?" She tutted, fork poised. "Mr Temple was a gentleman born."

"True. But I am his daughter, and I have been for more than six years a schoolmistress in a Bath academy."

"A schoolmistress! Oh, no, dearie, have you indeed?"

The shock was evident and Felicity caught a meaningful look from Lord Lynchmere. Realising her tone had been tart, she moderated it. "I beg your pardon, Mrs Dadford. I did not mean to distress you. You see, I know my father was not above plying a trade, for he used to sell stories from time to time."

The little landlady made a dismissive gesture. "His writing! That is a very different matter, dearie. A most genteel occupation and none could cavil at it." She looked to Lord Lynchmere. "His lordship will bear me out, I'm sure."

His lordship, taking no part in the conversation, merely gave his enigmatic smile. Not that it mattered, for Mrs Dadford was off again.

"Nan and I were used to look forward to reading one of his stories in the magazines, and sometimes dear Mr Temple would read them to us. Oh, such stirring tales they were! How he thought up such adventures I shall never know."

The word brought a constriction to Felicity's throat. Adventures! Papa's stock in trade. But this was getting her nowhere. She took a sip of wine and plied her fork for a few moments to give herself time. Lord Lynchmere, to her relief, filled the breach. Had he noticed?

"What Miss Temple is getting at, ma'am, is that her father engaged in excursions of his own. She understands that he had an allowance of sorts and that he used to see a Mr Rusper. Do you know if the man was a lawyer or something of the sort?"

Mrs Dadford frowned over it. "I cannot say I ever heard of such a man, sir. Nan may know, perhaps. It's true Mr Temple was apt to leave little Flissie with Nan and go off somewhere." Her eye brightened. "Marlborough! Well, he must have gone there, for it was where the accident —" She broke off, setting down her fork and shaking her head. She threw an apologetic glance across the table.

Felicity seized on the slip. "That is where he was killed? Don't fear to speak of it, Mrs Dadford, pray. I need to know."

The little lady sniffed and dabbed at her eyes with her napkin. "Forgive me, dearie, but it's brought it all back. Poor dear Mr Temple!"

Oddly, her distress proved strengthening to Felicity. "What exactly happened? I was never told the full sum of it. Only that a carriage was going too fast and he was knocked to the ground."

The landlady was shuddering. "Trampled by the horses! They bolted too, leaving poor Mr Temple crushed and battered on the ground."

The horror of it hovered somewhere above Felicity, waiting to descend. Yet she felt curiously detached, needing more. Someone was accountable. "Didn't the driver stop? Come back when he had his horses under control?"

"Not then, he didn't. Leastways, I never heard he did. But he was there at the inquest, for we read all about it in the newspaper. Accidental death, they said, which of course it was. But Nan will have it he paid his dues."

Felicity began to feel chilled, though still divorced from the harrowing tale. "How so?"

Mrs Dadford looked surprised. "Didn't you know that was the reason? Oh, I suppose you were too young to understand."

The coldness turned to ice as a snaking suspicion curled into her mind. Her voice felt alien. "The reason for what, Mrs Dadford?"

"Why he took care of you. That lord. I forget his name now. Nan didn't want to let him take you, but she said he was all remorse and meant to make it up to you and would adopt you and all. For there was no one else, and you were a gentleman's daughter and he was a lord."

Felicity's lips felt bloodless. The candlelight flickered in her vision, the scene before her fading into a dreamlike amorphous mass.

"My guardian ... you are speaking of my guardian, Lord Maskery."

CHAPTER TEN

From far away Felicity heard the voices, making no sense.

"Was that his name? Nan will remember."

"Steady, Miss Temple! No swooning now."

Too late. The darkness began to overwhelm her. She was in a carriage, coated and bonneted, staring into a void, only half aware of the man at her side. Her guardian. Guardian: a man to guard her, shield her, protect her. Like a father, like the father he had despatched to his maker. *Ah, cruel...*

"Miss Temple! Felicity! Wake up!"

A light slapping at her cheeks.

"Smelling salts! I'll fetch them, sir."

"Felicity, wake up, I said!"

The voice was insistent. She forced her eyes open against the pull that wanted to drag her down, buried forever in blessed oblivion. But it was not oblivion, not if *he* meant to inhabit her dreams.

"Come, drink this." Cold steel at her lips. "Open your mouth."

She opened and pungent liquid slid across her tongue. She choked, becoming aware of a supporting arm across her back, pushing her upright. Coughing, she lifted a wavering hand to push away the flask she could now see in his hand. His hand? Revulsion overcame her and she uttered a cry, tugging away from him.

"Behave! I'm trying to help you."

Familiar features came into focus. Relief claimed her and she sagged. "Oh, it's you."

Lord Lynchmere held the flask to her lips again. "A little more."

"No, pray."

"It's only brandy. Another sip."

She allowed him to tip another measure into her mouth. Ready for it this time, she swallowed the fiery liquid and sucked in a breath. The world around her came back into focus. Lord Lynchmere was leaning in beside her chair, a supporting arm around her, holding the flask ready.

Felicity gave him a wavering smile. "Thank you. I am better now."

He seemed to study her face for a moment. Then he nodded and released her, straightening and setting the hinged stopper back on the flask. He slipped it into a pocket.

Felicity watched his motions as from a distance, still a trifle disoriented. Remembrance washed her mind and she shuddered. "How could he? He never confessed. Then to use me as he did!"

His lordship resumed his seat at the head of the table, pushing away his plate. Her own was nowhere to be seen. Neither was the landlady.

"Where is Mrs Dadford?"

"She went to fetch smelling salts."

"Oh, dear." She looked at him. "I was not out, I don't think."

"Not entirely. You were muttering."

"Was I?" She drew a painful breath. "I don't know how to deal with this."

"Then don't try." He reached out a hand and laid it over one of hers. Felicity had not known her fingers were glued to the table. The warmth of his grip was balm. She looked at him.

"You are always coming to my rescue, Raoul."

His lip quirked. "I am at your service, Felicity, didn't you know?"

A tiny laugh escaped her. Realising she had used his given name, she withdrew her hand from under his, embarrassed. "I'm sorry. I should not have…"

"Not have what?"

Felicity hesitated. She still felt quite odd, not at all herself, as if she had sustained a blow on the head. "Your name. Too informal."

His smile twisted. "Don't you think we are well enough acquainted now to dispense with formality?"

"Do you wish to?" Why had she said that? Her inhibitions appeared to have deserted her.

"I already have."

Warmth invaded her from somewhere, but she was spared having to answer by the reappearance of Mrs Dadford, armed with a little vial she was waving in triumph.

"I found it at last. Would you believe it was buried at the very bottom of my dressing drawer?"

"Thank you, ma'am, but she no longer needs it. She is very much revived, as you can see for yourself."

Felicity did not feel wholly revived, but she dutifully smiled as the little lady twittered over her, lamenting the late contretemps and apologising for having brought it on. "Your dinner quite spoiled too! Margie, love, bring across the syllabub. You'll take some, I hope, dearie. Or perhaps a morsel of cheese. There's been no decent fruit in the market, but there's the remains of an apple pie if you should fancy it."

Allowing the words to wash over her, Felicity accepted the bowl of syllabub and toyed with it, spooning up a little at a time as Mrs Dadford turned her attention to her other guest, pressing cheese upon him when he refused the syllabub, and producing a little basket of savoury biscuits to accompany it.

"Then I'm sure you'd like a nice cup of tea, dearie, while we leave his lordship to enjoy a glass of port."

"In solitary state? No, I thank you. I will accompany Miss Temple to the parlour and drink it there while she takes tea."

Relieved that he did not intend to leave her alone, Felicity managed a few more spoons of the syllabub. She was glad to find herself, within a very short time, ensconced in the parlour with Raoul while the little landlady went off to supervise the making of the tea.

Loath to disturb her, Raoul regarded Felicity with residual concern as she sat with closed eyes, sunk against the chair-back. Her face was still pallid, her skin pearly in the candlelight which dulled the freckles. A few strands of that tantalising burnished hair had escaped from its pins, drifting down her cheek on one side and curling into her neck on the other. Conscious of a wish to twine one of them around his finger, Raoul tamped down his natural urges. She really was uncommonly seductive.

He thrust the thought away. Even had she not been in a vulnerable state, there was no going down that path. Yet if her background proved viable…

She stirred and his mind snapped back to the shocking revelation of Maskery's perfidy.

"Have you that letter?"

Her eyes were open. Raoul was thrown for a moment. "Which letter?"

"The one that made you think me as vile a creature as that slinking, slimy snake."

He could not suppress a flicker of amusement at the description. "I never thought you a slinking, slimy snake. You are far too warm-blooded."

A faint smile rewarded him, but she gestured to his clothing. "Did you bring it?"

"Why?"

She sat up straighter. "Amends. Do you not remember? He spoke of a history and amends. This must be what he meant."

His mind jumped. "I had forgotten that bit. But of course I have the letter with me. That and your father's journal are all the proof we have of any claim you may have."

She stared up at him, clearly without comprehension. "Claim?"

"Trustee? Devils in the woodwork?"

A gesture brushed this aside. "The letter, if you please, Raoul."

He slipped his hand into his inner pocket and brought forth the folded sheet.

She held out an imperative hand. "Give it to me!"

Her eagerness touched him, but the imperious manner could not but annoy. She had a thoroughly contradictory effect on him, wretched female. He passed the letter across and watched as she held it close.

"Oh, perdition, I can't read it! Not enough light."

Raoul rose and commandeered the two-branched candelabrum on the mantel, taking it across and setting it down on a little table beside her. Felicity bent towards it, holding the letter under the light and wholly ignoring Raoul.

A good deal chagrined, he straightened and leaned against the mantel, looking down at her bent head. He ought not to blame her for this single-minded obsession, but he was horribly conscious of feeling shut out. It came to him that he

182

enjoyed her attention, her reliance on his good offices. Damn it, he liked being responsible for her. How the deuce did that happen?

"Here it is! It is just as I thought."

Raoul's attention veered. "Well, what?"

"*If the history be opened, let the record show I did then and have here done what I might to make amends.* You see? He did then, he says. This is the history. He killed my father! And he thinks shoving me into a school and leaving me there unattended and unregarded for years is an adequate recompense?"

With some violence she threw the letter from her. It fluttered across the room. Raoul went after it and picked it up, refolding the leaf and stowing it in his pocket.

"I hate him! I always did, but this —!"

Raoul eyed her, his attention caught. "You always hated him?"

Her breath had shortened, her voice turning guttural and the expression in her eyes near vicious as she stared up at him. "He dumped me in that school. My father was dead. I had no one. He took me away from the only person who still cared. I wish he had not tried to make amends, as he calls it. Why could he not have left me with Mrs Kimble? It would have been kinder."

"Perhaps. Or perhaps he meant to do more and could not."

She paid no heed, her gaze dropping to the middle distance where no doubt a vision of Maskery hovered in her head. "He is evil. Guardian! Lying, scheming, *devil*. Even then he likely decided I could be of use to him. Yes, I'll wager that was it."

Raoul dropped into his vacated chair. There was little point in arguing with her in this state. She was looking for loopholes, a way to deal with the hideous truth. Raoul was not going to waste his breath either in expostulation or possible alternatives.

For his part, he believed Maskery likely was trying to make amends. At the time. Gamblers did not operate on future possibilities, beyond the present hope of enriching themselves. Maskery was ever a gambler. He may have had worthy intentions, but his feckless nature would make him lay them aside, find excuses to avoid the responsibility he had taken on. But there was no use saying as much to Felicity in her current mood.

She was still muttering under her breath, her fingers tangling with one another. The light from the candles beside her threw one side of her countenance into shadow, enhancing the other. The freckles there were visible again, and Raoul was conscious of a wish to see the dancing ants again, to see her laughing.

Sounds outside the room betokened the arrival of the tea. He got up and went across to retrieve the candelabrum, setting it back on the mantel just in time as the door opened. Mrs Dadford entered, bearing an urn, closely followed by the maid with a loaded tray.

"Here we are, dearie. It's Pekoe and just what you need to bring the roses back to your cheeks."

Felicity was visibly pulling herself together although her smile was strained. Raoul's feelings veered again to pity. The poor girl had sustained a severe shock. Scarcely surprising she had gone off into a comprehensive denunciation of her erstwhile guardian.

The bustle of setting down the makings for the tea upon a side table and Mrs Dadford's chatter as she proceeded to create the brew afforded, he hoped, an opportunity for Felicity to calm down a little. Though she would likely brood all night. Would he had the right to distract her.

The inappropriate images engendered by this thought faded as Mrs Dadford handed the cup and saucer to Felicity and turned to address him.

"And you, my lord? Would you care for a cup?"

He had long since finished the glass of port he'd brought with him and the idea of tea before retiring was welcome. "Thank you, yes, I will take a cup. Without milk or sugar, if you please."

"Here we are, sir." She lowered her voice to a murmur. "Is she a little less distressed, poor dearie?"

He nodded, unwilling to draw Felicity's fire should she overhear. He glanced at the clock on the mantel. "Is it ten already? An early night would not go amiss, I think."

The landlady threw up her hands. "Gracious me, so it is! I declare, I am at sixes and sevens myself." She swept back to Felicity and patted her on the arm. "Do you sit there quietly, dearie, and enjoy your tea. I've to see Margie takes up a warming pan and I'll light the candles in your chamber. Now, are you wishful of having Margie help you to undress, dearie, or can you manage?"

Felicity did not seem to have been paying a great deal of attention to these effusions, but at this she looked up with a frown. "Help me undress? Heavens! No, indeed. I cannot remember when I did not look after myself, Mrs Dadford."

"Well, there. Though I dare say Nan had the dressing of you once or twice in the old days. The rooms will be ready in a trice, my lord."

She got herself out of the room at last and Raoul looked back to find Felicity gazing after her, cup in hand.

"What has so caught your attention?"

She blinked, glanced his way and sipped at the hot tea before setting it down in the saucer in her lap. "A flash of memory. A

185

man — not Papa — attempting to button my coat. It was a blue one I had, double-breasted. He was unhandy. He got the buttons awry and had to begin again. I can't imagine why I was not doing it myself."

If her condition then had been anything like it was now, Raoul could well imagine why she had needed help. Maskery probably found the needs of a child disconcerting. He refrained from comment, not wishing to mention the name. "Drink your tea, Felicity."

She obeyed and he was led to hope her temper had subsided. It was quick to kindle, but he had noticed the fireworks did not last. A mercurial creature. One never knew what she would do or say. Was that the attraction? She would never drive a fellow to screaming tedium.

"I wish you would not stare at me in that fashion."

Conscious, Raoul took a deliberate swallow of his tea, but he could not resist responding. "In what fashion?"

Felicity's brows had lowered. "As if you expect me to break out in hysteria at any moment. I am perfectly calm, I'll have you know."

He hid a smile at the belligerent tone. "So I perceive."

"Well, I am. It would not be wonderful if I was at this moment lying on the floor and drumming my heels, screaming the while."

He did smile at that. "I must beg you will refrain. I should be obliged to empty a jug of cold water over you."

A tiny laugh escaped her. "Yes, I dare say you would, unfeeling wretch."

"Come, you begin to sound more like yourself. The tea is clearly efficacious."

She sighed and relaxed against the chair-back again. "To tell you the truth, I feel quite disoriented still. Almost as if it all happened to someone else. Does that make sense?"

"Perfect sense. Shock has that effect."

"True. I don't think I truly came out of it for months after I was left at the academy. It was strange to me to be among other girls. I'd had few playfellows. It was always Papa and I, you see. Mrs Jeavons was used to say I took time to adjust, which is why she was wont to put the orphans under my particular care. She supposed I understood. In fact I had little memory of the entire period. Now I think I suppressed it. I hated my guardian's visits for the reminder."

"Then he had the decency to visit you from time to time?"

Her expression changed, puzzlement entering in. "That's just what I can't fathom. I was trying to place him when I spoke of him to Silve and Hetty Latimer."

Raoul was glad her manner was calmer, but this was news to him. "You doubt him?"

"I'm not sure it was him. I did not recognise him when he came for me. Only vaguely. Though he had not visited, if it was he who came, since I took post as one of the mistresses."

"Intriguing." Raoul's mind raced across several possibilities. He was loath to voice them, not wishing to raise further spectres tonight. "In the morning, we will see what we can discover from Mrs Kimble. Finish your tea."

He spoke soothingly and was glad to see her obey without protest. She looked drained and no wonder. He was again beset with a wish to comfort her in a way that might drive off her demons and chafed at the necessities of rank. It would not do if her background proved inadequate. Yet, if it did and he must let her go, it was beginning to feel as if it would be a wrench. Had he made a mistake to keep Angelica out of it? She would have provided a buffer between them. It was to be hoped he would not be alone with Felicity for many days.

The arrival of Mrs Dadford in the role of mother hen relieved him from the immediate frustration. Bidding his self-imposed charge sleep well, he opted to take a cooling walk down to the Plough before seeking his own bed.

Contrary to her expectation, Felicity slept like the dead, waking to the rattle of the curtains around the old-fashioned bed being drawn back.

"Good morning, dearie, and I've brought you a cup of warm milk. We don't run to chocolate, sadly, but milk will set you up for the day, dearie, and put heart into you."

Smothering a yawn, Felicity uttered a sleepy greeting and struggled up. The elderly dame stacked pillows behind her and told her to relax back. A laugh escaped her. "You are spoiling me, Mrs Dadford."

"Well, and if I am, I dare say you deserve a little pampering. Take your ease now, for there's no rush. I'll send Margie up with hot water in a little while and there'll be bacon sizzling in the pan by the time you're ready. One thing we've plenty of around these parts is pork, and if his lordship should prefer ham with his eggs, we've a tasty piece of hock and there's fresh rolls in the oven too and my best raspberry jam."

She rustled out on the words and Felicity was left with an inordinate sensation of comfort. She could not remember feeling this well looked after since ... oh, since before Papa died. It was almost like dropping through a gap in time. Mrs Dadford's adoption of her as the child she had been then was curiously heartening.

She sipped at the tepid milk and looked towards the window where the drapes had been pulled back and the shutters opened to reveal a bright March day. For the first time since she had begun upon this quest, Felicity felt hopeful.

The shock of last night's revelation had diminished. Or perhaps sleep had enabled her to adjust her ideas enough to accept it. The past was past and there was no way to change what had been. Why fret herself to death over it when the more important question of her future was still ahead? Although even that reflection failed to pierce her newfound sense of peace. It felt fragile. She hugged it to herself, half afraid of losing it the moment she rose to face the challenges of the day.

The opening of the door brought young Margie, puffing in with a huge jug of steaming water. Felicity finished her milk and prepared to begin upon her ablutions.

Venturing downstairs to the dining parlour a short time later, she found Lord Lynchmere already seated at the table. He rose on her entrance, scanning her face as he moved to set a chair for her.

"You look a good deal rested. Did you sleep?"

Felicity smiled at him. "I did, Raoul, thank you. Like the proverbial log." She took her seat and he returned to his own, picking up a tall pot.

"Coffee? Food has yet to make an appearance, but Mrs Dadford promises it will be here in a jiffy."

Felicity laughed. "Yes, she recited a gargantuan menu to me when she woke me with a glass of warm milk. In fact I abhor warm milk, but I managed to finish it."

His brows rose as he poured dark liquid into a cup for her. "Why drink it at all, if you dislike it?"

"Because she took the trouble to bring it for me, of course. I could not insult her generosity by refusing it." She looked up as he set the cup down before her and found him regarding her with an expression she found hard to read. It was not his enigmatic look. Rather an appraising one. Felicity frowned. "Well, what?"

The oddity vanished. "Nothing. Cream and sugar?"

She accepted both, feeling strangely disconcerted. But the effect dissipated as the door opened to admit a procession of tray bearers: Mrs Dadford, the maid and even the fellow she called her "lad" with enough viands to feed an army.

There was time for nothing but attempting to unravel the plethora of offers proceeding from the garrulous dame's mouth. A piled plate before her, Felicity began upon her repast, accompanied by Mrs Dadford's monologue as, in addition to food, she plied her guests with news of the likely weather for the day and advice about the proposed visit to Mrs Kimble.

"Young Cissy gets her up, but it's no manner of use going before ten o'clock as Nan won't be fit to receive you. That's why I didn't wake you too early, dearie, for you'll be able to pop over there just as soon as you've finished your breakfast."

Felicity replied suitably in between disposing of as much as she could of the bacon and scrambled eggs on her plate. The marquis, contributing nothing to the conversation beyond a nod here and there, worked his way steadily through a veritable mountain of food, but even he was obliged to leave some.

At a moment when Mrs Dadford was out of the room, he set down his fork and sat back, blowing out his cheeks. "What we need is a dog under the table to whom we could surreptitiously slip pieces of ham and bacon."

Felicity eyed the remains on his plate. "Why in the world did you accept so much?"

He gave her an unloving look. "I am following your lead. We must not insult Mrs Dadford's generosity, remember?"

Felicity broke into laughter. "I did not mean for you to stuff yourself to death."

He pressed a hand to his stomach. "Now I know how the pig feels. And it's your fault."

"I won't be blamed. Did I say you must let her pile up your plate?"

He threw her a vengeful look. "It is of no use to cavil. I never eat such a breakfast as a rule and if you had not bleated about insults, I should not have dreamed of eating as much."

Amused, and considerably surprised, she eyed him with interest. "I am astonished you allowed yourself to be swayed by any words of mine."

His enigmatic look appeared. "It must be the schoolmistress in you."

"Affecting you? Ridiculous."

A faint smile was all she got by that. He picked up the pot. "More coffee?"

"I doubt I have room."

Raoul nodded towards the basket of rolls. "You'd better have at least one of those or Mrs Dadford will be feeding it to you herself."

"Lord, how right you are! I will have more coffee, if you please." She seized a roll and began to butter it as he refilled her cup. He picked up the jam pot and set it nearer to her. Felicity glanced up. "Are you not having one?"

"No, Miss Schoolmistress, I am not. I have done my share."

She giggled, feeling absurdly pleased by the nonsensical exchange.

He lifted an eyebrow. "You appear to have woken a new woman, Felicity."

"I have. It's most odd, but the way Mrs Dadford cossets me has made me feel like a girl again."

His wry look appeared. "You are scarcely more than a girl in any event, though I admit you have acquired a certain air of maturity."

"You think it spurious?"

"No. I believe the rigours of your existence have prematurely aged you. A female of your years ought to be on the threshold of the bloom of life."

Unexpectedly touched, Felicity eyed him, her roll forgotten in her fingers. He drank his coffee, apparently unaware of her scrutiny. Such an odd mixture of understanding and cynicism in him. His words replayed in her head and she found a flaw. "If I am to judge by the expectations of my pupils, at my age I ought rather to be on the threshold of triumphantly producing an heir for a husband."

To her consternation, Raoul choked on his coffee, setting down the cup and spluttering as he coughed, putting his napkin to his mouth.

"Oh, I do beg your pardon! Are you all right?"

"Do I look all right, you wretch?"

His voice had turned rough and it was a moment or two before he was sufficiently recovered to accept the water Felicity hastily poured into a glass from a jug on the sideboard and pressed into his hand. He took a few sips, grimaced and set the glass down. Felicity retook her seat and met the violence of his reproachful stare with raised brows.

"It is of no use to glare at me. What in the world was there in what I said to send you into a frenzy?"

"Frenzy? You made me choke, you little witch! What possessed you to bring that up?"

She gave a puzzled laugh. "Why should I not? I am two and twenty after all, and in other circumstances I dare say I would have been married by this time, assuming I could have attracted a respectable parti."

"Any parti foolish enough to take you to wife might count himself a lunatic. He would be lucky to survive the honeymoon."

The bitterness with which he uttered this sent Felicity into a fit of the giggles. Aware of his lordship's baleful regard, she tried unavailingly to hiccup them back. His lips twisted at last into that characteristic smile.

"It's well for you to laugh yourself into stitches, but if I don't end by strangling you, my girl, it will be a miracle."

"I am wholly impenitent, if you wish to know," she said when she could speak at last. "I have not laughed so much for an age."

"I am happy to have afforded you entertainment, ma'am."

She ignored the ironic note. "You should be after last night. As a matter of fact, I am feeling unprecedentedly optimistic this morning."

His smile lingered. "Are you? I wonder why."

"Oh, I don't know. I have every reason to be apprehensive, but being here in Middenhall and with Mrs Dadford so cosseting towards me, it is like…" Her voice became constricted and her lip trembled a little. "…like coming home."

He continued to regard her, his expression, as so often, unreadable. Felicity took refuge in nibbling at her roll and was glad when their hostess came twittering in to enquire whether they had finished.

The preparations for departure to find Mrs Kimble did not take long and presently, cloaked against the chill, Felicity was stepping out beside the marquis along the lane heading back towards the church. To her chagrin, all the questions she had thrust to the back of her mind crept back, together with the riffle of anxiety that had never been far away since the start of this adventure. The word brought Papa instantly to mind and her lighter mood began to dissipate.

"It's a pretty village."

Raoul's remark served for a slight distraction and she focused on the neat gardens and the picturesque little cottages they were passing.

"Yes, very pretty. Not that I thought in such terms as a child. It is becoming more familiar, though."

"Are you remembering it more?"

"It's not so much recognition of the place as that sensation of *déjà vu*." She made no mention of her returning feeling of apprehension.

Raoul pointed. "I believe we must take that path beside the church, according to the landlord of the Plough. I checked again last night to be sure I had it right."

Surprised, Felicity glanced up at his profile. "You went down to the inn last night?"

"I needed fresh air and a restorative."

He turned her in to a narrow, worn path which Felicity abruptly knew.

"I remember this. Mrs Kimble's house is just down on the left, past a massive chestnut. I used to play in its shade and gather conkers. Papa taught me to battle with them." She paused as the tree came within sight. "It has shrunk!"

"No, you have grown." Raoul took her arm to urge her onward. "Come, let us not waste any more time or you'll be on the fidgets again."

Felicity gave a small sigh. "I hoped you had not noticed."

He made no reply but led her inexorably to the little house beyond the chestnut. Little? She recalled the bright green door and the whitewashed exterior with dark wood beams set into the walls in the old Tudor fashion.

"It is just as I remember it, except for being a good deal smaller."

Raoul gestured to the front door. "Will you knock or shall I?"

Felicity's pulse shot into high gear as she moved to lift the knocker and sound a sharp rat-a-tat on the wooden door. Everything around her faded as she waited, her heart behaving in a fashion as ruthless as it was uncomfortable. The best and worst moments of her early life resided here. It was like plunging into a reality she had buried deep so it could not hurt her. But the agony was still there, curled in a ball that was now unravelling faster than she could contain it.

The door opened. A youthful female peered out. Her eyes widened. "Oh? Are you the leddy as wishes to see Gran?"

"You know?"

"Aye. Auntie Minnie sent Billy down early."

The girl's self-possession reminded Felicity at once of Mrs Kimble as she was all those years ago. She fought for calm, producing a smile. "You must be Cissy."

"Aye, ma'am."

"Have you — have you told your gran I have come to see her?"

Cissy's awed eyes had found Raoul standing a little way behind Felicity and it was a moment before she dragged them back. She shook her head. "No, ma'am, for Billy said as how Auntie Minnie charged him straitly to tell me I must wait 'til you come."

Felicity did not know whether to be relieved or sorry that her advent had not yet been announced. She glanced at Raoul, who gestured for her to enter.

"May I go in to her now, Cissy?"

"Aye, ma'am. I've settled her already and she's had a bite. She's in the parlour."

Stepping into the long hall, Felicity glanced at once towards the stairs where she had run up and down a hundred times, often with impatience to open the door in hopes of seeing Papa's energetic figure striding down the path on his way home. She followed Cissy past the door at the front and saw the open door towards the kitchen premises where she had run tame, bothering the woman who came to cook for a spare piece of pastry to make jam tarts or petting the kitten under the big table.

The memories filtered in and out, but her attention caught on the back parlour door, also open, from which a well-remembered voice called out.

"Who is it, Cissy love? Not that Billy again come a-courting, I hope."

"No, Gran, it's a leddy to see you."

Cissy passed into the room and Felicity hesitated on the threshold as Mrs Kimble's surprised voice returned an answer.

"A lady? What lady, love? What do you mean, Cissy?"

Torn between rushing into the room to reveal herself and an unnatural fear of she knew not what, Felicity glanced back to Raoul, waiting a little way down the hall. He was half a silhouette against the light emanating from the glass panel in the front door and she could not see his face.

"Go in, Felicity. I'll await you here."

The encouraging note put heart into her and she moved into the parlour. It was both cosy and spacious, light flooding in from a set of windows with French doors between to an open garden. A fleeting remembrance of playing there scooted across Felicity's mind, but it was superseded by her first sight of Mrs Kimble, ensconced on a day-bed set to catch the warmth from a crackling fire.

She looked a good deal older and smaller than Felicity remembered, her once plump cheeks thinned, her features worn. But the spectacles were the same, as was the frilly cap, its ribbons tied in a bow beneath her chin. She was peering towards the visitor, her head poking forward in a way that was peculiarly her own and so familiar that Felicity could not utter a word.

"Who is it?" Then the old lady uttered a gasp and clutched her bosom. "No! It can't be! You are not … not…"

Felicity found her tongue. "Yes, I am! I'm Flissie. Oh, Mrs Kimble!"

"Little Flissie Temple? Oh, my dear child!"

Felicity stumbled forward, falling on her knees beside the day-bed, throwing herself into the arms held out to receive her and weeping copiously into Mrs Kimble's bosom as that lady crooned quite in the old way.

"There, there, my duck … there, there. Find a handkerchief, Cissy love … there, there, my little duckling… Nan's here. Nanny's here now."

A wash of warmth swept through Felicity and she raised her head, half laughing through her tears. "Oh, Nanny, how much I've longed to hear you say that. All these years!"

"Never say so." She took Felicity's hands and squeezed. "Come, let me look at you, all grown up. I'd have known you anywhere, duck. The spit of your pa, you are!"

The beaming smile she remembered appeared on the old lady's face, the trace of her own tears visible. Old? Yes, she had aged more than she should.

"Dearest Nanny Kimble, what has happened to you? Mrs Dadford told me you were suffering with arthritis."

197

Mrs Kimble waved this away, releasing one of Felicity's hands to grab at the handkerchief held out by her hovering granddaughter. Armed with this, she wiped Felicity's cheeks, which made her giggle as she dug into her pocket for a handkerchief of her own.

"Just seeing you has made me a child again, Nanny Kimble." She sniffed and blew her nose. "There, I'm all better."

Mrs Kimble had removed her spectacles and was busy wiping the wet from her eyes. This done, she urged her granddaughter to pull up a chair for the lady. "Not that I can think of you as a young lady, duck. You'll always be Little Flissie Temple to me. How old are you now? Why, it must be years and years."

"All of thirteen. I am two and twenty, Nanny."

"Goodness! Two and twenty! Who'd have thought?"

Felicity found Cissy was holding a straight chair and rose from her knees. "Thank you so much, Cissy. How pretty you are!"

"Isn't she, duck? So lucky I am to have my Cissy to look after me. Set the chair down, love, that's it. Go and see if the coffee's boiling on the stove, there's a love. You'll take a cup, I'm sure, duck."

Cissy hesitated as Felicity sat down. "What about the gentleman, Gran?"

Mrs Kimble's bespectacled eyes popped. "Gentleman, Cissy?"

"Waitin' in the hall."

Felicity hastened to explain. "He brought me, Nanny."

A look of foreboding entered Mrs Kimble's face and she lowered her voice, grabbing at Felicity's arm. "It's not that horrid creature who did for your pa, duck? I should never have let him take you!"

"Lord Maskery? Heavens, no. Though it's about him I've come, Nanny. The gentleman with me is the Marquis of Lynchmere."

"*Marquis!*" The word was fairly shrieked and Mrs Kimble clapped a hand to her mouth. "Beg his pardon, but what are you doing with a marquis, duck?"

Felicity sighed out a breath. "It's a long story. He's helping me. I'd best introduce you."

Mrs Kimble started up. "Bring him in here? That you won't! And me in my old bombazine!"

Already on her feet, Felicity leaned down to press the old lady back against the end of the day-bed. "Don't fret, Nanny. He's not at all high in the instep."

She crossed to the door, through which Cissy had already disappeared, and found Raoul right outside. He grinned.

"Any height in my instep has been thoroughly dashed by you, Miss Schoolmistress."

"You heard that?"

"I could hardly fail to. Lead on."

She went back into the room and he followed, his tall person at once dwarfing the place. "This is Lord Lynchmere, Nanny. Mrs Kimble, that is."

He moved to the day-bed, his charm at the full, Felicity noticed. "How do you do, Mrs Kimble?"

Clearly flustered, the old dame took his hand. "You'll forgive my not rising, my lord, I hope. I've a horrid complaint as won't let me."

"So I understand. Pray don't concern yourself." He waved Felicity back to her chair. "I am persuaded I ought to leave you to converse with Miss Temple alone, ma'am."

"But you'll take a cup of coffee, my lord? Cissy is just seeing to it. She keeps the pot boiling for me, the love."

Raoul replied suitably, but insisted on taking a chair on the other side of the room. "You have not told her why you've come, Miss Temple."

She noted the formality and instinctively followed suit. "I've not yet had a chance to do so, my lord."

Mrs Kimble reached for her hand, clutching it tight. "You've come to see me and that's a miracle in itself, my little Flissie." She shook her head. "I can't get over you being quite a young woman. Your pa would've been so proud."

Her fingers tightening on those of the elderly dame, Felicity was hard put to it not to burst into tears all over again. Raoul's voice relieved her.

"She has only just discovered that it was Lord Maskery who ran her father over, Mrs Kimble. Until last night she thought of him only as her guardian."

Nanny bridled. "Guardian! I'd give him guardian if I was to see him now!"

"But he was my guardian, Nanny, or so I understood. Not that he did more for me than put me to school."

Mrs Kimble's eyes sparked beneath the spectacles. "He said as he would adopt you, duck, to make up for what he'd done. I thought as he meant to take you into his home and bring you up like a proper lady. That's what he said to the magistrate when he heard he'd left you an orphan. Him being a lord and all, Sir Bernard approved it. He was the magistrate then and he heard the case at Marlborough."

"Was that Sir Bernard Pitshanger?" asked Raoul.

"Did you know him, my lord?"

"I've heard of him. My home is not very far from here." Felicity caught his glance. "We might visit him, Miss Temple."

But Nanny waved this away. "You can't, my lord. He's dead and gone now and all."

Felicity's brain was reeling. "But did this man give order for me to go with Lord Maskery?"

"Not as such, duck. He recommended it and he told me private it was likely the best for you. There wasn't no one else, you see. Or I didn't know of anyone then." A darkling look accompanied this last.

The pitter-patter started up again in Felicity's breast. "Then? Do you mean someone came for me afterwards?"

The frill to Nanny's cap rippled as she nodded with vehemence. "Oh, yes, Flissie, he came all right. I hoped he'd found you and taken you back to where you rightfully belonged."

Her heart sounded loud in her ears. "The Beast! Could it have been the Beast himself?"

Mrs Kimble's astonishment was plain. "Beast, duck? Whatever do you mean?"

"It is what Papa called him in his journal. I've been reading it, you see. I don't know who he was, but perhaps a relative of some kind?"

"Well, it wasn't he who came. It was that Mr Rusper, as your pa were in the habit of popping off to see come quarter day."

CHAPTER ELEVEN

Felicity's gaze flew to Raoul, whose brows were raised in the very same realisation. "The very man we hoped to find!"

"Is that what you came for, duck? To find Mr Rusper?"

"And you, Nanny," Felicity said, warmly clasping her hand between both her own. "You most of all. I knew you would be able to help me, if anyone could. You are the only person with whom I can talk of Papa, and you were the one who looked after me when he died."

"I'd have kept you with me, duck, if you'd not been born a lady."

"I wish you had, Nanny."

"If that isn't your sweet nature to say so, duck, but it wouldn't have done, now, would it? Though it fair broke my heart to let you go, poor little mite, that I will say." Wrung, Felicity could only press her hand, her throat tight. Mrs Kimble was obliged to remove her spectacles and wipe her eyes again. "You'll forgive an old woman's sensibility, I hope, my lord. I'm knocked acock with seeing my little Flissie again."

"Very understandable, ma'am." Raoul was at his blandest. "But here is your granddaughter with the coffee."

The advent of Cissy bearing a tray afforded a much-needed respite, giving Felicity an opportunity to pull herself together and gather her wits. Under her grandmother's direction, Cissy put the tray down on a sideboard and set about serving the visitors. By the time everyone, including Mrs Kimble, had been provided with a cup of coffee and Cissy dismissed, she was sufficiently mistress of herself to ask the questions burning on her tongue.

"What did Mr Rusper say when he found me gone, Nanny?"

Raoul intervened. "Just a moment. Why was not this fellow Rusper at the inquest, Mrs Kimble? If Mr Temple went to him at quarter day, he must have had an interest in the business."

Nanny Kimble sighed. "It was most unfortunate timing, he said, for he was away on his round of visits to his clients. He only heard of the accident when he got back to Marlborough."

"Ah, so that is where we can find him, is it?"

"I should think so, my lord. You see, poor Mr Temple's accident was only reported in the local papers, and Mr Rusper said his clerk hadn't the wit to send to him. Not that he'd have got back any the quicker, he said."

"But when he found me gone, Nanny?"

Mrs Kimble sighed. "I don't know, duck. He's one of them closed types, who don't show nothing of what they're thinking, if you know what I mean."

Felicity could not help throwing a significant glance at Raoul. "Yes, I know exactly what you mean."

A flicker of a smile acknowledged a hit, but he did not rise to the bait. "Are we to presume you could not tell Rusper where Miss Temple had been taken?"

"No, my lord, for I didn't know. That lord had mentioned some name or other, meaning his home, but I was so put about at the time I found I hadn't asked him to put his address on the card he left with me."

"He never took me to his home, Nanny. He took me to Bath and put me in Mrs Jeavons' academy. I've been there ever since, first as a pupil and then as a teacher. Until Lord Maskery came to fetch me — oh, less than a week ago — I saw him only on one or two occasions in all that time."

Nanny Kimble's indignation was voluble and took some time to subside. Though it was balm to Felicity, she bore it with a touch of impatience, anxious to get down to the nitty-gritty of Mr Rusper's involvement. Fortunately, it did not occur to Nanny to enquire into Lord Maskery's reasons for fetching her from the academy, so upset was she by his failure to carry out the promises he'd made. As well, for Felicity dreaded to think how Mrs Kimble would react to his appalling scheme and subsequent abandonment.

At length, Raoul succeeded in redirecting the discussion to Mr Rusper. "Are we to assume this Rusper was acting for another, Mrs Kimble? He sounds to be a man of business."

The old dame looked regretful. "I've no notion at all. He's in the law, my lord, that's all I know. I took it as he knew Mr Temple's business for he came seeking our Flissie, and he was not best pleased as she'd been taken without a word vouchsafed to him."

A streak of indignation burgeoned in Felicity's breast. "What right had he to object? It is not as if he made the slightest effort on my behalf, either before or after Papa died."

"Well, he did come for you, duck, and he was right determined to track down that lord, however *inconvenient*." Behind the spectacles, Nanny's eyes kindled again. "Which made me cross as crabs, I don't mind telling you, duck. Inconvenient! And now you say he didn't do nothing for you after all. Unless he never did track you down."

But the vague confusion of identities was surfacing in Felicity's mind. "I wonder if he did? Someone came when I was still in a state of numbness. I thought it must have been Lord Maskery, but I begin to wonder."

"Not for long," came in a brisk tone from Raoul. "Have you this fellow Rusper's direction in Marlborough, Mrs Kimble?"

The bustle of the town forced Raoul's attention off Felicity and onto his team as he threaded a path through the traffic, keeping an eye out for the Corn Exchange. The landlord of the Plough had been able to offer directions from there to the street where Mr Rusper's business premises were situated. Leaving Felicity with Mrs Kimble, he had gone in search of Broome, with a promise to pick her up once the curricle was readied for departure.

Nevertheless, he had been held up for several minutes while Felicity dragged herself away from the elderly dame, and she had been distrait for the duration of the short trip to Marlborough. With his groom up behind, Raoul could not enquire too closely into what was holding her attention and a mild question produced no satisfactory answer.

"What is troubling you, Felicity?"

She had looked round, frowning as if she knew not what he said. "I beg your pardon, I was thinking."

"So I apprehend. About what?"

Her gloved fingers flicked in an aimless fashion. "Oh, this and that. You know how it is."

Raoul did not pursue it. Either she did not wish to speak of what was in her mind, or she could not do so in front of Broome. Yet he found himself concerned. Was she apprehensive about the coming meeting with Rusper? Assuming he was to be found. Or had Mrs Kimble divulged something to worry her?

It took some little time and several queries of passers-by to locate the right building, but at length his groom, who had jumped down from his perch to check at several doors of a line of yellowed buildings, returned with good news.

"This is the place, my lord. Leastways, there's a brass plate for Rusper & Son."

"Thank the Lord! Knock and ask for the fellow, Broome. There's no point in getting down if he isn't there."

Evidently this caught Felicity's attention, for she sat up, alert all at once, looking round. "You've found him?"

"It would seem so. Broome is finding out if he's in." She turned to look at him and he met her troubled gaze. He dropped his voice. "What is it?"

Her lip quivered. "The Beast, Raoul. I'm not sure I want to know about the Beast."

"Understandable." Although it was precisely what he did wish to know. "It can't hurt you to know, and perhaps it may be advantageous."

She did not look to be reassured. "I cannot think Papa would have wished me to make his acquaintance."

"You can't know that." He laid his gloved hand on hers. "You have come this far, Felicity. Don't fail now."

A wavering smile came. "I'm so glad you came with me."

He was conscious of gratification, and something more. Before he could identify it, Broome's voice cut into the thought.

"It appears he is within, my lord. I gave the clerk your name and he's gone off to inform Mr Rusper."

Raoul took his hand from Felicity's. "Excellent. Go to their heads. You'll need to walk them, I expect."

Within a short space of time of escorting his charge into a wide hall, a clerk was ushering them up the stairs and into a large office at the front of the house, where a much younger man than Raoul had expected greeted them with a bow. He was dressed with propriety, but a rather colourful waistcoat matched the evident cheeriness of his disposition. He greeted them with a bow and a smile.

"I am Rusper, my lord." He looked enquiringly at Felicity.

"This is Miss Temple, sir, on whose behalf we are here. But I fancy we are looking for your father. You, I take it, are Rusper the son?"

The young man grinned. "I am, my lord." He directed a small bow to Felicity. "Miss Temple. How may I serve you? I'm afraid my father no longer conducts very much business. I'm sorry to say he has grown frail."

Felicity spoke for the first time. "Then he is not here?"

"No, but I am conversant with all aspects of the business. What I don't know I can readily find out. Pray will you not be seated?"

Receiving an agitated look from Felicity as she took the proffered chair before the fellow's desk, Raoul struck in at once. "I believe it is doubtful you will know of the matters concerning Miss Temple, sir, since a great deal of time has passed since then."

"Thirteen years," Felicity said, her gaze now flickering on the younger Rusper's youthful countenance.

His brows drew together. "I see. May I know just what this is all about?"

Hesitating, Raoul looked at Felicity's profile. She was still regarding Rusper Junior with an odd sort of interest. To his surprise, she did not immediately speak of her affairs.

"Do you resemble your father, sir?"

He looked taken aback. "I believe there is a similarity. Hard to tell without examining old portraits, ma'am."

She drew a quick breath and let it out, her gloved fingers restless. "I beg your pardon. It is just that there is something familiar about you. I might have seen your father, years ago."

What was this now? Had she recalled more than she had told Raoul? Being in Middenhall had certainly broken through some kind of barrier to uncover memories of the past. But this fellow could not help there.

"The case, sir, is that Miss Temple's father was, we believe, a client of Rusper and Son."

"Jeremy Temple. My father's name was Jeremy."

This was news to Raoul, but he hastened to add helpful detail. "Mr Temple was used to visit your father here, at quarter day we understand, prior to his accidental death."

Rusper Junior looked a little blank, but he cast a reassuring glance upon Felicity and reached out for a hand bell and rang it. "We will have in Knowlton, our chief clerk. He has been with my father for many years and will doubtless be conversant with the business."

"Thank you."

Raoul eyed Felicity in some degree of concern as she fidgeted with the petticoats of the singularly unattractive gown she had chosen to assume for this journey. He had a sudden urge to see her clothed as befit the lady she was, but suppressed it as the door opened to admit the lad who had shown them up. Mr Rusper gave order to fetch his chief clerk and presently a spare, elderly fellow in an old-fashioned wig presented himself.

"Ah, Knowlton, allow me to make you known to Lord Lynchmere and Miss Temple. They have come about Mr Temple, who was a client here some thirteen years ago."

The elder man had arrived at the desk and executed a neat bow, but at this his head lifted and he directed a penetrating stare at Felicity. "Mr Temple? Mr Jeremy Temple?"

"Yes, that's right, Knowlton. You know of him?"

"Indeed, Mr Rusper." The old clerk flicked his junior a glance but his gaze appraised Felicity. "You have come from Bath, ma'am, I surmise?"

"No, from London," Raoul began, but he was interrupted.

"I knew it! He did come to Bath, did he not? Mr Rusper?" Felicity waved an impatient hand towards the younger man. "Not him. The other. He came once or twice perhaps, did he not?" Her bosom rose and fell. "Why did he leave me there? Why didn't he tell me who he was? Why didn't he speak to me of Papa?"

Raoul moved to set a hand to her shoulder, pressing it firmly, his eyes on the clerk, who was looking wooden-faced. He clearly knew the precise answers to these impassioned questions. "I imagine you can throw light upon these matters, Mr Knowlton, but answer me this, if you please. Is Mr Rusper some kind of trustee to Miss Temple?"

The clerk pinched his lips together. The younger Rusper was looking bewildered, as well he might. But he frowned at the man's silence. "Well, Knowlton? I certainly have no knowledge of such a thing. Is it so?"

The other's wooden expression intensified. "I cannot say, sir."

"Cannot or will not?" Raoul snapped.

There was a tense pause. Then Knowlton turned to his employer. "I believe it would be well to consult your honoured father, sir, if you don't object to it."

"I think so indeed, Knowlton. Better still, if he is up to it, conduct Miss Temple and his lordship into my father's parlour."

"Then you reside upon the premises?" Raoul asked as the clerk departed upon his errand.

"My father does. He likes to be within easy reach. It irks him to be unable to carry on with the business. I was used to live in the apartment when I was apprenticed, but we exchanged a few years back. Since I have a growing family and my mother has sadly left us, it seemed expedient for my wife and I to take over the house."

"It sounds to be a mutually satisfactory arrangement. Have you a son to take over from you?"

Rusper laughed. "That will be a few years yet, I fear. He is scarcely out of short coats."

Raoul had but a tepid interest in this history, but he encouraged the fellow to expatiate on his domestic affairs since it served to pass the time and allowed him to keep Felicity under surreptitious observation. That she was labouring under suppressed agitation was obvious. He only trusted she would not be induced to lose her temper.

It was not long before the clerk returned with an invitation to step into Mr Rusper's parlour which proved to be up another flight of stairs. Raoul found opportunity to murmur a warning to his charge. "Steady, Felicity! Don't go top over tail with the fellow. Leave it to me to put the pertinent questions."

She gave a nod, but entered a caveat. "As long as you ask the right ones."

"Just don't go flying into a pelter, that's all."

A faint smile rewarded him. "I will try not to."

Raoul was conscious of a sliver of disquiet. He could scarcely depend upon this assurance. The charm of Felicity's unpredictability was anathema in such a situation as this. He could only hope whatever information Rusper was able to impart would not infuriate her.

"This way, ma'am."

Arrived at the top of the flight, Knowlton opened a door to a bright chamber overlooking a square at the back of the building. The room was done out in a neutral shade, with paintings on the walls, a marbled fireplace and old-fashioned wooden furnishings.

The elder Mr Rusper was seated in a large chair by the window, with one leg resting on a footstool, but he removed it from there as the visitors entered, rising with the help of a stick and limping a few paces into the room.

"How do you do, Miss Temple? I have wondered when it would occur to you to seek me out." His voice was dry, a trifle cracked, and he looked to be indeed frail, unsteady on his legs. Despite these indications of a debilitated condition, the habit of command was evident in the beaky nose and the still keen gaze. It travelled from Felicity, who was staring at him in some degree of blankness — shock? — to Raoul's face. "My lord Lynchmere, I understand?"

"That is correct."

"Your interest in this matter, my lord?"

There was no impertinence in the tone, yet it put Raoul's back up and he became haughty. "I am Miss Temple's escort, sir, she having been deserted by Lord Maskery, of whom I am very sure you are aware, after his promise to introduce her to the *Ton*."

The man's brows lowered at mention of the name, but he said nothing of it, merely turning back to Felicity and indicating the chair his clerk was setting. "Will you not be seated, Miss Temple?"

She seemed to come out of a stupor. "Yes, I will sit, but I think you had better sit down as well before you fall down."

Surprise flickered in the fellow's eyes and a faint twitch attacked his lip. So Rusper had a sense of humour? Promising. The dry tone returned.

"I am not yet at my last prayers, ma'am. Pray be seated."

He waited for Felicity to take the chair, indicated another for Raoul, and only when both were sitting went back to his own chair, refusing the aid of his clerk in a testy fashion.

"Take the stool away, Knowlton. I don't need it. Fetch the file, if you please." He waited for the door to close behind the clerk and turned his gaze upon Felicity. "Now, Miss Temple, let us begin."

She was frowning. "You did come to Mrs Jeavons' academy, did you not? I recognise you. I couldn't recall if it had been you or Lord Maskery, but to see you here and now I have no doubt."

A thin smile twisted Rusper's mouth. "I am surprised. You were a slip of a thing, my dear."

The familiarity with which he addressed her rankled with Raoul, but Felicity did not appear to notice.

"It was a dark time for me, sir. My memories are vague, but I know it was Lord Maskery who left me there and I have believed all these years that he was my guardian. But it was not so, was it?"

The fellow's lips pursed. "As to that, Miss Temple, there was no named guardian. In light of the circumstances, however, my client wished to avoid the complications of your becoming a ward of court."

Raoul's senses came alive. "Your client? Some person other than Mr Temple, I surmise?"

"Indeed, my lord."

A glance at Felicity betrayed her feelings. She was white of face, the freckles standing out, her eyes fierce. "The Beast!"

Rusper tipped his head to one side. "I beg your pardon?"

"It's what Papa called him. In his journal. It must be him you mean. My father detested him. He came to Middenhall because he hoped the Beast would be induced to increase his allowance. By you, Mr Rusper. He meant to ask you … and then he was killed."

"A most distressing occurrence, Miss Temple. I have ever regretted I was on my travels at the time. Knowlton did what he could, but he had no authority beyond organising the funeral. He sent an express to my client, but that too was received too late to be of immediate use." Another slight smile appeared. "However, we must do *the Beast* the justice to own that he did take an interest in your welfare."

"Interest?" Not much to Raoul's surprise, Felicity fairly exploded. "He left me in Bath to rot! Much he cared if I was alive or dead all this time. No, nor if I had so much as a sou to my name, which I may tell you I haven't now, thanks to Lord Maskery. I am quite destitute, and if it had not been for Lord Lynchmere and his cousin, I don't know what would have become of me. So pray do not talk to me of doing him justice. Whoever he is, Mr Rusper, he is a beast indeed!"

The lawyer took this tirade without a blink, merely surveying Felicity as if he had encountered a rare specimen. On the point of saying something soothing to her, Raoul was prevented by the re-entrance into the room of the elderly clerk, who was carrying a file of yellowed parchments tied up with red tape. These he brought to Rusper, who set them on his knee.

"Sherry for my guests, Knowlton. You may take one yourself and remain, if you please. I might need your elephantine memory."

A sour smile creased the other man's mouth, but he said nothing, merely crossing to a cabinet to one side of the room, from where he extracted a decanter and several glasses. Raoul withdrew his attention from the fellow's proceedings and found Felicity was focused upon the file in the lawyer's lap.

"Is that all?" Her voice was shaky. "What became of my father's property? All his clothes? His books? Papers? I have only his journal and I don't even recall how I came by that."

"I may be able to enlighten you, Miss Temple," said Rusper, waving his clerk, who was hovering with a filled glass, towards Felicity. "But take a sip or two, if you will. I feel sure you are in need of a little restorative."

She took the glass with a gesture rather grudging than gracious and drank a little. Done to appease? Raoul sipped with approval from the one handed to him. Rusper had taste and could clearly afford the best.

"Well, sir?" Impatience sounded in Felicity's voice.

Rusper was taking a glass himself. He nodded to the clerk, who effaced himself somewhere behind them. "Mr Temple's hostess, Mrs — hm, memory fails me. What was her name?"

"Mrs Kimble," Felicity supplied. "We have just come from there."

His brows lifted a fraction. "Ah, indeed. She has been your informant?"

"She told us where to find you. Also that you had come for me and you meant to find where Lord Maskery had taken me. That is all she knew."

Rusper nodded. "Quite. As to your father's property, Knowlton cleared the rooms and packed it all up and held it here for my decision."

Felicity looked to be half hope, half fury. "Then where is it?"

"I am coming to that, ma'am. My first priority was to discover your whereabouts. Lord Maskery's progress was erratic and it took some time to catch up with him. I located him at length in Brighton, by which time, I regret to say, his remorse had somewhat diminished." A faint look of distaste entered the fellow's face. "His lordship appeared to believe he had discharged any obligation to his victim's daughter and could not be expected to do more."

"Scoundrel!" Raoul's rage with the fellow revived. "Did he pay down his dust for Miss Temple's education?"

"He had, he said, the intention of so doing. However, he took my advent in good part, expressing himself as happy to think there was a relative, and one with means too, who had Miss Temple's interests at heart."

Glancing at Felicity, Raoul saw her fingers clench on the glass, but she did not speak. He transferred his gaze to the lawyer. "In sum, he washed his hands of her, I take it?"

Rusper looked dry. "With every expression of regret and goodwill."

This proved too much for Felicity. "Regret? He had none! Besides, he could not have been ignorant of my remaining at the academy since he came for me just last week, claiming to be my guardian."

A collection of recalled tidbits she had let fall swept through Raoul's mind. "Did he say that? Or was it your assumption?"

She looked at him, meditatively sipping from her glass. Did she even realise what she was doing? "I thought it. Perhaps he did not say it. I can't remember now."

"It is of little consequence, ma'am," interrupted the lawyer. "Suffice to say that once I had your direction, it behoved me to consult with my client."

Felicity's gaze veered back. "This so-called relative. Who is he, sir?"

"He is Sir Arthur Temple, a baronet of Wotton Basset, and your great-uncle."

Memory kicked and Raoul exclaimed aloud. "That stiff-rumped old recluse? Good God!"

"You know him, my lord?"

"Not personally. My own father was a little acquainted with him, I believe, and called him an old curmudgeon."

That faint twitch attacked Rusper's lip. "He is not a bonhomous type, it is true."

"Bonhomous!" Raoul turned to his charge. "Believe me, Felicity, you may thank your stars he did not choose to take you into his household. From all I have ever heard the man is a mean-spirited, irascible near lunatic and cordially disliked by the entire neighbourhood."

This description proved Rusper's undoing. He gave a bark of laughter, hastily smothered, and took refuge in his sherry.

Felicity glanced from him to Raoul and back again. "Then Papa was right to call him the Beast. No wonder he did not wish to go anywhere near the man." A frown creased her brow. "But why was he so horrid to my father? Papa often spoke of having expectations, but he only had his allowance."

Recovering himself, Rusper nodded. "That is correct. Your grandfather having died when Mr Temple was still at school, he grew up under his uncle's aegis along with your grandmother. She did not live to see her son become a man, and Mr Temple was wont to claim her spirit had been crushed by Sir Arthur's distempered manner."

"No wonder Papa loathed him."

Rusper's dry look appeared. "I regret to say the feeling was mutual. Your father escaped as soon as he could, he told me. Needless to say, Sir Arthur disapproved violently of his marriage. Respectable, but of no particular worth. Mrs Temple was, I understand, the youngest daughter of a vicar with a numerous progeny, whom your father met when he was up at the university."

"They married in secret, did they not?" The eager note in Felicity's voice touched Raoul. "I remember him telling me. Also that the Beast forbade him the house when he knew."

Rusper gave a tiny smile. "That, I assure you, Miss Temple, exactly suited your father. He had no desire to set foot in the place ever again, he was wont to say. Except under circumstances that would permit him to do as he pleased there."

Raoul caught the inference. "He would have succeeded Sir Arthur?"

"Had he lived, yes. Sir Arthur did marry, but his wife perished before giving him an heir. When his brother died, he did not trouble to marry again for the purpose of making one. Failing your father, there is a cousin. In any event, the property is merely a comfortable competence."

"Evidently not very comfortable while Sir Arthur occupies it," said Raoul with a flickering look of humour towards Felicity.

She smiled. "I had not thought to be glad of being abandoned, sir."

Rusper's features tightened. "You should not have been, Miss Temple. Sir Arthur behaved ill towards you. He might have smoothed your path, but he chose merely to grease the wheels of your education. When I came a second time, it was to negotiate with the headmistress there —"

"Mrs Jeavons, you mean. Negotiate what, sir?"

"For a position as schoolmistress at the academy for you, Miss Temple."

Felicity's shock was apparent. "You mean that was the Beast's doing?"

He nodded. "He maintained that he was too old to take on a young girl's future. Nor had he the inclination to do the pretty, as he phrased it, to his neighbours in hopes of *turning you off.* He had, he said, done enough by Jeremy's whelp — his word, not mine — if he saw to it you had means of making your way in the world."

"Generous!" Raoul's dislike of the man was growing. "If I understand you, sir, Miss Temple can hope for no financial assistance from that quarter?"

Felicity's sharp little intake of breath told him this had touched a nerve. Unsurprising, since she had not exaggerated when she said she was destitute.

Rusper did not answer immediately, his gaze steady on Felicity's face. He held up a finger as she opened her mouth to speak. "One moment, Miss Temple."

A puzzled glance came Raoul's way, but she remained silent as Rusper set down his glass and at last tugged at the ties of the tape binding the file still reposing on his knee. He sifted for a moment and glanced up, looking past Raoul.

"Thornbury, do you recall how far back is that final account?"

The clerk came from behind, accepted the parchment and set the whole lot upon a convenient table resting against the wall behind his employer. While he hunted through the aged parchments, Rusper's faint smile appeared as he once more turned his gaze upon Felicity.

"Mr Temple never did receive his allowance upon that last quarter day. The accounting for those expenses arising from his demise was paid separately by my client. As also subsequent expenses relating to your education. Moreover, your Mrs Jeavons, a scrupulous lady in her financial dealings, sent me always an exact account instead of the Dutch reckoning I expected."

Guessing what was coming, and seeing the mix of bewilderment and burgeoning hope in Felicity's countenance, Raoul cut short the suspense. "You have saved something from the wreck, is that it?"

Rusper did not look best pleased by the interruption, but acknowledged it. "My client provided a general sum and the discrepancy between this and Mrs Jeavons' accounts has accumulated over the years into a tidy little saving."

"But it does not belong to me," Felicity burst out.

"It was provided for your use. My client had neither interest nor desire to know how it was spent. He understood there were expenses beyond your school and boarding fees, for clothing, for instance."

"Then you kept the — the discrepancy, as you call it?"

Rusper's smile grew. "My responsibility in the matter ended when you joined the staff of Mrs Jeavons' academy, Miss Temple. I have long expected, however, that you would one day seek me out. And here you are."

Raoul was ready with a question he was very sure would occur to Felicity, but he was forestalled by the clerk, turning with a paper in his hand.

"This is the final account, sir."

Rusper took it and ran his eyes down the sheet. Felicity's gaze was fixed upon the thing, her fingers tensely held in her lap, curling like claws. Keeping his question back for the moment, Raoul waited, finding in himself almost as much eagerness as he guessed Felicity was feeling. It was unlikely to prove an independence, but any amount was better than the zero of her current state.

The lawyer touched the paper with his finger. "Ah, I thought as much. I could not recall precisely, but if we add this to Mr Temple's last allowance, I believe you may count upon some four hundred pounds, perhaps a trifle more. There will be an accumulation of interest, of course."

Raoul grunted. A paltry amount, though better than he had expected. But Felicity appeared to be wholly bereft of speech. She was gazing at the lawyer open-mouthed, more shocked than Raoul had before seen her. He slid into the breach.

"What I wish to know, Mr Rusper, is why you did not, perhaps when Miss Temple came of age, seek her out instead? You held these monies for her. You knew where she was. Surely you must have known she was in need?"

Rusper looked conscious, but before he could answer, Felicity spoke at last.

"*Four hundred pounds?*"

Had she even heard his question to the lawyer? Impatient, Raoul cut in. "It is scarcely a fortune, Felicity. But it might have made life a deal easier for you in Bath."

She turned on him. "It may not be a fortune to you, but it is more money than I have ever seen in my life! I thought I had none at all, and now —" She leaned from her chair, putting out a hand towards the lawyer. "I cannot sufficiently thank you. You have given me hope and a chance to find a way to live again."

Rusper touched his fingers to hers briefly, the natural austerity of his expression softening for an instant. "My dear Miss Temple, I only wish it were more. I was fond of your father. He amused me, little though he suspected it. I have rarely met with another with such a zestful approach to life. He had a generous spirit."

"He had, hadn't he? I adored him."

Felicity's voice quivered and Raoul glanced quickly at her. Her eyes were both glowing and glistening.

The lawyer, perhaps with an intention to give her time to compose herself, turned his gaze upon Raoul. "To answer your question, my lord, I judged it kinder not to intervene in Miss Temple's life. The monies in my possession were and are to be used at my discretion." He turned to address Felicity directly. "Without having it in my power to change your life in a radical fashion, Miss Temple, as I should have wished to do, I thought it less cruel to leave you in ignorance of your great-uncle's involvement. I may have made the wrong choice, but I stand by it."

Raoul would have hotly disputed the choice, but Felicity smiled warmly at the man.

"You chose right, sir. It could not have added to my comfort to know that the Beast rejected me as he had done my father. I grew up to the tune of Papa's remembered maxims and learned to value my independence. It would have irked me horribly to be obliged to kowtow to the whims of a despot."

The lawyer's dry look reappeared. "Like father, like daughter?"

Felicity laughed, the most carefree sound Raoul had heard from her in days. His heart warmed, but as she and Rusper exchanged a reminiscence or two, he cast his mind back across the discussion and found one answer wanting. He broke in at the first lull.

"You did not say what happened to Mr Temple's effects, sir."

"Ah, that, yes." Rusper cast a grave look towards Felicity. "There I had no choice, ma'am. All that Thornbury had packed up was returned to Sir Arthur. I have no knowledge of what he did with it all."

Raoul inwardly cursed. He had hoped to avoid having to make contact with Felicity's great-uncle. Unless she wished for it, which seemed unlikely. She looked a trifle disappointed, but she spread her hands.

"I dare say it makes no matter. I only thought of consulting his papers to see if I could learn something of his family."

Thornbury, hovering at his employer's elbow, leaned to murmur in Rusper's ear. The lawyer's eye brightened. "Ah, yes, I had forgot. Fetch them, if you please." He turned back to Felicity as the clerk hastened from the room. "There were some papers we kept back, Miss Temple. Call it intuition, if you will. I did not think your father's whimsy would sit well with my client."

"Whimsy?" For a moment Felicity looked puzzled. Then delight spread across her countenance. "His stories! You kept them? Oh, Mr Rusper, thank you!"

The fellow looked as pleased as punch. Raoul was amazed at the change in him. "I well remember your father describing to me, with much embellishment, your reactions when he entertained you with his tales, my dear. Several of them were published, you know."

"Yes, I do know. He was used to indulge us in a treat or an adventure whenever he sold a story."

Rusper smiled. "There now, I knew I was right to keep them. To be truthful, my dear Miss Temple, I could not risk the possibility that your great-uncle might destroy them."

When the clerk returned with a fat package, carefully wrapped in cloth, Felicity and the lawyer spent some time examining its contents together. Raoul, his mind busy, played no part in this beyond smiling at her exclamatory comments as she looked at both printed and hand-written effusions from her father's pen, reading out snatches of what appeared to be particularly fantastical, fey and even some gruesome tales.

His attention centred on the recognition that Felicity's antecedents were indeed perfectly respectable and presented no bar to the scheme he had in his head. Nor did he think it incumbent upon him to approach the irascible Sir Arthur upon the matter. Once the thing was done, he might inform him, perhaps. Felicity was of age. She needed no one's permission but her own. Which was where the water stuck.

Would Felicity see it in the same light of convenience that Raoul did? Or would he be balked by her streak of independence?

CHAPTER TWELVE

Felicity came away from Mr Rusper's establishment happier than she could remember to have been for an age. She clutched the precious package of Papa's stories, which were almost of more value to her than the draft on the lawyer's bankers now reposing in an inner pocket of Raoul's coat.

She still felt stunned by the amount and was relieved to have him take charge of it for the moment. He had promised to cash it on her behalf at the first opportunity. Although how would she look after such a sum? One could scarcely keep it under the mattress.

"Besides, I don't have one."

"One what?"

Surprised, she glanced at Raoul, who was concentrating on weaving a path through Marlborough's traffic. "Did I say that aloud? I mean I don't have a mattress."

A disbelieving laugh came her way. "A mattress? What in the world are you talking about, you absurd creature?"

She glanced back at Broome on his perch behind and lowered her voice. "I wish you won't cash that draft, Raoul. Not yet. I can't think how I am to look after such an amount when I could not even hold on to a few measly guineas."

She received an amused look. "You are scarcely to blame for their loss. Have no fear. We will arrange to keep the bulk of it safely in the bank."

Puzzlement followed the sliver of relief. "But how? They won't let me have an account."

"No, but I have one."

"But…" A host of objections leapt to Felicity's tongue, but she forced them back. Such arguments could not be engaged upon in an open carriage. Yet they gave rise to so many questions in her mind she did not know which to tackle first.

She had not had time to think of the vista of future that had opened out before her. Her whole object had been to discover a way back to a situation where she might have sufficient means to find another post. But need she do that? Could she not live quite comfortably with upwards of four hundred pounds at her disposal? Not a house, perhaps. That would rapidly dissipate her funds. But a room with Nanny Kimble? It must alleviate poor Nanny's lot to have her there, though she could not replace young Cissy. Only what would she do in Middenhall?

"I could set up as a teacher."

"Wool-gathering, Felicity?" Raoul's wry look was in his face. "I shall not again question your remark, for I don't think I wish to know what is in that butterfly mind of yours."

"I wouldn't tell you if you did ask," Felicity said, goaded.

"Thank God for that! Would you care for refreshment before we leave Marlborough?"

"Yes! No! I need to think."

"Well, you won't do that with Mrs Dadford fussing about you. We will repair to a suitable hostelry."

Remembrance of Angelica's warnings kicked in Felicity's mind. "But we are supposed to be circumspect. What if someone you know sees us?"

"I hardly think it matters now. Nor were you concerned in Middenhall."

"No one knows you in Middenhall."

"They do now."

"Oh, you know what I mean, Raoul."

"You are worrying needlessly." He was already drawing into the yard of the Lamb, a substantial coaching inn, where he brought his equipage to a standstill. "We'll bait here, Broome. Get the team into the warm and rubbed down."

"Aye, my lord."

The groom leapt down and went to the horses' heads and a couple of ostlers came forward to assist in removing the animals from the traces.

Felicity forebore to argue further. She was too elated to be considering the proprieties. But as Raoul handed her down, she belatedly recalled his promise to return her to Angelica's care. It seemed so long ago now, though in reality it was a mere couple of days. Less? Probably. Her life had changed so radically with the revelations of the journey, it felt as if an eon had passed.

"I feel quite disoriented," she said as she accompanied Raoul through a bustling hallway.

"Hardly surprising. Let me procure a private parlour and you will have an opportunity to settle your mind again."

Felicity doubted the buzzing in her head would soon dissipate. Her mind was darting this way and that, seemingly out of her control. She abandoned all efforts at logic and let the wandering thoughts free as she was conducted into an upstairs room with a window overlooking the street. She watched the comings and goings below without taking them in, her imagination painting images of long walks in Savernake Forest with her sketching pad to hand, interspersed with memories of riding on Papa's shoulders or scrambling over rocks and climbing into a low-branched tree. Raoul's voice recalled her.

"I have ordered a light repast, since I have no doubt Mrs Dadford is preparing another gargantuan feast."

She turned from the window to find him setting a chair for her at the cloth-covered table. Failing the window seat, there was no other place to sit. Raoul smiled at her and an odd flip in her bosom took her by surprise. She eyed him as she came to take the chair, feeling baffled.

He lifted an eyebrow. "What is that look for?"

"Nothing." Her cheeks warmed a little and she hastily sat down.

He did not persist, merely taking the chair opposite, setting it at a casual angle and leaning back at his ease.

Felicity began to feel fidgety, unaccountably flustered as she had never been in his presence. Was it because they were alone? In just the situation Angelica had warned against? "I suppose we are safe from interruption in here from anyone who knows you?"

His brows flew up. "Are you at that again? You may cease to nag at it. Within a short time it will be of no consequence."

Blank incomprehension stilled her mind. "Of no consequence? How?"

"That you shall see." His enigmatic face was in place. "They are bringing coffee at once. I thought you might be in need of a restorative."

She felt in need of a new brain altogether. What had got into her to be abruptly conscious of Raoul and the fact of their isolation? He was oddly different. His gaze seemed to appraise her, dropping to the neckline of her gown. His expression altered and Felicity read disapproval in his eyes.

"The first thing is to be rid of that abominable garment. Surely you could wear one of the gowns Angelica sorted out for you?"

Startled, and considerably ruffled, Felicity pulled at her gown, straightening it. "Neither is suitable for travelling, especially in a curricle."

He grunted. "Well, we can remedy that. Not that there is likely to be a suitable modiste in this town."

"It is scarcely a matter of urgency —"

"It will be."

"— and I have no intention of wasting my funds on fripperies." Belatedly taking in his interruption, Felicity blinked at him. "What do you mean, it will be? Until I decide just what to do —"

Raoul put up a finger. "If you are thinking of that ridiculous scheme of yours to return to a life of drudgery, forget it. I won't permit you to do any such thing."

"You won't permit me?" A blaze swept through her. "If you think, merely because you helped me to come here, you can dictate what I do with the rest of my life, my lord, let me tell you —"

To her utter astonishment, he burst out laughing. Felicity eyed him, bewilderment chasing away the spurting fury as she waited for his mirth to abate. He held up a hand in a placatory gesture.

"I haven't run mad, I promise you. Forget I said it."

How could she possibly forget? He was behaving in a most peculiar fashion and Felicity had no idea how to deal with it. Fortunately, a waiter entered the room at this moment and she was able to recover herself as he set down a silver coffee pot and its accompaniment of cream and sugar.

"The rest will be here directly, sir."

Raoul nodded, already upending a cup. Felicity watched him pour and set the filled vessel down before her. He put the cream jug and sugar bowl within her reach.

"Thank you." Aware her voice was frigid, she became incensed again at his amused look. "I hope you know you are ruining my enjoyment of the day."

He was busy with his own coffee. "Accept my apologies."

She sipped, still feeling aggrieved as she recalled his animadversions upon her gown. A thought occurred and she gave it voice at once. "That's one thing I can do now. Pay you back for those wretched gowns."

He lifted an eyebrow. "As far as I know, I have not expended any money on your gowns."

"You know very well Angelica charged them up to you."

"Ah, did she? Then my secretary will deal with any such bill."

"Then you can reimburse yourself from the monies you are holding for me."

She received one of his bored looks. "No doubt, if I were the least bit interested in so doing."

"You may not be, but I do not care to be beholden."

"You won't be."

Felicity set down her cup. "I wish you won't be so cryptic. What in the world has come over you?"

The corners of his mouth twitched. "Oh, I am thinking of your future, Felicity, can you doubt it?"

A trace of alarm trickled through her. "You mean me to fall in with Angelica's scheme? I am not sure that I shall. I need time to decide what I wish to do. Everything is topsy-turvy, Raoul, and I won't be rushed."

He sipped at his coffee, regarding her over the rim of his cup. Consideringly, she thought. Another frisson attacked her. Had he some other scheme in his head?

He lowered the cup. "Perhaps I am too precipitate. I dare say Rusper's information has been a trifle overwhelming."

"To say the least. To be frank, I do not know if I am on my head or my heels."

"Then let me set you upright again. You need time? Then we will repair to Ruscoe Hall."

"Ruscoe Hall?"

"My seat. It is not far from here, but we won't attempt the journey today. You will wish to take your leave of Mrs Kimble, and I imagine our hostess will take it unkind in us if we depart without doing justice to her hospitality." A wry grin appeared. "You see how I am learning from you already?"

Felicity could not answer at once. She was thoroughly taken aback, and not a little dismayed despite a sliver of unnamed feeling snaking into her bosom. Apprehension? No, not that. It felt more like nervous anticipation. How she had felt before one of Papa's treats. How was that either possible or sensible?

Raoul was still watching her, an odd light in his eyes. "What, I wonder, is going on in that head of yours, Miss Independence?"

"I don't know."

His brows flew up. "This is something new. I have never known you at a loss before."

Instinct loosened Felicity's tongue. "How should you? You scarcely know me at all."

"Oh, I think I know you well enough."

"Well enough for what?" He did not answer, the enigmatic blankness she so much disliked curtaining his thoughts. Felicity set down her cup and leaned forward. "I hate it when you do that."

"Do what?"

"Look at me in that — that annihilating fashion. As if you don't choose to reveal yourself. It is horribly alienating, if you wish to know. Worse even than the bored look."

His countenance became a trifle rigid, but the despised look did not abate. "I beg your pardon. It was not my intention to alienate you. On the contrary."

Felicity was prevented from answering by the re-entrance of the waiter, bearing a tray. Relieved to be able to turn her eyes from Raoul, she watched the man setting out a platter of cold meats, bread, a board of cheeses and a dish of sweetmeats. She took in the viands only vaguely, preoccupied with the worsening oddity of Raoul's manner. What in the world had come over him? He had been so supportive she had felt inordinately at ease with him. Then, just when she ought to be basking in her triumphs, he began behaving in this elusive and peculiar way.

The moment the door closed behind the waiter, she looked across at him. "Why are you being like this, Raoul?"

For a moment he looked as if he might explain, his gaze meeting hers. Was that actual apprehension in his eyes? Or merely hesitation?

Abruptly he smiled. "Let us eat. All this delving into your history has made me hungry."

Felicity felt unaccountably disappointed as she accepted the ham with which he served her and opted for a slice of bread which he cut for her from the fresh loaf. His manner became far more normal as he began upon his own more substantial repast, accompanied by a jug of ale.

"Do you mean to tell Mrs Kimble of your good fortune?"

"Of course I will tell her. She was most anxious for me and will wish to know how I fared."

She refrained from mentioning her half-formed notion of residing with her old landlady. She was by no means sure it was what she wanted to do. Although she might sound Nanny out. After all, there was no saying she would be anything but a burden, even if her contribution would augment the household income.

Unexpectedly, the notion of resuming the sort of nomadic life she had lived with Papa all those years ago held no attraction for her. She had been for too long settled in a situation at least predictable, if far from ideal. On the other hand, the longer she allowed herself to continue in a sphere of life to which she could not aspire, the harder it would be to leave it. As leave it she must. She was not equipped for the sort of society Angelica enjoyed, far less Raoul. The thought at once found its way onto her tongue.

"If you mean to take me to Ruscoe Hall, it must be only for a day or two."

"That is as you please."

He sounded cold. Felicity found herself oddly anxious. "Was that rude? It was not meant to be. I only meant I must not allow myself to become too accustomed to your sort of lifestyle. I cannot deny it is very comfortable to have everything arranged for me and not to be obliged to consider how to pay for my food and lodging, but it will not do, Raoul."

He set down his fork and seemed about to speak, but she hurried on.

"No, pray don't argue the matter. You of all people must realise this windfall is limiting. You can afford to lose your winnings from Lord Maskery, so you cannot possibly consider it other than paltry. Indeed you said as much."

"Felicity —"

She held up a hand. "Let me finish! You mock at me for being independent, but necessity has made me so and I have been obliged to practise economy. Now I have means beyond anything I supposed possible and I intend to live within them. Do you see?"

His smile was wry. "I see. You must forgive my arrogance. But you need practise no economies while you are under my protection. Is it agreed?"

She gave him a wavering smile, abruptly beset by a ridiculous desire to weep. Why the notion of having Raoul's protection should have that effect she could not fathom. Her voice, to her dismay, became husky. "You have looked after me very well indeed."

"A trifle. I could do more, if you will let me."

Unable to speak, she shook her head and dived for her coffee cup. Finding it empty, she reached out a trembling hand for the coffee pot just as Raoul did the same. His fingers brushed hers and a jolt shot through her.

Felicity snatched her hand back, glancing at him in shock. His attention was on the coffee pot and he did not appear conscious as he poured dark liquid into her cup. Had he not felt it? All too aware of the tremble in her limbs, Felicity eyed him in a jumble of suspense and disbelief. How had that escaped him? What was it? A mere touch to make her feel as if she had suffered the sort of shock one got from banging an elbow? Only in her bosom instead.

What in the world was happening to her? Recalling the several occasions upon which Raoul had touched her, even held her in a comforting embrace, she could find none to which she had experienced a similar reaction. Disoriented all over again and utterly bewildered, she added cream and sugar to her coffee and drank it, horribly conscious of Raoul and fearful of giving herself away.

In a minute or two, he pushed away his plate. She watched him pick up his tankard and down the rest of his ale, fascinated by the motion of his throat, the tilt of his head and the strength of his fingers about the handle.

He set it down and grinned. "That is a good deal better. Let us repair to Middenhall and inform Mrs Dadford that we are off tomorrow. You could visit Mrs Kimble too, perhaps, so we won't be delayed in the morning."

Due to Raoul's insistence on an early start, the curricle entered the environs of the grounds surrounding Ruscoe Hall a little after noon. Informed of this fact by her escort, Felicity dragged her mind from its preoccupation and looked about. They were rolling through a village bordering a low wall, beyond which lay a bank of woody trees with here and there a break showing distant greensward and a glimpse of water.

The undercurrent of anticipatory nervousness that had beset her from the moment of waking sprang to life. She was about to enter Raoul's home where the vast disparity between them must inevitably oppress her. In the concentration of her quest, his status had never intruded on her mind. Indeed, she had cared nothing for it. But the consideration of her future, coupled with his odd behaviour, had forced it to the forefront of her mind.

Admittedly, he had reverted to a more normal manner, but Felicity found it impossible to relax in his company, aware all the time of his maleness in a way she had not been before the shock of her reaction to his touch. Every time he took her hand to aid her to climb up into or down from the curricle, Felicity experienced a flitter in her pulse at the feel and strength of his fingers. Her own tingled for minutes after he let her go. It was utterly disconcerting and she had no idea how to combat such an unprecedented reaction.

"The country hereabouts is dense with my peers, I regret to say, but most are thankfully fixed in the Capital at this season. So you need not fear to be obliged to do the pretty."

Startled at the very thought, Felicity could not forbear a relieved laugh. "I should hope not. How would you explain me?"

He gave her a sidelong look. "You are an acquaintance of my cousin's, remember? You are here to — let me see — yes, you are here to meet with Lucille."

"Your sister? But I don't know her."

"I dare say you met her when she was staying with Angelica. She has often done so."

Felicity balked. "That may be so, but it scarcely explains why you should be driving me. Nor why I should be visiting Lucille."

"I did not drive you. You arrived by hired chaise, accompanied by your maid. Ah, yes, you have come to chaperon Lucille while Miss Wimbush visits a sick relative. However, by the time you arrived, she had received comfortable tidings and need not make the trip. How does that sound?"

"Highly unlikely."

"But plausible, don't you think?"

"It is inventive, I'll give you that."

He laughed and gave a mock bow. "Let us hope we are not obliged to employ the subterfuge. Ah, here we are. Those are my gates."

He turned the vehicle into the dip towards a wide drive and pulled up before a closed wrought-iron barrier. An elderly man came hobbling out of a small lodge to one side, exclaiming at his master's unexpected appearance as he hastened to open the gates.

"Thank you, Samuel. Is Lady Lucille in the house?"

"Aye, her ladyship's there right enough, me lord. Had a drive around the estates in her little gig earlier, but she's been inside fer better nor an hour now, me lord."

Lady Lucille? Well, of course, she must be so titled. She was the daughter of a marquis. Felicity's oppression deepened as the curricle moved forward and rooftops became visible, poking above the trees. Why had she agreed to come here? She would be much more at home in Nanny Kimble's little house, although her tentative probing had elicited a clear signal that a sojourn with her old landlady would not do.

Once the exclamatory discussion of Felicity's news had died down, Nanny was induced to loosen up about her situation. It became obvious that Cissy, dealing with a woman in need of care almost around the clock, could not possibly cope with the extra burden of a visitor. Even were Felicity to take care of her personal needs, the necessity to provide additional meals as well as the extra washing and cleaning would be untenable. Felicity's means would not for long run to providing extra help. She must think of something else.

If she was honest, the prospect of living in such cramped conditions did not appeal. She'd had a small room at the academy, but it was a large establishment with several parlours, including one for the teachers as well as Mrs Jeavons' own to which she was often invited. But where she would go and what she was to do she could not decide. It began to look as if necessity might force her to accept Angelica's invitation.

The thoughts faded as a turn in the sweeping drive brought Ruscoe Hall into sight. It stood on a height, a massive square building of three storeys, seeming to go on forever as the curricle climbed, skirting an ornamental lake. Felicity felt hollow and perfectly dwarfed as the curricle came to a standstill in front of a lengthy pillared portico with a sweep of stair leading up to an arched doorway.

"Well? What do you think of it?"

An oddly eager note sounded in Raoul's voice. She struggled for adequate words. "It is — it is *big*."

He gave an odd laugh. "That's all?"

She flicked a glance at him. "No, I — I had not thought ... expected... But of course it was bound to be a mansion."

"Don't let that worry you. It's still a home."

His tone was clipped and Felicity felt horribly guilty. She rushed into speech. "I don't mean to disparage your home. It is extraordinary. Awe-inspiring really."

His lip twisted in a wry look, but he said nothing, merely preparing to alight as his groom was at the horses' heads.

Felicity turned her gaze back upon the huge façade and was immediately distracted by a flurry of activity at the entrance as the double doors were flung open and an elderly fellow in livery, accompanied by a couple of acolytes, came out onto the porch. Then Raoul was handing her out, the pair of footmen extracting luggage, the butler greeting his lord and bowing to Felicity as her name was given and within seconds she found herself ushered into a vast hall, its walls a mass of light and shadow, surrounding a wide central staircase. A plump, motherly woman took charge and swept her up the wooden stairs.

"I am Mrs Astwick, ma'am, and I will show you to your bedchamber."

"My bedchamber?" uttered Felicity, finding her voice. "But you cannot have known I was coming."

"No, ma'am, but we will scarcely be incommoded. I think the Blue Room will suit, and I will set the maids to prepare it for you. But you will wish to wash away the dirt from the roads and perhaps change your gown."

Talking gently all the time, Mrs Astwick led her along a wide gallery and through a door at the other end where they turned the corner and began walking through a series of rooms along the side of what she called the West Wing. Two were evidently parlours, but those at the far end proved to be bedchambers and the housekeeper stopped at the second one where a huge four-poster, hung in blue velvet, dominated the room.

Mrs Astwick moved to close the far door. "You'll be private enough once everyone knows it's occupied, ma'am. Now let me take your cloak."

Barely had she allowed the woman to remove it than a procession of servants turned up. A footman bearing her portmanteau, a maid with a jug of water, another carrying towels and a sturdy creature armed with a bucket of coals who proceeded to make up the fire. The footman placed the portmanteau on a chest at the foot of the bed and retired, bowing and closing the door behind him so that the room immediately became more private.

With the housekeeper directing operations, Felicity, completely overwhelmed, was stripped of her outer garments by one of the maids while the other unpacked, busily stowing her belongings in a japanned and inlaid commode at one side of the room. Mrs Astwick poured hot water into a basin on a dressing stand.

"You will wish to wash, ma'am, and I will arrange for tea while Jenny presses your day gown. When you are rested and ready, I will conduct you to the family drawing-room."

She went off without waiting for a reply beyond a stammered thank you and Felicity, standing in her shift before a glowing fire, was left to begin upon her ablutions with one maid standing ready with a towel. Felicity smiled at her.

"What is your name?"

"Easter, miss," said the girl, dropping a curtsy.

"Easter. Both pretty and unusual."

The maid giggled. "They does tease me, miss."

"Oh dear, do they?"

"Yes, miss, but I don't mind."

The exchange served to make Felicity feel a little more like herself and she smiled at the girl and dipped her head towards the bowl to wash her face.

Presently, wrapped in her large shawl, which the maid Easter unearthed from the commode, she was sitting against the banked pillows in the massive bed, sipping a restorative cup of tea brought up by a footman. Easter, who answered the knock at the door, would not let him in, but took the tray herself.

"You shut that door for me, Andrew," she ordered primly, and setting the tray down, she set about pouring tea from the pot, fussing over Felicity in a motherly way that amused her. Easter was barely more than a child herself.

"Does everyone who visits here receive such a —" Felicity struggled for a word that would not convey her utter ignorance of this kind of life. "Such a welcome?"

"Oh, no, miss," said Easter, busy brushing Felicity's discarded old gown. "Leastways, of course we look after a guest proper, but mostly they have their own servants, miss."

Felicity felt her cheeks warm. "I see. Mrs Astwick saw that I did not have one."

"Oh, but you come with his lordship, miss. Mrs Astwick knew straight as you was special. His lordship wouldn't bring just anyone into the house, miss. 'Sides, Mr Sholden likely tipped the wink to Mrs Astwick as you was an honoured guest. Mr Sholden always knows his lordship's mind, he does."

A vague recollection of the flurry of names as she came into the house surfaced. "The butler, is it?"

"That's right, miss. Mr Sholden has been here for years and years, with the old lord and all."

Felicity's fascination increased. "Is it only Lady Lucille who lives here now?"

"Yes, miss, and Miss Wimbush, who is her governess."

Felicity's mind went to the chattering girls at the academy. "It must be very lonely for her."

Easter, who was now carefully folding the gown into a drawer, looked surprised. "Her ladyship don't complain, miss. She has lots of friends round these parts, coming and going. She's one as enjoys company, her ladyship does. Lady Lucille ain't the least bit like his lordship." Then Easter gasped, putting a hand to her mouth and growing red in the face. "Ooh, I do beg your pardon, miss! Mrs Astwick would have my head, speaking out of turn!"

Felicity was obliged to crush a pressing urge to pursue the subject. "Don't worry, I won't tell her."

But Easter's confidences were at an end. She became prim all at once, wondering aloud when Jenny would bring the pressed gown and retiring to the commode to look, she said, for anything else that might need pressing.

Sipping her tea, Felicity contemplated the sky outside the un-shuttered windows. From where she sat, she could see only a vista of parkland where the ground rose sufficiently to present a bank of trees, at this distance indistinguishable one from another. She would have liked to look at the nearer prospect, but her view was restricted to the room itself.

On a more leisurely examination, and with the doors closed, it was not as imposing as she had at first thought. The walls were papered in a flowered pattern on a blue background with blue velvet pelmets to the windows, and a couple of landscape paintings provided more colour. Besides the commode, which now had her toothpowder and toiletries atop, and the washstand, there was a small escritoire on the other side of the bed into which Papa's journal and her meagre collection of books had been put along with the few personal items she possessed. The only other pieces of furniture were the chair by the desk and a long mirror set in the corner, behind which one of the maids had stowed her portmanteau. Felicity was, to all intents and purposes, installed in the room for the duration.

She was just beginning to wonder what sort of accommodation the head of the house enjoyed when Jenny came in with her pressed gown. For the first time since her childhood, Felicity was dressed by another and was shocked to find she enjoyed the attention. Easter requested her to sit down while she brushed and dressed her hair and Felicity, enjoined to look in the long mirror, was startled to see how different she looked in a fashionable gown and with her hair piled on top of her head, a couple of ringlets coaxed to sit either side of her face. She hardly recognised herself and was still feeling acutely unlike Felicity Temple when Mrs Astwick arrived to conduct her to the drawing-room.

"The girls will make up your bed fresh, ma'am. You need not fear damp sheets."

"Thank you, Mrs Astley, you are very good."

"It's no trouble at all, ma'am, and while you are here I hope you will allow young Easter to wait upon you. She's a good girl and she learns fast."

Felicity smiled. "I found her quite charming and I should be happy to have her services, although I am quite used to looking after myself, you know."

The housekeeper's voice became a trifle pinched. "That will not be necessary in this house, ma'am."

From which Felicity took it that she would infallibly offend Mrs Astwick's sense of what was fitting if she insisted upon her independence.

The housekeeper led her back to the start of the West Wing, across the entire gallery to the East Wing and through a large and rather formal saloon with gilded chairs and sofas set against the walls to a parlour with a much less formal feel. Chairs and a sofa were grouped about the fire. A couple of bureaux, a table and a pianoforte hugged the walls and a card-table with straight chairs around it occupied the open area opposite the fireplace. Standing before the mantel and leaning one arm along it stood Raoul, looking very much the marquis in a mulberry coat over a cream waistcoat, immaculate buckskin breeches and a fresh and intricately tied neck-cloth.

He smiled as she spotted him, flicking a glance down her gown and back up to her face. "Come in and sit down, ma'am."

Ma'am? Felicity's stomach dropped. He looked very much less approachable than he had throughout their unconventional journey, and she was attacked with both shyness and a flutter of butterflies in the stomach.

"I have put Miss Temple in the Blue bedchamber, my lord. If you will ring when the lady wishes to go there, I will send up one of the maids to conduct her."

Raoul nodded. "Very proper."

Felicity, her voice jumping, chimed in. "I think Mrs Astwick has realised I won't be able to find my way by myself."

He glanced from her to his housekeeper's carefully neutral expression. "I am sure Miss Temple will very soon learn her way about. Or her ladyship may show her. That will be all, Mrs Astwick."

The excessive formality was quite as oppressive as Felicity had feared, and she watched the housekeeper's retreat with the oddest sensation of apprehension. Was she afraid to be alone with Raoul?

CHAPTER THIRTEEN

Felicity rushed into speech as she moved to take a chair as removed from where Raoul was standing as possible. "When may I meet your sister?"

"Presently." He waited for her to be seated and dropped into the nearest chair, crossing his legs and leaning back, very much at his ease. "Lucille is at her lessons, I believe. I've sent a message up, so I daresay she will cajole Miss Wimbush into letting her curtail them directly."

Felicity wanted to say she could wish Lady Lucille to arrive at once, but it would scarcely be polite. Her mind balked. Since when did she consider politeness when talking with Raoul? Only he looked so much a stranger in this environment, she hardly knew how to talk to him at all.

He was eyeing her with his enigmatic expression. "I am glad to see I will not be wasting my money." Bewildered, Felicity blinked at him. He gestured towards her person. "The gown. It becomes you. I will say for Angelica that she has excellent taste."

"In fact, I chose it," snapped Felicity, unaccountably goaded.

His lips twisted in amusement. "Then I applaud your taste, ma'am."

She flung up exasperated hands. "For heaven's sake! I wish you won't call me ma'am in that horrid way. It is bad enough without that."

He raised an eyebrow. "What is bad enough?"

"All this!" She described an arc with her hand. "This grandeur!" She saw his brows draw together and leaned a little

244

forward. "I don't mean to disparage it, Raoul, but I can't — I am not — It's all so —"

"So grand? So formal?"

"Yes! I feel utterly unlike myself. And you are like a stranger! I've never been so uncomfortable in my life."

He did not speak for a moment. His measured regard seemed to weigh her. He uncrossed his legs and sat up, leaning his arms along his knees, a frown creasing his brow. "Do you think you might perhaps be able to grow accustomed?" He threw up a hand as she opened her mouth to speak. "I do understand it is not what you are used to. But any new experience is bound to be difficult at first. Will you not give it a little time?"

"Time? But we only came here for a day or two."

"To give you an opportunity to decide what you wish to do, exactly so. Well, there is no rush, is there? Allow me to spoil you a little, Felicity. You have not been well used and you deserve a trifle of consideration. Or don't you think so?"

His tone was perfectly matter-of-fact, but Felicity could not listen to the words unmoved. Indeed, her eyes pricked and she was hard put to it not to burst into tears. Her voice was husky. "How is it you manage to be so kind, a man as provoking as you are?"

A smile twisted his lips. "Now you begin to sound more like yourself. Come, relax! I will engage to provoke you at every opportunity and you will very soon find the alien environment becoming all too familiar."

She had to laugh, a little of her oppression dissipating. She did not answer him directly, instead fixing upon the portrait above the fireplace. "Is that your mother?"

He nodded and his face softened. "It is indeed. My father commissioned her portrait as soon as she was installed in the

245

house. It is a Lynchmere tradition. She will give place to the next marchioness."

His wife? The oddest stab afflicted Felicity's bosom. A snatch of memory presented her with the animadversions of Silve and Hetty upon the prospect of either becoming Raoul's wife, despite his undoubted eligibility. He was the bar. But they did not know him, not as she had come to know him.

She caught herself up. Where were her thoughts tending? He was speaking again and she snapped her attention in.

"There are later portraits in the gallery, along with past Lynchmeres and Ruscoes. I will show them to you."

"Is there one of you?"

He made a face. "Several, at various ages. The last was done when I came into the title, some five years ago. These things are expected, you know. It is not pomp."

"Tradition?"

"Exactly. One has certain inescapable duties and tradition is one of them."

A light footstep sounded from the direction of the saloon and Felicity turned to see a youthful creature trip into the room. She swept one glance across and her face lit up.

"Raoul!"

With a shriek of delight, she ran across the room and threw herself at the marquis, who rose to receive her in a startling and comprehensive embrace, lifting her quite off her feet. "Have a care, little sister! You'll have me over."

The girl was laughing in a delighted fashion as he set her back down. "I didn't expect you for ages! Why didn't you send a message? Are you staying long? Has something happened to bring you?"

"I will tell you if you will stop trying to strangle me." Raoul extricated himself from his sister's clinging embrace and bodily turned her to face Felicity. "I have brought Miss Temple to see you. Felicity, this is my graceless little sister, Lucille."

An indignant Lady Lucille dug him in the ribs with her elbow. "Graceless! How horrid you are!" She smiled at Felicity, who had risen, and moved to take her hand, dropping a curtsey. "How do you do, Miss Temple? Pray don't heed my brother. I am perfectly well behaved in company as a rule, only he gave me a shock arriving out of the blue."

Felicity warmed to her straight away. "Pray don't pay any heed to me either. I had been feeling quite a stranger here, but you have made me feel at home at once."

"Miss Temple has been a schoolmistress, Lucille. She is used to dealing with hoydenish young ladies."

The vivacious creature threw him a mischievous glance but her concentration remained on Felicity. "You can't be a schoolmistress. You aren't old enough."

Felicity laughed. "I have been one for six years." She looked from Lucille to Raoul. "How like your brother you are!"

Lady Lucille shrieked a protest, but the resemblance was marked. She had the same dark hair, and similar cast of countenance, although softened by youth. But it was easy to see her features would be commanding in time, though attractive. She was not a beauty in the conventional sense, but her personality was instantly taking.

"She is not in the least like me in temperament, however," said Raoul, with a teasing look at the girl. "A more pert and bouncing female I hope I may never meet."

This unflattering description sent her ladyship into a peal of laughter. "You make me sound like a dog." She turned to Felicity. "He is a perfect beast to me, you see?"

"On the contrary, I am excessively indulgent and am forever incurring Miss Wimbush's displeasure for spoiling you to death. Where is your duenna, by the by?"

His sister made a dismissive gesture. "Oh, she will be here all too soon. I could not come at her dawdling pace when I was longing to see you. And you haven't answered me!"

"Well, sit down and stop fidgeting Miss Temple."

"She isn't fidgeted. Besides, if it's true she is a schoolmistress — not that I believe it for a second — she must be used to being fidgeted."

"You're fidgeting *me*, wretched child! Sit down!"

"Yes, but you must sit with me, Raoul," the creature said gaily, seizing his hand and dragging him to the sofa. But no sooner had he consented to sit beside her than she swung about to Felicity, patting the space on her other side. "You too, Miss Temple! Quick, before old Wimby comes, and then she won't dare try to drag me away if I am parked between you."

Felicity could not help laughing, but she declined to join them. "I can talk to you much more comfortably from here, I thank you. I shan't be able to look at you if I sit there."

Lucille put her hands to her face, peeping between her fingers like an infant. "I was used to play peep-bo with Raoul, like this." Her merry smile was cast upon her brother. "Didn't I?"

"I'm supposed to remember all the tricks you played as an infant?"

He was leaning comfortably back, his legs once more crossed, regarding his sister with a good deal of affection in his face. A pang smote Felicity. Was it because of the recent reminders of Papa? She hardly heard Lucille's rejoinder, beset by an inexplicable yearning. The fondness between brother and sister was patent, showing a side of Raoul she had not been

248

privileged to see. He had been carelessly kind, amusing sometimes, but too often enigmatic and cryptic. Felicity had not before seen him show this wholehearted enjoyment in anyone else's company. She had ample opportunity to observe it while Lucille was present, that young lady proving irrepressible.

A faded lady of middle years came clucking in and was immediately persuaded by Raoul to allow her chattering charge free rein. "Lord knows why I have this effect on her, Miss Wimbush, but I can endure it for a short while."

"Oh, my lord, you are so very… Indeed you should not. Her ladyship is very naughty to plague you," fluttered the duenna.

She was a wispy female who, to Felicity's experienced eye, was clearly no match for her charge. Nor for Raoul, who introduced her and bade her take a chair in an authoritative way that evidently overawed her, although she clucked away as she hovered by a chair.

"Well, for a little perhaps, my lord, but her ladyship —"

"Oh, Wimby, don't keep on her ladyshipping," pleaded Lucille, jumping up and going across to give her preceptress a hug. She pushed her into the chair. "Sit, sit, sit, or I shall never get to ask Raoul all the questions in my head."

"Heaven help me! If you are going to ask me again to let you come out next year, the answer is no."

Lucille flitted back to the sofa, plonking down and seizing her brother's hand between both her own. "Dearest Raoul, I shall be nearly seventeen by then, and you know very well you want me off your hands as soon as possible; you are always saying so. If I have to wait for years and years, I shall be on the shelf before I come out at all."

Amused, Felicity watched Raoul roll his eyes as he looked across at her.

"You see what I am obliged to endure?"

"Well, when I am married, you won't have to endure it," Lucille pointed out.

Miss Wimbush tutted. "Really, my dear, you should not speak to his lordship in that impertinent fashion."

Lucille twinkled. "How else am I to speak to him when he insists on being so obstinate?"

Raoul wagged a finger at her. "He'll be more than obstinate if you don't behave, you little wretch."

His sister giggled. "No you won't, when you've neglected me for weeks and I haven't uttered a word of complaint."

"Yet."

"Well, I won't, but —"

"Be quiet, you little monkey! I won't yield. In the first place, you won't be seventeen until next summer, and in the second, Angelica won't bring you out until you can behave properly. Furthermore," he added, ignoring a squeak of protest, "I've a very good mind to send you to school instead of allowing you to drive poor Miss Wimbush into her grave. From what I've learned from Miss Temple here, a spell in a strict academy would do you a great deal of good."

Lucille turned horrified eyes upon Felicity, who entered at once into the spirit of this.

"Yes, indeed. A few days on bread and water in the naughty attic will do wonders, what with the cold and the rats. If that doesn't do it," she went on as Lucille's eyes grew rounder, "there is always the dungeon. We were used to keep a number of persuasive instruments down there to —"

She broke off as the girl broke into peals of hiccupping laughter. "Oh, you are f-funning! I thought you m-meant it about the attic at least."

Felicity smiled. "Well, no, though we did have a naughty room where there was nothing but an improving book or two to read. But no one was sent there for more than an hour at a time. Usually our pupils got so bored, they were begging to be allowed out within ten minutes."

Raoul pounced on this. "Now that is an excellent idea. Miss Wimbush, we should certainly find somewhere to put a naughty Lucille, don't you think?"

"Raoul! How can you be so cruel to me? In any event, it is far too late to change me now. You should have thought of it when I was too little to object."

Raoul pinched her chin. "As far as I can recollect, you were never too little to object." He looked across at Felicity. "She's been a handful from the hour of her birth. I can't imagine how the devil I'm to find a man competent to control her."

"I shall find one myself. I refuse to marry anyone unless they are just like you and let me do just as I wish."

"And there, in a nutshell, you have the utter failure of my guardianship, Felicity. Five years of subjugation. God help society when I do unleash her at last!"

Lucille evidently found this hilarious, protesting however that she knew very well how to behave and would become a pattern-card of virtue when the time came. Abandoning the subject, she then turned a bright smile upon Felicity. "I do like you, Miss Temple! Have you come to stay?"

Watching Felicity coping easily with his little sister's inconsequent chatter, Raoul was conscious of a measure of relief. He had not bargained for the deleterious effect upon her of Ruscoe Hall. He ought to have anticipated some such reaction from one who had lived in a very different style. It was natural to him to live as he did and he had been eager to show her his home, hoping, if he was honest, for a very different response.

He must be grateful to Lucille for breaking the ice. Felicity, relaxing with the child, was much more the woman he had come to know and appreciate, as she had not been since the visit to her father's lawyer.

Raoul blamed himself. His candour was ill-timed. Not that he had the slightest intention of allowing Felicity to do anything other than fall in with his scheme, but it might be politic to let her see for herself the utter ineligibility of any plans she might be revolving in her head. When she found herself at *point non plus*, when nothing could compare with what he had to offer, she would, he was certain, capitulate.

When Lucille conceived the notion of showing Felicity around the house, he rose at once.

"An excellent idea. I must see my steward and attend to a trifle of business. I will leave you in my sister's capable hands, my dear. Don't let her deafen you."

"Of course I won't, horrid creature!"

"Don't exhaust her either." Ignoring Lucille's protests, he smiled at Felicity. "We dine early, so you won't be plagued by her for too long."

"I am very happy to be plagued, I thank you," she returned, "and if Lucille means to drag me all over this pile of yours, I shall certainly need her help to find my way back to my room."

Even as Raoul laughed, he regarded her narrowly. Was there a resurgence of her earlier disquiet? Or was he imagining it? Perforce, he turned to the governess. "I suggest you seize the moment, Miss Wimbush, and take a little time to yourself. Miss Temple is competent to chaperon Lucille."

Felicity was rising. "We will chaperon one another." She linked her arm through Lucille's. "Where would you like to take me?"

Raoul left them, beset by an unreasoning surge of feeling as he headed for his library headquarters. Jealousy, was it? Of his sister? Absurd. He was glad to think Felicity and she had made friends so readily. He could use it to strengthen his argument. But the riffle of unaccustomed annoyance did not leave him.

Why could not Felicity feel as much at ease with him? He recalled how she was apt to call him provoking and balked. He had shown her far more attention and generosity than he had to any other woman. By his own choice, it was true. Yet she persisted in an unreasoning resistance. Miss Independence indeed! He liked that in her, but there was a limit. One had no wish for a clinging female, but a trifle of submission to his wishes would not go amiss. Did she even like him?

He recalled instances of laughter, moments of shared intimacy, but had there ever been warmth in her eyes? Of gratitude, yes. A flitter of unaccustomed fury snaked through his veins. He did not want her damned gratitude! He wanted...

The thoughts faded as the realisation of what he truly wanted from Felicity surfaced. His spirits dropped upon the swiftly following thought that he was baying for the moon. But once unleashed, there was no shoving it out of sight. He wanted Felicity's affection.

Her first panic and dismay had abated somewhat by the time Felicity was at last conducted back to the Blue Room by her vivacious guide. She still found the place inspired a good deal of awe, but Lucille's light manner was infectious. Having been brought up in the environment, she was naturally at home there, but it was plain she had no inordinate sense of superiority. She greeted every passing servant by name and even addressed the immobile footmen who sprang to life to open doors.

A very little of this insouciance served to make Felicity feel a good deal more comfortable, and only when she met Raoul at dinner did a glimmer of apprehension return. She was glad of Lucille's presence, along with Miss Wimbush. Felicity took pains to draw the governess out while her charge chattered to her brother, feeling kinship with one whose sole purpose was the fashioning of an educated and well-behaved young lady.

She was relieved that the meal, though well cooked and presented, was not overly sumptuous, and was able to do justice to her portion of chicken pie and a pork olive, though she rejected the artichokes and contented herself with omelette and stewed mushrooms for the second course.

At length Miss Wimbush rose, signalling to Lucille to do the same.

She made a face. "Oh, must we go now? I am having such a good time."

"You may remain with Miss Temple until I join you," said Raoul, rising and turning to give Felicity a look she was at a loss to interpret.

A flurry disturbed her pulses as she quickly got up. It was decidedly odd to be 'leaving with the ladies' as she knew was customary. The unconventional journey had not included the formality and it had not before been a feature of her existence. It had the immediate effect of making her feel alien again as she glided out of the dining-room behind Miss Wimbush and Lucille. She was tempted to look back, convinced Raoul's eyes were boring into her back.

The room they retired to was a formal apartment situated off the main gallery, but with Lucille's hand once more tucked into her arm as they climbed the stairs together, her unease dissipated.

"Do you ride, Miss Temple?"

"I'm afraid I don't."

"Then tomorrow I'll drive you in my gig. As long as it doesn't rain. You will like to see the grounds, I expect. I'll show you all my favourite haunts, if you like."

Felicity replied suitably, but her mind was dwelling on the inevitable tête-à-tête with Raoul. If he meant Lucille to go off to bed the moment he appeared, she would be alone with him again. The prospect was unaccountably unnerving.

Fortunately, she had not long to build it into an ordeal. She had barely taken in the opulence of her surroundings with straw-coloured upholstery to the white painted and gilded sofas which matched the yellow stripe on the papered walls, when his tall figure entered the room.

"It is dull work drinking alone," he said with a singularly charming smile bent upon Felicity.

It had the effect of sending her pulse into a frenzied dance and she was relieved when he turned at once to his sister so that he might not notice the tell-tale warmth she felt in her cheeks.

"Off with you, baggage! I should think poor Miss Temple must be longing for a trifle of peace and quiet."

"Oh, Raoul, can't I stay for a little? I promise I will behave. It will be practice for my come-out." This said in an artless tone of innocent cajolery which had no effect upon her brother.

"You will have ample opportunity to practise next year. Besides, I wish to talk to Miss Temple."

"Oh! Are you hatching secrets?" Lucille's eyes sparkled and she clapped her hands. "How exciting!"

Raoul cast up his eyes. "Nothing to interest you. Miss Temple has decisions to make and I am going to help her with them, that is all."

Oddly, this declaration did nothing to soothe Felicity's nerves. But it deflected Lucille.

"Oh, how dull! Why must she make decisions?"

"Don't be inquisitive! Miss Wimbush, take her away, if you please."

The governess, twittering and clucking, began to usher the girl away, but she refused to go without first subjecting her brother to a ruthless hug and giving him a kiss on the cheek.

"I love you, best of brothers, even if you are perfectly horrid to send me to bed."

His face softened and he grinned. "I am flattered. Sleep tight, little sister. Don't let the bugs bite."

Lucille giggled and turned from him to skip up to Felicity, seizing her hands. "I'm so glad you came. You won't run away, will you?"

"Not immediately. I have enjoyed today, thanks to you."

Lucille was about to speak, but Miss Wimbush called to her from the doorway. "Coming, Wimby!"

With a quick goodnight to Felicity and a jaunty wave to her brother, she was finally persuaded out of the room, leaving a breathless silence behind her. Felicity studied her hands, wishing there were not quite so many candles so that she might hide her inner disquiet.

As if he read her thought, Raoul picked up a snuffer and moved to extinguish those in two of the wall-sconces. "That is better. They will insist on keeping the rooms ablaze with light." He smiled as he turned to Felicity, moving across to where she sat on a long sofa set against the wall. He perched sideways at a little distance. "This is not the place I would have chosen for this discussion. Would you prefer to remove to the family parlour?"

"No, indeed, I am quite comfortable here," Felicity said, her voice distressingly tight.

"You don't look comfortable." She made no reply and he grimaced. "I wish you won't be shy of me, Felicity. I'm the same man, you know, despite all the trappings."

She ventured a look at his face and found a disturbing expression there. She hurried into speech, saying the first thing that came into her head. "It's not the same. Here, I mean."

"I'm all too well aware of it." A faint smile came. "But needs must. This is my inescapable world and there is no reason why it cannot be yours too."

An odd buzzing crept into Felicity's mind as she stared at him, his words revolving in her head. Her throat felt like sandpaper as she forced herself to speak. "Mine? How so?"

Raoul looked away, his fingers shifting where they rested on his knee. Was he nervous? What turn was this? His gaze caught their movement and he clenched his hand quickly, shifting his glance back to Felicity's face.

"You heard Rusper. Your background is impeccable."

Her unease grew. "My background?"

"Your father was Sir Arthur Temple's nephew. Your life ought to have been very different. It can be still. You are young yet, Felicity. Do you truly wish to condemn yourself to years of drudgery?"

Confused, she avoided his intent gaze. Had she expected something else? She drew a breath and let it out, trying for calm. "I don't have a choice, Raoul."

His hand reached out and captured hers and he shifted a little closer. "I'm giving you a choice. I'm offering you a better life."

His clasp about her fingers sent slivers of heat through her and she found it hard to concentrate. She struggled to make sense of this. "Are you thinking of Lucille?"

"I am thinking of her, yes, but —"

"She has Miss Wimbush already." The protest was immediate and strong. Felicity snatched her hand away. "You can't supplant the poor woman. How do you think I would feel to be the means of her losing her employment?"

He looked thoroughly taken aback. "Supplant her? Good God, no! But Lucille likes you and she needs a younger woman of good sense to emulate."

She blinked at him. "You propose to employ two governesses? Is not that unnecessarily extravagant?"

Raoul let out a disbelieving laugh. "Is that what you think I meant? Felicity, I don't want you for a governess for Lucille. I want you for a wife!"

CHAPTER FOURTEEN

Felicity could not move or think. A slow thumping started up in her bosom as she stared at him. He looked anxious and his cheeks were darkening as he waited for her to speak. She found her voice.

"Have you run mad?"

His flush deepened. "No, of course I haven't."

"Then you are jesting."

"I'm perfectly serious. If you must have it, I've had this in mind from the start."

Felicity's breath seemed to have become caught up in her throat. A vague, unformed hope living somewhere deep within her perished before she understood it, superseded by the unflattering significance of Raoul's words. Fury lodged in her bosom. "You had it in mind? You actually thought of this? When, Raoul?"

He spread his hands. "I can't be sure exactly. Certainly by the time we set out on this journey."

"But you scarcely knew me!"

A muscle twitched in his cheek. "It's not unusual for men of my rank to be little acquainted with a prospective bride. Besides, I knew enough. I knew you did not bore me. I knew you were a woman unlike the parade of debutantes to which I've been subjected year on year."

"Am I supposed to be flattered?"

He flung up his hands. "I'm doing this all wrong!"

"I can't imagine how you could possibly do it right." She was up on the words, pacing away to the mantel. "I knew there was something. You wouldn't say. You treated me to your enigmatic front." She turned on him and found he had risen. "You waited to see if I was worthy, didn't you?"

"Yes, I did. Of course I did." He took a hasty step towards her. "I had to, Felicity. I have a duty to my name, to my title. A marquis cannot marry to please himself."

"But you are pleasing yourself, Raoul. From a worldly point of view, I could not be more unsuitable."

"By birth you are perfectly suitable."

"Is that all that matters?"

"It's the one consideration I can't ignore."

"But you can ignore the fact I have been a schoolmistress for six years. You can ignore the fact Lord Maskery intended me for your mistress. Not your *wife*, Raoul. You must have windmills in your head!"

He came up to her, and triumph lit in her as she saw the blaze of anger in his eyes. "You ought to be glad I don't think of you in such terms, for heaven's sake! Why are you behaving as if I've insulted you? I'm offering what I have never done to any other woman."

Felicity struggled with herself, aware of the justice of his words. She forced her voice to a semblance of calm, but it came out clipped and frigid. "Sensible as I am of the honour, *my lord*, I must regretfully decline your very flattering offer."

The effect of this was not at all what she had expected. The fire in Raoul's eyes died and amusement took its place. "You idiotic girl! You are not in the least little bit sensible of the honour, though it is a considerable one. However, I can scarcely complain of that since it is your very lack of toadying to my rank that made me like you in the first place."

Disarmed, Felicity felt obliged to apologise. "I should not have flown out at you like that."

His lips twisted. "That sounded all too grudging. Never mind. I'm going to ring for tea and then we'll start again."

He crossed to the bell-pull and Felicity watched him, beset by a sudden yearning for a very different sort of approach. He tugged on the bell and gestured to the sofa.

"Come." She hesitated and he smiled. "I won't bite. Let us discuss this calmly, shall we?"

Felicity did not want to discuss it at all. An unaccountable wave of misery attacked her. She crossed to the sofa and sat down again, her spirits rapidly dropping while he settled beside her.

"Let me spell out the advantages."

Heavens, not that! "There is no need."

He waved her to silence. "It seems to me there is every need. I must obviously explain myself a little more."

A catalogue of reasons? The last thing she wanted to hear. She said what came into her head in a bid to deflect him. "This is useless, Raoul. You must know it's impossible."

"You underrate me. I am in the habit of making the impossible possible."

She could not repress a giggle. "Now you are talking nonsense."

The wry smile came. "One of the charms of your society, my dear Felicity, is the unpredictable. I never know how you will respond."

"And that makes you want to marry me?"

He laughed. "It is of more value than some conformable creature who will behave perfectly and drive me to the point of unutterable tedium. That, you know, is why I have resisted all Angelica's efforts to plant on me whatever creature she happens to think suitable."

Felicity pounced on this. "She won't think me suitable. She knows everything."

His brows rose. "What gives you the idea I care tuppence for Angelica's opinion? Besides, she likes you."

"That is beside the point."

"I agree. What matters is that I like you."

Felicity's temper rose again. "Indeed? What I like has no bearing on the case, I take it?"

"Don't be ridiculous!"

"It's not ridiculous! What matters is whether you like me? I've never heard such arrogance. As if your wishes are paramount!"

"Well, they are." His voice was a snap. "You could hardly propose to me, could you? And in my position —"

"Thank you, I understand your position, Raoul. You are a marquis. You can't marry just anybody. You've already said so. Well, I am nobody and I prefer to stay that way."

"Then you're a very silly girl! Improvident too. Have you forgotten that until a day ago, you were penniless and wholly dependent on my charity?"

In one swift movement, Felicity was up, heading for the door, too furious to think what she was doing. It opened before she could reach it and one of the ceremonial processions of servants entered with the tea.

Veering off, she crossed to the nearest picture on the wall and stared at it, blinking back tears and struggling to contain the sobs choking in her throat, her thoughts chaotic.

How could he taunt her? How dared he use her poverty against her? Did he think that would make her yield? Stupid, arrogant man! How she hated him! She must leave here at once. Not one night would she remain in this terrible museum of a house. With its monster of a master! Marry him? She would rather throw herself in the lake!

The clink of crockery and murmurings of the servants began to penetrate. She recalled that Raoul was still in the room. What was he doing? She was not going to look. Then he spoke.

"That will do. You may leave now."

There was an edge to his voice that cut through Felicity. She felt quite sick, dreading the exit of the servants. She heard the door close and a hasty footstep behind her. His hands were on her shoulders and she turned perforce at his urging and looked up.

He was pale, his face taut. "Felicity…" His eyes appeared to burn with something she did not recognise. His finger came up and brushed gently under her eyes. "Don't weep! Forgive me. I should not have said that. It was cruel of me. I didn't mean it."

She could not speak. There was a tender note to his voice that struck at her heart. Realisation crept into her mind and the secret longing she had not recognised took form. God help her, but she had fallen in love with Raoul! At once she knew why she was resisting his truly very flattering offer and the words escaped without will.

"You are proposing a marriage of convenience."

His hands dropped from her shoulders and his face changed. "Yes, of course. Did you suppose it could be anything else? One cannot command affection at will, I realise that."

But one could slide irrevocably into it without will or realisation. Felicity did not say it. She had no words. Deflection was all that was left. "I would like that tea now, if it is not too much trouble."

Without a word, he crossed to the table which had been opened out, the tea kettle, steaming now, placed upon it along with the rest of the accoutrements required for the beverage.

Someone had evidently made the tea already. Felicity watched him pour, all too aware now of why his movements had that disturbing effect upon her.

She crossed to one of the chairs that had been set near the table and sat down.

"Cream and sugar?"

His very voice set her trembling, the words too ordinary for her to bear. She hardly knew what words she wanted to hear — but cream and sugar?

"I will take it with one lump of sugar, if you please."

He obliged and passed her the cup. She stirred absently, watching him pour his own, which he took without either addition. He sat on the other chair and drank without looking at her.

Felicity's gaze devoured him, as if she saw his features anew. He looked abstracted, frowning. She wanted to smooth the frown with her finger. She wanted to tell him he had already commanded her affection without even trying. She wanted...

Forcing her gaze away, she sipped at her tea, trying to still the tremor of her fingers by gripping the handle of the cup. Her dilemma was total. She loved him. How could she possibly agree to a marriage of convenience? It was not in her nature to live a lie. To hide her feelings while she daily lived within his sight? And what of the nights? The enormity of that pretence hit her.

"Oh, I could not!"

He did not at once speak, but his gaze lingered on her face for a moment. He set down his cup with an air of finality. "I shall importune you no further. When you have decided what you wish to do, you may command my services to take you wherever you wish to go."

The coldness of this utterance chilled Felicity. She could not look at him as he rose and crossed to the bell-pull.

"One of the maids will show you to your chamber. Good night."

Felicity heard his steps. Her heart in tatters, she looked up in time to see the door close softly behind him.

He hardly knew where he was going, only that he could not remain in the same room with her. Her words echoed in his head. *Oh, I could not.* Inwardly cringing, Raoul sped up, his steps taking him through the candlelit gallery. He ignored the night candles waiting on a side table and the footman ready to light them, and hurried down the dark of the stairs into the hall where the moonlit slivers of light from the high windows streaked the marble and the shadows thankfully covered his unutterable shame.

There was no bearing the knowledge she regarded him with revulsion. She had called him arrogant. How true. How despicably correct. Yes, he was guilty of arrogance. In supposing he had only to hold out against her arguments to force her to his will. He had not bargained for the demon of hurt that scourged him now.

Without the aim of going there, he found himself in his library, the decanter kept in a cabinet there in his hand. He poured a measure of brandy and knocked it back. Its fire burned his gullet, pooling heat into his chest as it went down. It was balm, of a sort. But the corroding sense of injury and loss did not leave him.

Pouring another measure, he replaced the stopper in the decanter and returned it to the cabinet, slamming the door. He moved to one of the leather chairs and sat, staring into the embers of the tamped down fire smouldering in the grate.

Oh, I could not.

How had he got it so wrong? He thought she liked him at least. Yet she had not even paused to consider the proposition. She had shied away from it at the outset. Shied away from *him*. As if he was some kind of monster!

Someone came quietly into the room, bearing a candle. Raoul hardly noticed the footman who set the candle down on a table at his elbow and withdrew as silently. He was struggling with an unpalatable realisation.

Ever since the visit to Rusper, Felicity had changed towards him. She had been edgy. Nervous? Apprehensive? With the resolution of her search, she had changed altogether, now he thought about it. And he, determined on his own course, had not even allowed her time to reflect. Had not thought of her wishes at all. Had she not accused him of it?

Lord, but he had made a complete hash of it! Had been justly served too. Felicity could not endure the idea of marrying him. She had made that abundantly clear. A bitter pill. He had no choice but to swallow it. There was no marrying a woman who plainly could not stomach him for a husband. He would have to let her go.

Yet the thought of Felicity blundering into the sort of life she had endured was anathema. At least let him deflect her from that. Angelica! Remembrance of his cousin was productive of a tiny thread of hope. What if Felicity stayed with Angelica for a space? Might he persuade her to that at least? She would not go altogether out of his reach. Given time, might she recover a little of the former ease between them? It might grant him a chance to woo her, perhaps. Or was he baying at the moon again?

An odd yearning superseded the hurt. If only they might go back a couple of days. There had been intimacy. At Mrs

Dadford's, she had been so easy with him, had she not? Might she be so again if the threat — Dear Lord, but that was how she saw it! — if the threat of his offer were removed?

But he had removed it. He had told her he would take her where she wanted to go. Which meant she was effectively still dependent upon him.

He remembered the bank draft from Rusper and withdrew it from his pocket. He examined it in the light of the single candle, unable to make it out clearly beyond the writing and the lawyer's signature. What should he do? It was useless to Felicity without his banking facilities. She could cash it, of course, but he would have to take her to a bank.

He made up his mind. Let him give it into her charge. That would show her he did not mean to stand in her way.

The decision made, he slipped it back into his pocket and rose, picking up the candle. But as he made his way up to his apartments, he became prey to renewed yearning for a very different outcome to his abortive attempt to make Felicity his marchioness.

The night was interminable. Snatched sleep, filled with unquiet dreams, felt momentary, bringing no relief.

Felicity turned and turned again, ruffling the bedclothes and increasing her discomfort. Being in the bed at all was anathema, reminding her too much of the distressing notion that had prompted her outburst. She had not meant to speak aloud. A bad habit, got into when her mind was churning.

She recalled the times Raoul had picked up her words, laughing at her apparent inconsequence. Not this time. He had shut like a door, alienated. Felicity felt it, in his voice, in his bearing, in his very words. He would not importune her further, he said. He withdrew the choice, the fateful offer. A marriage of convenience? Highly convenient for her it would have been, and Raoul was ready to spell out advantages which could not have been more obvious. She had balked because she wanted more from him, more of him. She wanted what he could not give. Fool!

What right had she to demand the moon when he was offering the stars? What, would she have none of the night sky if she could not have it all? Now she had lost her chance and she must dwell in the dark without him for the rest of her days.

This melancholy thought held for some little time while her imagination painted a night such as she had never dreamed on, until she remembered it could never have been like that. Useless to regret an impossibility. Convenient wives had an inescapable duty which had nothing to do with tenderness.

Oh, but he would have been kind. He had been. Gentle, even. That very first night he had shown compassion, holding her while the shock of her abandonment made her tremble. He had proffered his help every step of the way.

Yes, said her evil genius, because he hoped for a wife who would not bore him!

Groaning aloud, Felicity turned again, burying her face in the pillows and longing for the dawn. When it came at last she woke to the chink of crockery and Easter pulling aside the curtains around the four-poster.

"Morning, miss. I've brought your hot chocolate."

Bleary-eyed, Felicity struggled up, blinking in the brightening light as the maid dragged all the bed-curtains back. The shutters were open and sun was spilling into the room from the wide windows.

"Let me bank your pillows, miss, and then you can be comfortable."

Easter banged the pillows back into shape and dropped them at her back. Felicity leaned thankfully into them and accepted the cup the girl handed her. The steaming aroma curling up into her nostrils was both appetising and comforting. She sipped and the rich sweetness rolled across her tongue. For a few minutes, she indulged in the unaccustomed luxury, grateful for its cushioning effect. But the unbidden thought of the might-have-been sneaked in to taunt her. This could have been her life from here on.

At this instant, exhausted from her restless night, Felicity felt as if she would sell her soul for a lifetime of morning chocolate and being waited on hand and foot. She wriggled her toes as the heat between her cupped hands permeated all the way down her body, pooling in her loins. All for a bargain of pretence!

"Ooh, I forgot, miss. There's a note from the master on the tray."

Felicity almost dropped the cup. She clutched it, gazing at Easter, who set down the gown she was shaking out and hurried over to the press where she had left a tray. With a soar of hope, Felicity watched her pick up a folded sheet and hurry across, holding it up.

"Here you are, miss. Mr Bilting give it to me. That's his lordship's valet, miss."

Felicity set down the half-empty cup of chocolate on the bedside table and held out a shaking hand. She took the missive with a word of thanks, her bosom a riot of dread and longing. The folded letter was sealed and Felicity turned it over and read the superscription of her name, written in flowing black letters. Raoul's hand? It must be.

She waited for Easter to busy herself with the gown again and broke the seal, unfolding the paper. Another piece of paper fell from it to the coverlet, splitting in two. Felicity snatched up one, but stared at the other. It was a bank note for ten pounds. Confused, she looked at the one in her fingers. Mr Rusper's bank draft?

Her eye went back to the letter. It was short and to the point.

Felicity —

You should take charge of this yourself. I am advancing you a little on account so that you need not apply to me. I know how you value your independence. Hugh Summerhayes can bank the draft for you as well as me if you will go to Angelica for a space. I do not presume to dictate to you, but you might with advantage stay with her while you decide how to proceed. Say the word and I will convey you at your earliest convenience.

Lynchmere

Her heart dropped. He wanted her gone. He did not even want the responsibility of being her banker. She was to be shuffled off onto his cousin, like a parcel. He could not wait to rid himself of her. Oh, what had she done?

Lynchmere. He had signed with his title, not his name. Alienated indeed. All the intimacy of their journey — the closeness, the quarrels, the laughter — was thrown away as of no account.

The words jumped out at her as she read them again. *A little on account? Ten pounds?* So that she would not have occasion to ask him for money. Then he need not hear her voice or speak to her again. But he said he would convey her, did he not? What did that mean? Surely he would not drive her himself? No, more like he would send her in a carriage with a maid for chaperon, only to satisfy Angelica. After which, she would never see him again.

Her heart rose up in rebellion. It was not to be borne. She would not let him cast her aside, like a worn glove.

"I must get up!"

Easter turned from the press, looking startled. "Now, miss?"

Felicity was already throwing off the covers. "Yes, now."

"But I've to fetch your hot water first, miss," said the maid, hurrying to the bed as if she would prevent Felicity from getting out. She peeped into the cup on the bedside table. "And you've not finished your chocolate, miss."

"I don't want it. Fetch the water at once, if you please." Easter looked crestfallen and a sliver of conscience pricked at Felicity. She forced a smile. "I will finish the chocolate while you fetch the water." The girl brightened and began towards the door. "And hurry!"

Easter threw another startled look over her shoulder and broke into a skipping run. Felicity watched her leave and then grabbed up the letter again. Absently, she picked up the cup and drank as she read, hardly tasting its contents for the concentration of her thoughts.

How dared he treat her so dismissively? After all they had been through together. Even if he hated her, he need not write as if she was of no account. Oh, he knew she valued her independence, did he? Well, he would discover how much. It was not merely a question of finance, my lord marquis, and so he would find. What of independence of spirit? Independence of choice? *I do not presume to dictate to you...* She should think not indeed! But of course he meant it for sarcasm, did he not? She could just see that twist of his lips in the wry look he wore when he made one of his cryptic observations. Exactly like that one.

You wait, my lord marquis! He and his palatial residence would not intimidate Felicity.

271

She tipped the cup to her lips and found it empty. As she set it down, her eye caught on the bank note, discarded to one side. She snatched it up. Ten pounds? He had paid twenty for the privilege of her company at the wretched auction. A bagatelle to him, as had been obvious from the start. Ten pounds? It was nothing short of an insult.

But the anger that had buoyed her to this moment had begun to dissipate, giving way to a feeling of corroding humiliation. Would ten pounds get her to Middenhall? To Nanny Kimble? A longing for that ample bosom overtook her. She wanted to sink her head on it and cry her eyes out. What in the world had she been thinking? Had she really thought she could beard Raoul and tear him to pieces in his own home?

She wanted to. Oh, she did — so much. But for what? He was not going to renew his offer, was he? He wanted nothing more to do with her, and if she screamed like a banshee, which she would dearly love to do, he would just laugh in that heartless way he had and throw her another careless bank note.

By the time Easter reappeared with a jug of steaming water, listlessness had overtaken Felicity and she had no idea in the world what she was going to do. Instead of racing through her ablutions as she had intended, she made a desultory job of washing, forgetting her face and then starting all over again when she remembered.

Easter, standing patiently with the towel ready, tutted at her. "You ain't got your mind on what you're doing, miss. Here, let me."

Felicity found herself being vigorously towelled and stood still, beset by a sudden memory. Papa, lifting her out of the tub and rubbing her down while she giggled at the childish ritual he recited. *Rub-a-dub-dub, three men in a tub.*

Yearning for the sort of close intimacy that allowed for such nonsense attacked her. To be loved and to love in return was all it took. Exactly as was evident between Raoul and his young sister. The boon of affection permitted so much. Felicity had forgotten. Too many years, starved of the like. And here she had wantonly thrown away her chance to feel it again.

Lost in her thoughts, she allowed Easter to dress her in the day gown provided by Angelica. She ought to wear her own horrid schoolmistress gown, ought she not? She had condemned herself to it. But she could not bring herself to make the change. While she remained in this house, she would have pride enough to look presentable in a milieu to which she had no longer any aspiration. After all, there was no saying when she might encounter Raoul. She could not bear to see the condemnation in his eyes if he should find her inappropriately dressed.

"There, miss, that'll do. You look a picture, if I do say so myself."

Easter was holding up a hand mirror and Felicity perforce looked at her reflection. She hardly noticed the neat arrangement of her curling autumn locks, caught by the shadows under her eyes and the tragic look within them.

In haste, she pushed the mirror away. "Yes, thank you, very nicely done." The maid looked disappointed and Felicity captured the hand holding the handle of the mirror. "Forgive me, Easter. It is excellent and I'm grateful. I am afraid my mind is all over the place at the moment."

The girl tutted, looking distressed. "I thought so, miss. It's that letter from the master, ain't it?" She shook her head. "Don't you pay no mind, miss. He's one as gets into them moods of his, the master is, but it don't mean nothing. He'll come out of it, you'll see."

Felicity had to smile at the motherly note, though the reminder stung a little. Young as she was, the girl sounded for all the world like Nanny Kimble in encouraging mode.

But a moment later, Easter caught herself up, blushing. "Ooh, I done it again! Mrs Astwick will have my head, she will, speaking out of turn. I do beg your pardon, miss."

"You need not. I am very glad to have a friend who cares enough to try to help."

The girl's cheeks went even pinker and she dipped her head in a bashful way. "Good of you, miss, but I'm not supposed to speak so free. Me tongue runs away with me, that's what Mrs Astwick says."

"It will be our secret, Easter. If you wish to know, this is all very new to me and perfectly overwhelming. There, now you have a secret about me to keep too."

"Ooh, I won't say a word, miss," promised the girl, round-eyed.

"You may call me Miss Flissie if you wish. It will make me feel very much more at home."

Easter's young bosom visibly swelled and she lifted her head and dropped a curtsy. "That I will then, Miss Flissie. Shall I show you to the breakfast parlour now?"

To Felicity's combined relief and disappointment, Raoul was not present in the sunny room where Lucille was discovered, partaking of the morning meal in company with her governess.

"There you are, Miss Temple! I'm so glad. I was wishing you would come, for I mean to show you the grounds in my gig. I promised, remember?"

Felicity took the seat the butler was setting for her and accepted a cup of coffee. "Thank you, yes, I do remember."

"You will need a cloak, for it is chilly out." She called to the maid who was just leaving the room. "Easter, bring Miss Temple's cloak to the hall."

Easter curtsied and went off, leaving Felicity without an excuse to refuse the treat. She did not in the least feel like going for a drive, especially around Raoul's grounds when she knew herself to be unwelcome. The fateful letter, with its accompanying bank draft and note, was reposing in the pocket beneath her petticoats where she had stowed it with care. She could not leave it in the bedchamber where anyone might find it. The precious bank draft could only be kept safely upon her person. If she lost it, she would be adrift all over again.

Lucille began to chatter of the treat in store as the butler proffered a dish of baked eggs. Felicity nodded without thinking and then stared at the portion on her plate, feeling quite sick.

Lucille noticed. "Don't you want it, Miss Temple? Have a warm bun instead. These are spiced and very tasty. Pass Miss Temple the butter, Sholden."

Felicity made no demur as her hostess insisted on plying her with buns, honey, jam and oat cakes. Perforce, she buttered a bun and nibbled at it, washing it down with copious draughts of the sustaining coffee.

Lucille talked all the time, thankfully relieving her of the necessity to do more than utter a word of enquiry or agreement. Just as well, for the frequent introduction of his lordship's name caused her to wince.

"I am not yet allowed to drive a pair, for Raoul is not convinced I can manage them on my own. Of course, he won't let me attempt his team. Raoul taught me, you know. He says I have light hands, but I'm not strong enough to manage four horses. Raoul drives superbly, does he not? He can ride the boldest of the stallions, even Buffalo, who is such a beast." She trilled with laughter. "That's what I call Raoul sometimes, when he is beastly to me. Beastly Buffalo!"

Here Miss Wimbush tutted. "Now, that will do, Lady Lucille. That is not at all a proper way to speak of his lordship."

"Oh, don't fuss, Wimby! You know I never speak hardly of Raoul outside the family."

"I know nothing of the kind. You are speaking to Miss Temple at this moment."

Surprise flickered in Lucille's eyes. "Oh, but Miss Temple is practically family already, aren't you? Raoul brought you himself and he never brings females here, unless it's in a party. Not that he does that often because he hates having to do the pretty. Raoul says it bores him."

"Yes, I'm very well aware of that," snapped Felicity before she could stop herself.

"Oh, but he can't be bored with you here, Miss Temple. Are you going to marry him?"

"Lady Lucille!"

A wash of heat swept through Felicity and she gave an involuntary gasp. The governess twittered with annoyance.

"This is what comes of chattering, my dear young lady. If I have told you once, I have told you fifty times: think before you speak. No, don't say a word! No excuses, if you please." Felicity saw Lucille close her lips tightly, but her eyes were bright with speculation and resentment both as Miss Wimbush turned to the guest. "Miss Temple, I beg your pardon on behalf of my charge. You must be thinking I am perfectly ill fitted to be her mentor. She always becomes over-excited when her brother is home. I do hope you will forgive her."

Felicity forced a smile. "There is nothing to forgive. It was an understandable error."

A flush overspread Lucille's face and she burst out, "Oh, no! But I like you so much, Miss Temple! Don't you like Raoul? I quite thought you did."

"Lucille, did you not hear me? I said be quiet! If his lordship could hear you!"

Heavens, but she must put a stop to this! Felicity held up a hand towards the twittering governess. "Let her be, if you please, Miss Wimbush." Summoning her old schoolmistress manner, she turned to Lucille. "You are mistaken, Lucille. Your brother has been helping me with a difficult problem, that is all. There is nothing else to make out of my visit here. It was expedient because I had decisions to make and Ruscoe Hall was conveniently placed."

"Oh." Lucille's disappointment was palpable. "I wish it was so. I am quite dreading Raoul marrying some horrid creature who will think me too pert and be beastly to me."

"I am quite sure he won't allow anyone to be beastly to you, Lucille. He regards you with a great deal of affection."

Lucille's eyes were suddenly swimming and her voice became choked. "I know. He's the best brother in the world and I love him dearly." She gazed hopefully at Felicity. "Couldn't you bring yourself to marry him? I just want him to be happy, and I know you would make him so. He likes you a lot, I can tell."

It was too much. Felicity dropped her roll, pushed back her chair and got up. "I cannot! I know it's foolish of me, but I can't!"

She left the table precipitately, hardly hearing as both Lucille and Miss Wimbush broke out behind her, and ran out of the parlour. With no idea where she was going, her vision blinded by tears, she raced along the set of rooms opening one into the other.

Stumbling to a halt at last, she found herself in a large apartment lined with bookshelves. Out of breath, she glanced around and stood stock-still in shock.

Raoul was standing behind a desk, his startled gaze on her face.

Embarrassment gripped Raoul, compounded by the jolt that hit him at her unexpected appearance — impassioned and eminently desirable. Blood shot to his loins and his breath caught. Inappropriate and unwanted, for he knew her mind too well. He fought to school his countenance. Before he could command his voice, Felicity's expression changed, her pale cheeks beginning to show colour.

"Well met, my lord marquis!"

Her tone was clipped and furious. Raoul braced as, in one convulsive movement, she came to face him across the desk, digging a hand into her skirts.

"Here!"

The hand reappeared and she flung a folded sheet upon the desk. It broke apart and Raoul recognised his letter with its accompanying enclosures. Confusion superseded all else.

"What the devil —?"

Felicity grabbed up the bank note and flourished it. "This is my worth, is it, my lord? Dismissed with a matter of ten measly pounds?"

What in heaven's name was she talking about? Acutely conscious of his steward standing off to one side and evidently unnoticed by Felicity, Raoul signed to him to leave them.

She glanced at the man as he headed for the door, her flush deepening. "I did not realise you were not alone."

"Evidently." He waited for the door to close behind Chesterford and then picked up his letter. "Didn't you read this?"

The glare in her eyes raked him and he all but winced.

"Read it? Of course I read it. To my cost. What is it, my lord? You've never been rejected before and so you must needs insult me?"

Good God, she had it all wrong! But his temper was too quick for him and he hit back. "What in Hades do you mean, coming in here and accusing me of insults? How have I insulted you? And I wish you will stop my lording me in that ridiculous fashion!"

She came back like a tigress. "You deserve it! How dared you treat me like an unwanted servant? Throwing money at me!"

"I did not throw money at you," he retorted, stung. "I only thought you might need a little cash, since you can't bear to be dependent upon me."

"No, and you don't want the bother of attending to my banking either, do you?"

"What nonsense is this?"

But she ignored him, raging on. "Is it too much trouble to you, my lord? Just as I have been from the start, is that it? Well, I did not ask for your interference, if you remember. It was no scheme of mine to drag you all over the country in search of my past."

"Have you run mad?" Raoul began to feel utterly disoriented. "Why are you ripping up at me like this? I was trying to help, for God's sake!"

"No, you weren't," she blazed. "You wanted to be rid of me, and this —" she threw the bank note at him — "is what you think of me! Even at the auction you thought I was worth twenty, you arrogant, hateful —"

279

About to answer in kind as she broke off, Raoul caught the husky note and his chest caved in. She was not angry. She was distressed. He could not bear it.

"Felicity, don't!"

He came around the desk and tried to catch her by the shoulders. She evaded him, backing off and throwing up her hands.

"Don't touch me! I can't have you touch me!"

A resurgence of hurt cascaded into his chest and he paused. "That's why you refused me, isn't it? Felicity, do you find me so repulsive?"

"Repulsive?" Was it bewilderment in her face? "Of course not."

A thread of hope flickered. "Then why do you shy away from me? Tell me, pray. Let me understand."

"Because I can't be *convenient*, Raoul. To live without affection? Without feeling? I couldn't do it."

There were tears in her eyes and he wanted more than anything to catch her up in his arms, but her very words held him aloof. He hesitated, but the yearning forced him to try. "That's why I let you go, Felicity. I hoped, if you went to Angelica that you might, in time, learn to feel some affection for me."

The film in her eyes cleared as she stared at him. "Learn to?"

"Is it asking too much?" Anxiety rode him. "I don't expect you to feel as I do, at least not all at once, but in time —"

"What are you talking about? Feel as you do? You don't care for me! You wanted a wife who would not bore you, remember?"

He recalled his words with an odd feeling of distance. Had he said so? It seemed impossible he could have been so stupid. He passed a distracted hand across his brow. "Yes, perhaps I did think it. At the start." He tried to remember back to the previous evening, before his world had been turned upside-down. "When first I broached the subject, if I am honest, I did think that was it."

Felicity's eyes flared again. "I knew it! Then when I said I would not, you went cold on me and threw me out of the house!"

Exasperated, he flung up his hands. "I wish you will stop talking nonsense, you idiotic woman! I think I must indeed have windmills in my head to be falling in love with such a shrew!"

Felicity's mind blanked. She stared at him, quite unable to believe she had heard what she thought he'd said. Her tone was hushed. "Falling in love?"

His mouth twisted in that wry look. "Yes, God help me! Though indeed I did not know it until you pierced my heart with your affirmation that you couldn't marry me."

Felicity blinked at him. "What?"

He eyed her with an intensity she found painful. "*Oh, I could not.* That is what you said. With so much revulsion in your tone, Felicity!"

Stunned, she gazed at him, a wild hope fluttering in her bosom. She struggled to get the words out. "I said it because I could not bear the thought of — of being obliged to accept your — your caresses without — without responding as I wished to."

It was Raoul's turn to blink. "Why in the world would you not respond? If you wanted to, I mean."

Felicity sucked in a sobbing breath. "Convenient wives are not expected to … to be affectionate in … in that kind of situation."

"But I want you to be affectionate!"

"Well, I couldn't be if I was only convenient, could I?"

His gaze softened into amusement. "You idiot woman!" But then his features became once again suffused with anxiety, his voice rough as she had never heard it before. "Felicity, does this mean —? If you are saying this, if you want to be affectionate, does it mean —? Do you feel *anything* for me? Any tenderness at all?"

Her brain was still whirling at this unexpected turn, but her heart was thumping so heavily she could feel it in her throat, half choking the words as they sobbed out. "T-tenderness? Oh, Raoul, you d-drive me to d-distraction!"

"That is no answer, for that I know already. For heaven's sake, Felicity, don't keep me in suspense!"

She tried to smile, but it went awry as the tears choked her. She struggled to speak, to tell him what was in her bursting heart. "I d-didn't know. I didn't think of it. Only I h-had become so shy of you and then, when you asked me to m-marry you, I knew I just *couldn't*, not if I had to hide how I felt. And that's when I *knew*."

The intensity of his gaze deepened, and Felicity thought a flare of something new appeared. Something strong and passionate that spoke to the deeps within her.

"You knew *what*? Let me have it in plain words or I dare not believe what I'm hearing."

Her lip trembled. "Can't you tell? Must I say it indeed?"

"On pain of my deepest displeasure if you don't." But a smile of great tenderness was quivering on his lips and Felicity could not speak at all. She caught her breath on a sob. "Oh, come here, you impossible creature!"

She was seized and held so tightly she could scarcely breathe. The thud of her heart was echoed in his chest where her head was resting and at last she began to believe. The aroma of maleness permeated her senses, making her weak. She sagged in Raoul's hold and he felt it. He relaxed his grip a trifle, leaning back and lifting her head so she had to look at him.

"Can you say it now? Quickly, before I am driven to kiss you into submission."

At that, she reared up. "Submission! That you will never —"

Raoul silenced her in the only way he could. It appeared to be highly effective, but in the rising heat he straightaway forgot everything beyond the delicious feel of her lips under his.

Felicity's limbs shook as fire streaked down her veins. A melting sensation engulfed her and thought became suspended. For the life of her she could not refrain from responding with a fervour she had not known she possessed. Raoul's groan was accompanied by a tightening of his hold so that she was tugged against the hardness of his body in a way that made her nearly lose her senses altogether.

But all at once, he released her mouth, almost pushing her away. "Oh, my God!" Her legs jelly, Felicity stumbled. Raoul caught her and swept her up in his arms. "Steady, my dear love!"

She threw an arm up about his neck, catching at his shoulder with her other hand. "What are you doing?"

He grinned. "Carrying you to somewhere where we can sit down."

So saying, he walked with her in his arms through the open door at the far end of the room and into yet another saloon. Felicity found she enjoyed the feeling of helplessness and utter dependency and was faintly disappointed when he set her down on a long sofa. But he settled beside her and, with an arm about her, drew her close again.

"That's better." Lifting up her face, he kissed her again, more gently, brushing his lips across her mouth and kissing her cheeks too. Felicity's heart melted.

"Oh, stop, Raoul! You are making me cry again."

He laughed down at her. "You are allowed to cry as much as you wish." But he found a pocket handkerchief and gave it to her. Felicity dried her cheeks and sniffed. "Better?"

She nodded, smiling at him. "I still don't think I believe this is happening. Are you sure I am awake and not dreaming again?"

His wry look appeared. "Don't speak of dreams! The nightmares I had last night! You ran away and I could not find you."

A sigh escaped her. "I wanted to run away. I could not decide whether to ring a peal over you or escape at once. You made me utterly miserable."

Raoul's arm tightened. "I'm glad. It is nothing to what you did to me."

She pushed up and turned on him. "How do you know? How can you be so cruel? I've a very good mind not to tell you how much I love you!"

A grin split his face. "You are a terrible woman! That's what it takes to make you say it?"

Felicity could not withstand a giggle. "I did say it, didn't I?"

"Yes, and I shall hold you to it, so don't dare think of escaping me. You are my prisoner for life, I hope you know."

But Felicity's mind had leapt. "Just think if you had indeed taken me for your mistress as Lord Maskery intended, Raoul."

"For God's sake! Are you crazy? You know I —"

"No, listen! The outcome would have been just the same, don't you see? I mean — I mean the passion there is between us." She felt her cheeks grow warm. "Don't frown at me.

284

Shouldn't I say it? You know I have no social graces. I can't imagine how you expect me to behave like a marchioness."

Raoul groped for her hand and kissed it. "You will be exactly the kind of marchioness I need. If I was frowning it was because I couldn't bear you to think I would use you in such a way."

"I don't think it. I know you would not." She released her hand and pressed a finger to the crease between his brows, smoothing it. "Don't frown at me. I only meant..."

She faded out as amusement reappeared in his face. "I know what you meant, and you are perfectly right. For which reason, we had best get married right away."

Happiness flooded her. "Can we? Without fuss? I should like that of all things."

He grinned. "I can't quite believe you are so eager for it today after the way you behaved last night."

"Don't! That is all forgotten." She remembered the bank draft now reposing on his desk. "I should not have thrown the money at you. But you may bank the draft now after all. It will serve for a dowry, though I know it is not much."

"Don't be ridiculous! Dowry indeed. That is yours, Felicity, to do with as you wish."

She was touched. "Thank you, Raoul. I shall use it to help Nanny Kimble. She could do with a maid and —"

"That you won't. If you wish to help her, I'll stand the nonsense. I could find her a cottage on the estate, perhaps."

Felicity balked. "Oh, no, no. What, take her away from all she knows? From her friends? That would not do at all."

Raoul's wry smile appeared. "You see how I need my schoolmistress bride? You will teach me how to think of these things."

She could not help laughing. "And what will you teach me, my lord marquis?"

"How to say I love you fifty times a day," he said without hesitation.

Felicity giggled. "You are importunate, sir. I shall ration you to twenty. After all, that is all you were prepared to pay for the pleasure of my company in the first place."

"Ha! How very true, yes. I paid good money to win you. Don't you forget it!"

Felicity drew herself up, but before she had a chance to tell him just what she thought of him, her unscrupulous love fastened his lips to hers again and everything but the pleasure of his attentions went out of her head.

A NOTE TO THE READER

Dear Reader,

The germ of this story began with the idea of the auction where it was essential that my heroine would be unknown and know nobody herself. Next came the horrible predicament of being abandoned and stranded, with no money, no home and no protection. Even in our day, as we see with the homeless on the streets, this would be a frightening proposition. For a genteel female in the Regency, it was disastrous.

In some ways, women of a lesser class were better off. There were several ways they could earn a living though the work was inevitably hard, the pay poor. Domestic service, a difficult life but relatively secure, was common for females. They might work in manufacturing, farming or trade of all kinds. They were less hedged about with restrictions and could go about unchaperoned, although there was always the danger of running into unscrupulous men and finding themselves "on the streets" as a prostitute.

Consider, on the other hand, the situation of the genteel female. Born a "lady", she was expected to conform to the very strict rules and shibboleths governing the conduct of women. Trangressions earned you condemnation from men and women alike. If she had no husband and no relatives to take care of her, your Regency lady had to work and her choices were limited. Companion, governess or schoolmistress, the latter being a cut below the other two. Anything else was impossible, unless the woman was prepared to lose her status.

Thus, for Felicity to find herself out of a job, devoid of both money and chaperon, was the worst possible fate. Worse for a female as independent and strong minded as this one. More than capable of holding her own, she yet finds herself in desperate straits. She becomes literally a beggar, unable to survive without Raoul's assistance, which she has no choice but to accept. Perfect material for a Cinderella story!

I hope you have enjoyed this excursion into another adventure for one of my brides by chance as much as I enjoyed writing it.

If you would consider leaving a review, it would be much appreciated and very helpful. Do feel free to contact me on **elizabeth@elizabethbailey.co.uk** or find me on **Facebook**, **Twitter**, **Goodreads** or my website **www.elizabethbailey.co.uk**.

Elizabeth Bailey

Sapere Books is an exciting new publisher of brilliant fiction and popular history.

To find out more about our latest releases and our monthly bargain books visit our website: **saperebooks.com**

Printed in Great Britain
by Amazon

37489079R00165